Khaled Khalifa was born in Aleppo, Syria, in 1964. A founding editor of the literary magazine *Alif*, he is the author of four novels, including *In Praise of Hatred*. He has also written numerous screenplays for TV dramas and films, a number of which have won awards. He lives in Damascus, Syria.

No Knives in the Kitchens of This City won the Naguib Mahfouz Medal for Literature in 2013 and was shortlisted for the Inter~~~ ` Prize for Arabic Fiction in 2014.

Leri Price is a translator (ler translation of Khaled Khali   or the 2013 Independent Prize f   ζ.

"Critically acclaimed . . . [*No Knives in the Kitchens of this City*] traces the degrading and destructive impact of Syria's dictatorship on the lives of a family from Aleppo."

—Financial Times

"A searing indictment of the Syrian regime."

—The National

"Required reading for anyone who wants to better understand the roots of the uprising and current conflict in Syria."

—Literary Hub

"Intricately plotted, chronologically complicated and a pleasure to read. . . . The writing is superb—a dense, luxurious realism pricked with surprising metaphors. It is lyrical, sensuous and so semantically rich that at times it resembles a prose poem. . . . A sad but beautiful book, providing important human context to the escalating Syrian tragedy."

—The Guardian

No Knives in the Kitchens of This City

Khaled Khalifa

Translated by
Leri Price

hoopoe
AN IMPRINT OF AUC PRESS

SPOTLIGHT
ON RIGHTS

This book has been published under the Spotlight on Rights initiative of the Abu
Dhabi International Book Fair

First published in 2016 by
Hoopoe
113 Sharia Kasr el Aini, Cairo, Egypt
420 Fifth Avenue, New York, 10018
www.hoopoefiction.com

Hoopoe is an imprint of the American University in Cairo Press
www.aucpress.com

Exclusive distribution outside Egypt and North America by I.B.Tauris & Co Ltd.,
6 Salem Road, London, W4 2BU

Dar el Kutub No. 25804/15
ISBN 978 977 416 781 2

Dar el Kutub Cataloging-in-Publication Data

Khalifa, Khaled
      No Knives in the Kitchen of This City / Khaled Khalifa.—Cairo: The
American University in Cairo Press, 2016.
          p.   cm.
          ISBN 978 977 416 781 2
          1. Arabic Fiction –Translation into English
          2. Arabic Fiction
          I. Title
          892.73

    3 4 5   20 19 18 17

Designed by Adam el-Sehemy
Printed in the United States of America

The Lettuce Fields

ON MY WAY HOME I recalled that my mother was not yet sixty-five when she died so suddenly. I was secretly glad and considered it ten years too late, given her constant complaints of a lack of oxygen. My uncle Nizar told me that she rose in the afternoon from her putrid bed and started writing a long letter to an unknown person, who we thought may have been a lover or an old friend, and with whom she passed long hours talking about days past that no longer meant anything to anyone—days into which my mother had settled during her final years and had no wish to relinquish. She didn't believe that the President, like any other mortal being, had died, despite the funeral ceremonies and the national state of mourning. The television broadcast his image and past speeches; it hosted hundreds of people who enumerated his qualities and cited his innumerable honorifics with great humility, their eyes filling with tears as they referred to the virtues of the Father-Leader, the Leader of War and Peace, the Wise Man of the Arabs, the Strongest of Athletes, the Wisest of Judges, the Most Gifted of Engineers . . . Great were their torments that they could not refer to him as the First among Gods.

"Power and oppression do not die," my mother would say. "The blood of his victims won't allow the tyrant to just die. The door has been left ajar, and will keep closing until it chokes their murderer." She meandered through her favorite stories about the past, selecting just the right words.

Rapturously, she would describe the elegance of her friends, fragranced by perfumes redolent with hope; she would show us photographs of them where they looked like unpicked cotton bolls, snow-white beneath the setting sun. She perpetually extolled the past and conjured it up with delight as a kind of revenge for her humble life; she described how the sun used to be, yearned for how the dust used to smell after the first rain. She made us feel that everything really had changed, and how utterly wretched we were for not having lived during this beautiful era when lettuce was at its most succulent and women their most feminine.

She had left her scribbled notes on the table for days, and we paid them no more attention than we had the others. Dust piled up on the lines written in the special Chinese ink she had brought for twenty years from Uncle Abdel-Monem's bookshop at the entrance to Bab al-Nasr. She would visit him and ask for lined paper which smelled of cinnamon. Accustomed to her question, he no longer exchanged memories with her of the Streetcar Era, as they termed their barb-ridden childhood and complicated relationship; instead, in silence, he would hand her a sheaf of white pages and return her money, not hearing her when she implored him to be stoic. He would go back to sitting in his shadowy corner, where he gazed steadily at a faded photograph of his family. In its center stood his son, Yehya, smiling, his hair gleaming with oil. The arms of his brothers Hassan and Hussein encircled him, a powerful articulation of the ambitions of brothers in perpetual harmony with one another.

All Uncle Abdel-Monem saw in the photograph was Yehya, whom he had last seen as a corpse laid out in the morgue of the university hospital. His face was charred and he had no fingers; his body bore the marks of electric cables and suppurating knife wounds. One glance was enough to identify him, after which the forensic doctor, as if carrying out a routine task, had closed the iron box and wouldn't listen to the other man's wild pleas to be allowed to touch his son's face. Instead, the doctor coolly asked him to collect the body and bury it without the usual mourning rites, guarded by six of the paratroopers who patrolled, armed and in full riot gear, the corridors of the morgue.

Abdel-Monem had arrived at the hospital with Hassan, Hussein, and a friend, and been mercilessly turned out again, all before the dawn prayer sounded. They carried the body to an ancient Volkswagen being used as a hearse, lifted it inside, and squeezed themselves in around the coffin. They stared at each other and wept in silence.

Death was spreading through the desolate streets of Aleppo, oppressive and unbearable. They arrived at the family tomb and the soldiers asked them to carry the coffin inside so that the sheikh waiting there could pray over it. Abdel-Monem just nodded as if he were demented and muttered something incomprehensible. The sheikh prayed hastily as my cousins lined up behind him. They didn't raise their eyes from the coffin as the soldiers lifted from it a fleshy lump wrapped in a filthy shroud. They weren't allowed to look into the extinguished eyes or to embrace him as one should when burying a loved one. Their tears petrified in their eyes and they simply looked at their father who was still crying silently, muttering words no one cared to decipher.

My mother woke from her long coma and sat at the brokendown dinner table beside Nizar, who hummed quietly like a fly. She read him a line of the letter to the man she described as a dear friend: "Everything is finished, I no longer hold you to your promise to dance the tango with me on board an ocean liner." She abandoned the encrypted tone of previous letters as she stated plainly that it was impossible to trust men who smelled of rats. Unafraid of the possibility of her letter falling into the censor's hand, she went on to announce in a final moment of courage that it was all the same to her, and approval was no longer any concern of hers. She didn't for a moment consider herself to have committed any sin; rather, she felt that to face death head-on befitted the grand dreams which had died before she had, and she no longer had anything to hide about her defeat. In the months before my mother's death, Nizar became accustomed to sitting alone on an old wooden chair night after night listening to his sister's ravings whenever she woke from her bouts of torpor, as she did from time to time. She spoke to him about her hallucinations with utter conviction, as if she had watched a film that wasn't visible to anyone else. She would speak candidly about the ghosts which haunted my brother Rashid and asked Nizar about the state of the country. Before returning to her silence, she would converse with him for hours at a time, lucidly and fluently, with a force that astonished him, about such topics as the price of vegetables and her memories of nights spent with my father in that old stone house on the outskirts of Midan Akbas. She laughed as anyone might, recalling with a sigh how she had prepared coffee for Elena and taught her how to make apricot jam. To someone who didn't know them it was a perfectly normal scene: a brother and sister choosing to spend their old age together, chatting and frying seeds, settling their accounts with a family past which had never let them be. Both were immersed in reexamining characters from days gone by, and when they realized that everyone had long since died or fled, they fell silent and brooded over a history which, for all its beauty, had granted them nothing but misery.

Rashid had disappeared in her final days, and she couldn't bear his absence. She spoke about him whether coherent or delirious, and told us that he hadn't died, that he would come back. I stayed silent. I couldn't bring myself to weave tales to explain away his disappearance, convinced as I was that she had experienced enough chimeras in her life; there was no need to wound her further with yet another lie about my missing brother. For myself, I was sad that Rashid wouldn't see my mother's body laid out peacefully. He would shed no bitter tears over the loss of all our dreams. I hoped he would be found so that, for the first time, he would assume his share of our joint responsibility and stand at the door of the hall used for the mourning rites, the hall Uncle Nizar had rented to spare us the embarrassment of people seeing our house. Just one look was enough for everyone to know how our family's dreams had been crushed.

Uncle Nizar asked me to look for irrepressible Sawsan and drag her back. He burst out crying but his voice stayed resolute, reminiscent of my mother's when she told us that my father had gone to New York, leaving us for an American woman named Elena who was thirty years his senior. She told us nothing else; just that he hadn't died, but there was no reason to ever expect him to come back. She laid out a piece of English broadcloth, three stuffed eagles, a few of his striped shirts, some threadbare trousers, and the badge and distinctive felt caps of the railroad employees. She told us carelessly that we could divide up his bequest between ourselves. When she slammed the door behind her we heard her sobbing and smelled the scent of the oncoming disaster.

I thought I would have plenty of time after my mother's death to leaf through her photograph album. Its gazelle-skin binding had never faded and remained soft to the touch; it had acquired a certain sanctity, being the sole fragment of our household which hadn't completely disintegrated. I was supremely comforted at the thought of looking at my sister Suad, whose pallor we could no more explain than her screams in the night like a lone jackal in the mountains.

Suad's ceaseless delirium in the weeks leading up to her death caused us to reflect on our fate. The family picture hanging in the living room became a psychological burden we tried to avoid, a lie, an obscenity we couldn't conceal: a father who fled from us with an aging relic-excavator my mother had taught to make jam, and a miserable sister driven mad by an unknown cause, whose mouth gaped as she struggled desperately to breathe. We loved her, although my mother considered her a private shame to be hidden from the world.

I had just turned ten at the time and knew nothing about death, or shame. Sawsan shook Suad roughly, as she did when they fought, but Suad didn't move. My mother waited until dawn to carry her to the family tomb wrapped in a woolen blanket, helped by her friend Nariman and Uncle Nizar. That night she informed us that Suad would never come back, and explained curtly that death meant going away forever. She didn't add anything about what it felt like to bury your shame with your own hands.

We didn't believe that sweet-natured Suad would stay away. I told Sawsan that we had to find her—perhaps she was hiding in the lettuce fields like she often did, or by the train tracks which ran nearby. She used to take railroad spikes and make them into swords, brandishing them at invisible passengers.

Whenever a train passed by our house and whistled its heart-rending cry, Suad would fling open the door and hurry after it. She would count the train's cars, and cheerfully inform us that the driver could fly, assuring us she had seen his wings. We nodded credulously, imagining that after disappearing from sight around the bend, the train would fly over the fields and soar through the sky. When we asked her where it would eventually land, Suad explained seriously, as if she had expected just such a question, that the driver wouldn't stop flying until he died. She pointed with childish glee to her own slight body and concluded: "Just like me."

We walked through the lettuce fields and eventually arrived at the cemetery, and when we asked the caretaker if he knew where Suad was, he pointed to a mound of dust. Sawsan beat the dust with both hands furiously, and then collapsed in exhaustion. I ordered her to stop crying, reminding her we had to be back before dark. We walked home through the pouring rain, and without a shred of remorse I told Rashid that Suad hated us and would never come back, all because he had stolen her wooden train. Sawsan agreed gleefully. That night I dreamed of Suad. She was driving a long train carrying a flock of birds with long beaks and no wings who sang to her sweetly. Her hair was long and white, and she smiled as she looked ahead of her, an angel no one could see.

The only person I told about my dream and the recurring image of Suad with her long white hair was Sawsan, who laughed and took me back to the cemetery. We brought wildflowers and stood next to the blank gravestone, and I listened to Sawsan as she told me solemnly that here Suad couldn't laugh or breathe, and that the worms were eating her up. From her lengthy explanation, I came to understand death as the absence of those we love.

Years later, I saw Sawsan by chance in the cheap Bar Express and reminded her of those long explanations. I told her that death was a completion of memories, not an eternal absence, and she agreed with a boozy nod of her head. She asked me if I still saw Suad, and I lied and said I saw her every day. She bowed her head sadly and took my hand, and added that thirty years should be long enough to forget anyone. I suddenly realized she was repeating the very same words my mother used about death and, like our mother, was using slow, affected hand gestures. I felt sad that Sawsan had begun to imitate our mother; I nearly asked her what it felt like to resemble a woman she hated so much.

Rashid convinced me that Sawsan had lied when she said she wouldn't remember me, adding that thirty years weren't enough to forget anyone you love. I realized later that to forget was to completely rework the small, hidden details of things, until finally we think they are true and don't believe they are the figments of our own imaginations. At the time I had started to enjoy walking in the stillness of King Faisal Street, where I would reflect that Aleppo itself was as ephemeral as the act of forgetting; anything which remained of its true form would become a lie, reinvented by us day after day, so as not to die.

Suad's death made us think about escaping death. Rashid and I took our family's one blanket and spread ourselves out next to Sawsan who clung to us, afraid of Suad's ghost which Rashid swore he saw hovering around the closed window every night. He became engrossed in the details of his description, using terms he had learned from music harmony and the titles of violin pieces. The three of us seemed to be fleeing an inevitable fate which lay in wait for us when dusk fell and the house was submerged in quietness. Sawsan would tell us to be quiet and we would fall silent and draw closer to her warm body. She put her arms around us as if she too were seeking solace in us from her fear.

I don't know why twenty years later my feet brought me to visit Suad's grave one last time. I scattered the olive branches I had cut from our garden and sat close to the small grave for hours, weeping for her loss. It was the first time I had ever done so, unlike Rashid who had cried for a whole week after she died, before he wiped away his tears and waited for her to come back and play with him. My tears freed me from the dreams that had turned into unbearable nightmares, in which Suad appeared as an old woman, with her face daubed with cheap and garish make-up, looking like Sawsan's friends, and not the child who had asked me if I knew whether dead people got older.

I sought out the caretaker to ask him the usual questions about whether he had taken care of her grave and he told me casually that the tombs would soon be transferred out of the city, and my brother Rashid had taken possession of Suad's remains in the proper way. I was horrified at the thought that I had been weeping over nothing more than a pile of dust. I told my mother, who at that time lived with us at the house, what had happened to Suad's remains and she was astonished that I still remembered her. She made no comment on the reappearance of this old shame and merely looked into my face as if it were that of a stranger, at the marks on my right cheek made by a sharp razor and my clothes with their sour smell of sweat.

They were nothing like those of the child she had taken firmly by the hand on his first day of school, pointing out the familiar landmarks which would lead me along a safe path. She explained that big hulking men with moustaches would lie in wait for young children who were succulent as lettuce leaves, so they could violate them in the deserted cherry orchards. She looked hopefully at the distant horizon and, laughing, repeated school songs to herself. When we arrived at the school, she went inside and sat in the head teacher's office where she introduced herself as a respected colleague and explained briefly that my father had emigrated to America, where we would join him in a few years. His searching glances reminded her that she was now an abandoned woman, and easy prey for shameless men.

She drank her coffee coolly, recovering her strength, then in a ringing tone reminded the headmaster that she had been a teacher who won the respect of her pupils and tried to teach them to listen to themselves. Finally, she added that she had returned to her beloved Aleppo on account of her children, and in a series of contradictory phrases she both praised and cursed the inhabitants of the village she had just left. When she saw that the head teacher comprehended her suffering, she added that the ascent of the military inspired anything but confidence. He agreed that the future would be bitter as old turnips. He shook hands approvingly with me, the new pupil wearing a clean school uniform that smelled of lemon cologne, with an embroidered lace handkerchief tucked into my top pocket, my nails trimmed, and my hair fixed in place with perfumed henna. The head teacher bid my mother a deferential farewell and nodded as he repeated how hard it was to live without a free press. He reminded her to look out for the *Evening Standard*, and to read the articles which called for a separation of religion and state.

The head teacher led me to my classroom through a long corridor. The school had been built by a French engineer and was originally intended as a tuberculosis sanatorium whose patients, before they melted like ice cream on a scorching summer afternoon, could meditate on its high ceilings and wide rooms, or the windows overlooking flower beds filled with crimson roses which gleamed in the spring sunshine.

My first teacher welcomed me warmly after the head teacher whispered a few words in his ear. He sat me in a chair at the front next to a young boy who looked like me; I reached a hand out to him and we became friends. His name was Jaber and he lived on a backstreet near our house. I told him about my siblings at the first chance I got and invited him to our house where we played together and swore eternal brother-hood in a scene which made Sawsan, who observed the blood oath, laugh out loud. We became friends easily and passed most of our time in my room, listening attentively to Rashid, who played us our favorite songs on his violin.

I no longer listened to my mother's reproaches; I walked shamelessly in dusty roads, I had no fear of perverts. Jaber and I were more interested in the narrow lanes of the alleys where we gathered offcuts by the cotton gins of Ain Tel, or pilfered copper wires and exhumed empty glasses from rub-bish heaps. We exchanged our wares in the nearby Sunday market for a few coins, enough for us to spend the afternoon in Cinema Opera. We were ardent fans of Egyptian and Bol-lywood melodramas about good-looking, impoverished lovers who triumphed at the end of the film.

I would slide into the seat next to Jaber and savor the cool air and the breath of the few patrons who attended the daytime showings, waiting for my adored Naglaa Fathi to strut onscreen in a mini-dress that showed off her charms. I would say to Jaber that when I grew up I would travel to Egypt and find her to tell her that he sent her his regards, whereupon he would dig an elbow into my side to shut me up. When I turned to him he'd have dissolved into tears, cursing the director who had ended the film without telling us how she would be delivered from her travails. Our amorous heroes and heroines lived out the sheer magnificence of love, and we tried to finish the film's story for ourselves as we gobbled our falafel sandwiches from Arax and walked back to our alley across Suleimaniya Street, whose shops smelled of wine and meat. I would try and convince Jaber to wait for the evening train but, laughing, he would wave at me and curse the trains, and I was left alone. I would put large nails on the tracks and wait for the iron wheels of the seven o'clock train to transform them into swords. Jaber would drill a hole into them using the lathe from the metal-turning shop of his uncle the turnerji, and we hung them around our necks like highwaymen.

My mother looked at the swords hanging around my neck. To her, I looked like a beggar with my filthy clothes and ragged nails. I read in her eyes that I was straying from the path, a misstep that would destroy the ascendance of the house she depended on for protection from the hubbub of the street, and from men who smelled of pickled turnips.

But the tranquility of the house didn't last long; it was soon surrounded by the shouts of Party Comrade Fawaz's relatives and the lowing cattle and bleating goats they brought with them from the villages. They built a large chicken coop before apportioning a large number of rooms among themselves. Over the summer, wives of village cousins spent their days frying eggplants and wiping snot off their multitudinous children who loved stomping around, calling on Comrade Fawaz, their big brother, to notice that they were following in his footsteps by glorifying the Leader. At night they would sing Party songs in an uproar of revolutionary passion, but songs alone weren't sufficient; they also turned up a tape recorder which broadcast the President's speeches, and would hail and applaud him along with the crowds on the recording.

The noise caused my mother much frustration, and her desperation only increased after she discovered that most of her childhood friends were now Party members. On the first page of their notebooks they would write an aphorism attributed to the President Leader, and they had committed to memory all the songs which glorified him. For the first time, my mother realized that they had started to resemble seals, wearing identical clothing and using the same cheap perfumes. She withdrew into herself and began to weave an imaginary world, in which she recovered the voices of her old friends, who strutted about, and interwove them with the snatches of distant music. She convinced herself that living a parallel life was not so bad, and concluded that it wasn't necessary to be a friend to your enemies.

She looked at me sadly. I had begun to resemble the neighbors' sons, my clothes dirty and my hair matted. She dressed me in a bathrobe and dedicated herself to a thorough cleansing of me, rubbing me with cottonseed oil whose smell reminded me of mice caught in a trap. Meanwhile Rashid and Sawsan gleefully tore up whole pages of my books and flung them into the air so they would fall like the snowflakes Sawsan used to dream of walking beneath, at the side of a lover who would lead her by the hand over the bridges of a faraway city and kiss her tenderly as evening fell.

We loved our new house. It was built of white brick and bore an inscription of a Quranic verse with intertwined letters over the door. My mother didn't object when the mason expressed a wish to engrave it on the stone arch. She left nothing to chance. She bought copper beds in the classic French style from the Sunday market and mended their posts and polished their ornamentation till they gleamed. She put them in our bedrooms and kept the large bed for her own room where she tossed and turned by herself all night, going over her remaining memories of my father. The story of her marriage and his flight seemed like a film to her now, some implausible melodrama. She hadn't understood the cruelty my father had often spoken about before he left with Elena the American, not until she was an abandoned woman who, with her children, lived a life parallel to the Party which continued to impound any remaining freedoms. Permits to print newspapers were suspended and new ones blocked, the parliament was suspended, and a new constitution was imposed granting The Beloved President unlimited powers. Following the coup d'état, these powers were put to immediate use in the arrest of His friends and the president Nureddin al-Atasi, all to die in jail some years later. The Party alone retained the right to lead the country now fuddled by emergency rule and 'exceptional' court cases. The President, whose death in June 2000 my mother couldn't believe, had appropriated for himself all potentially sensitive offices, from President of the Republic to Party Leader and Commander-in-Chief of the Armed Forces, along with the right to appoint the judiciary of the constitutional courts, to name the head of the government, and to dissolve parliament.

When my father used to come home drunk he would knock everything in the room over and wake us up, not caring if he frightened us. He would spit on the family picture hung reverently on the wall, and ask, "What is the point of the same moments being repeated over and over in the same place?" He complained of being suffocated and heaped bitter indignation on the train station where he worked as well as on the Party and its informers. Even after the strong coffee my mother brought him, he would not be calm. She would convince him to go out into the courtyard where there was a refreshing breeze, stroke his hand gently, and wait for him to finish ranting about anything and everything. As usual he cursed God for having flung him into a Godforsaken station that stank of bleach and idiot railroad workers, insisting that he deserved a better place where he could realize his dreams.

At dawn he would fall silent and bury himself in my mother's arms, and she would lay him on the bed like a small child. After a few moments she would hear him snore, and felt relief that the troubles were over for another night. Sawsan, Rashid, and I gave a sigh of relief when he didn't kick Suad as he usually did. She would look at him as if he were a being from another world and cry whenever he approached her, hurrying to Sawsan and hiding her head in the warm embrace that surrounded us all like a little mother. There was no way we could have ever forgotten its scent.

My mother brought her old sewing machine from my grandfather's house as part of her inheritance. From cheap fabric she made colorful curtains and pillowcases, and from scant money she created our new, magical world. She spent a lot of time with a friend of hers, Nariman Siraj al-Din. Together they would scour the souk for some neglected object, haggling over the price as any impoverished woman would. The hands of these two sorceresses would bring these objects back to life: old Mamluk lanterns whose owners hadn't noticed their splendid ornamentation, an Italian chest of drawers whose front panel was engraved with a melancholy serpent and a naked woman like the maidens found on Renaissance paneling, a set of Louis XVI sofas for the guest room which were reupholstered with striated fabric. In the living room there was a cheerful living room set with walnut frames that she had collected from a pawn shop that sold second-hand things in Bab al-Nasr. Its maker had carved his initials on the sofa, and she would claim to her visitors that he was a famous Italian designer. She would stand in front of it for hours, dreaming of the new colors she would upholster it with, of how she would recline upon it during long winter nights when the rain was pouring down, a wood-burner beside her and her perfume intoxicating a man whose features were vague and known only to her, and to whom she would coquettishly reveal the secrets of her body. She thought it would be an iconic scene, and that anyone who had such an experience would need an entire lifetime to recreate its bliss.

She loved feeling that people liked her work, and was extremely irritated if her ideas were ignored or received no courteous acknowledgment. Love of praise accompanied her all her life, along with a few other things which gave her indescribable happiness. She had succeeded in escaping Midan Akbas and returning to her beloved city, where she ordered us to hush and walk on tiptoe so as not to disturb the silence. She would lie on the sofa in the evening, a woman dreaming, sipping tea, her thoughts wandering for long periods of time over a distant horizon; then suddenly she would remember that she was alone and her eyes would silently well up. Holding back tears, she would rise to go to her closet and pick out an old nightdress, soiled with memories of my father, whose flight she had not forgiven. She never mentioned him in front of us until her very last years, when she started cursing him vindictively for having chosen to save himself and flee.

Ever tactful, Nizar would bring her cassette tapes overflowing with songs from the Nahda era. They would listen to them together and talk slowly and laboriously. He was waiting for a question which she never asked, so he told her about his dream of traveling to Paris, retelling the story of their shared dreams of wandering the alleyways of Montmartre. Together they had amassed so many maps and paintings by impoverished artists that they knew its every detail and entrance, and had imagined living an entire life within its quarters.

She asked Nizar to teach us the violin after she realized that we had started stomping around and lustily singing school songs which glorified the Party and the Leader. She bought a violin and Nizar began his tutelage. My mother adored the scene of us all wearing clean clothes, sitting on the bamboo seats and echoing musical notes after Nizar. In that image, we more closely approximated the exemplary family she was resolved upon. In her daydreams, she longingly traced a picture of our future: either doctors or engineers, both celebrated and refined, we would listen to classical music and wear expensive ties and magnificent shoes. Every day we would gather in a circle around the dinner table at which she would preside, and she would look after her grandchildren.

No one took to the music lessons except Rashid; after five months he could play several challenging exercises with ease. Sawsan and I would flee at five o'clock, saying we didn't feel well. As the hour approached, Sawsan would speak with increasing earnestness of her afflictions, which included total paralysis and a bout of coughing that only ended after the music lesson was finished. She was made to stay in her room and tend to Suad. Sawsan drew pictures for her—of outstretched tongues, houses on which the sun never set, goats, horses—which horrified my mother. Any hint of Midan Akbas which clung to us was a nightmare for her; however much she fled it and tried to efface all traces of it, it reached out its tongue to mock her. She tore up Sawsan's pictures, who then, furious, would leave us to spend time with Suad in her little room under the stairs, trying to escape the odor of death. She told us that Suad would soon turn into a dog with no bark, and in fact her face did begin to look like that of an animal no one could identify, something like a squirrel or a decrepit puppy. Every night it came as a relief to us when Suad fell into a deep, semi-permanent sleep under the influence of the Diazepam my mother administered to her in a single cup of tea whenever she woke up suddenly. Sleeping pills no longer had any effect on her. She would take them while staring into empty space, half insensible, emitting feeble whimpers like a rabbit lost in the desert.

Whenever Rashid resumed his violin practice I would leave our room with a gravity that made Sawsan laugh. She would steal his violin and hide it in her wardrobe among her clothes. She believed in not taking life so seriously, and told me that Rashid's excessively serious nature would turn him into a complicated person who couldn't be trusted to keep a secret. I crossed the living room to slink out and sit in the street, walking on tiptoe to avoid drawing my mother's attention as she sat in her little studio in the corner. She was painting watercolor landscapes which she would bring to a shop in Manshiya in exchange for a few coins that paid for the medicines which kept Suad alive. I would go out with the friends my mother had banned from the house so they wouldn't dirty her cushions. I cursed the suspicious silence of our house and my mother's mania for sterilizing everything—crockery and teacups, corridors and beds and pillows, clothes and shoes—on a quest that would doubtless never end, seeing as everything that came from outside was contaminated.

My mother complained to Nariman, who agreed with her, that walking in the streets had become a terrifying experience. Rough, uncultured countryside smells lingered in the air and corrupted the breeze of their city. She added that most of their colleagues were in the Party and wrote in their reports that we were bourgeois, reactionary, and slightly condescending. Nariman was desperate to emigrate to Canada, and my mother fell silent so as not to encourage her into listing the advantages of flight and fear. They both felt that their destinies were proceeding into the unknown. My mother had felt this when I was born the same week that the coup that brought the Party to power happened. She thought that my birth, even though it did not coincide exactly with the day of the coup, had been severely mistimed and that, like the many military coups in Syria, would soon be forgotten.

She again felt that her life was a collection of mistakes that could never be resolved. She was determined not to give birth to me like one of the peasants from Midan Akbas; when they went into labor, they serenely lay down in the pomegranate fields and gave birth with the aid of their friends, who would cut the umbilical cord with a blunt knife or a stone without interrupting their discussions about the upcoming harvest. She would not allow the village midwife to touch her; superstitious after Suad's birth, she would often repeat that the midwife had caused Suad's disability.

When my mother went into labor she picked up a clean bag embroidered with yellow flowers and went to the state hospital in Aleppo. She sold her gold bracelets and bribed the nurses so they would give her a private room. The nurses tried to meet her wish that the surgical implements be sterilized more than once and the bedsheets changed no less than once every day, but after a few days they became irritated by her demands, despite her lavish bribes. They sympathized with her when they saw my feeble face and the gestures I made to them with my small hands. Meanwhile, the streets of Aleppo were empty following news of the coup. Baath Party officers had seized the General Staff building along with the radio and television stations, and Statement Number One was broadcast.

My mother got up from her bed and looked out the window and saw that the streets were completely empty. She considered the coup and the military's return to power a bad omen for a child born just a few days earlier, his eyes as yellow as dried lemon peel. A few hours after Statement Number One, soldiers burst into the corridors and chaos spread through the hospital—surgical instruments disappeared from the operating rooms, the store cupboards were emptied. My mother got up despite her pain and looked for milk to give me after hers had dried up. She begged for some milk from the nurses who stared at her, amazed that she had stayed and was determined not to leave before being assured that I would live. They whispered about her and giggled with each other as if she were an alien. The following day they asked her to leave and accepted no excuses. They picked up her numerous bags and put all her things in the corridor. They said that an Emergency Law had been announced, and as a precaution against said emergency the new head of the Party wanted the hospital empty in preparation for any casualties.

My mother uttered a few incoherent words and groped for my father's hand. The warmth of his palm slipped into her heart, giving her the courage to declare that it would be preferable to die than live under the rule of moronic peasant officers who couldn't distinguish between the scent of lily-of-the-valley and the smell of pumpkin. My father considered this speech about peasants, which she offered up with unrelenting disdain, to be a grave insult to his family that had supported the coup from its first moment. Over the following nights they did not return to their disagreement over whether there had been a revolution or a military coup. My father recovered the scents of the wife he loved, a dreamy woman with long, soft hair, large, dark eyes, and a white, elongated face that betrayed her upbringing among the city's aristocracy.

"Love at first sight" was how my father described it. He had fallen in love with her the second he spotted her at the annual dinner of the Railway Institute, which had appointed him to the station of Midan Akbas after his graduation from the Institute of Electrical Engineering. The dinner was a special function to honor the first employees of the Institute—my grandfather, Jalal al-Nabulsi, was among the earliest. A companion of Monsieur Henri Sourdain, my grandfather was one of the remaining few who had witnessed the founding of the Syrian railways, and could narrate the heroism of his colleagues who had cleaved the horizon of the mountains of Rajo to cross the German border in the early 1930s.

It was an elegant celebration in which the honored workers strutted around in their official uniforms, their proud families exchanging glances and discreet smiles. My grandfather Jalal al-Nabulsi, who was entering his seventieth year, spoke in a hoarse and affecting voice about his old colleagues, most of whom had passed away, and lavished praise on Monsieur

Henri who had left Paris and fallen in love with Aleppo, settling down in the new district before being executed by the occupying French authorities who accused him of being a German spy. My grandfather's eyes filled with tears more than once as he talked about the plan to excavate the German border in the Rajo mountains. His proud family—my uncles Nizar and Abdel-Monem, my aunt Ibtihal, and my mother, the youngest—applauded eagerly, glorying in the picture taken of my grandfather with Monsieur Henri which hadn't been moved from its place on the cabinet in the living room for fifty years.

My mother rose like a butterfly and took my grandfather's arm to accompany him to the head table. He was greeted by the minister, who proceeded to hang a Railway Institute medal on his breast and award him a bonus and a certificate signed in green ink. The employees who were being honored stood in a line and a commemorative picture was taken of them with the minister, who was all affability, attending to the honored employees and greeting their families. From his place at the table, Zuhayr, infatuated, was gazing at my mother in the manner of a newly appointed rank-and-file railway employee. She turned from the throng of admirers around her, who were each jostling to salute her respectfully, introduce themselves, and tell her their family names. Like a dove soaring skyward, she returned Zuhayr's look with her own gaze of admiration. She was captivated by his bold eyes, his tanned face, his carefully groomed moustache—the classic image, in fact, of an ambitious public official from the sixties, everything about him inspiring confidence.

Ignoring her family, Zuhayr shook her hand and asked where she went to school. She did not stop him from holding onto her hand for a few moments longer than necessary while a strange warmth and power slipped from his hand into her heart. She told him softly that she was a student at the school in Mahabba, and saw him seize the opportunity to wave to her before he left.

Visions of his face haunted her and she sighed. She wasn't expecting to see him the very next day, waiting in front of her school and following her like a teenager. She dawdled coyly with her friends in the alleys of Jamiliya, glancing furtively behind her. She surmised that he was waiting until she was by herself so he could speak to her. Her face flushed. She shuddered from this bliss that she was feeling for the first time in her life, and feared that Nariman, her best friend and neighbor, would realize what was happening and scold her for being yet another schoolgirl hanging around a handsome young man.

He was waiting for her the following day. On the seventh day he was still waiting, and on the eighth day and the days after that, she waited for him and he didn't come. She stopped looking behind her. She hated Nariman. She didn't know where to look for him. She was absent-minded at the dinner table. Emptiness crawled down her spine, chilling her to the bone. She searched the photographs from the dinner and scrutinized all the people surrounding her father but she couldn't see him. She was afraid that his image would be wiped from her memory. When she recalled the warmth of his fingers as he introduced himself to her with such confidence, she loved him.

She fled from Nariman and went to Souk al-Telal by herself where she plunged into the crowds to look for his face, and picked out photographs of singers who resembled him. She stared shamelessly into cafés reserved for men and inspected the faces of the customers staring into space, and endured being approached by men who came out of the café and followed her, thinking she was looking for customers. She looked for him in every likely place, and when it rained she got depressed. She went into Nizar's room and curled up beside him like a housecat, sunk in silence, as he practiced Vivaldi on his violin. When he finished his exercises she told Nizar that she couldn't find him and Nizar nodded sympathetically.

When they heard the door slam and Abdel-Monem's footsteps creak, Nizar picked up his violin and his music and went into the kitchen to finish practicing, leaving the room to Abdel-Monem who called him an "insect," never missing an opportunity to insult his brother.

Nizar and my mother conspired together, and went out in the evenings to walk in the quiet streets around Baghdad Station; they ate ice cream and returned to the house in silence. He left her free to look into the faces of each passer-by in a desperate search for the man she found so difficult to forget. For her sake, Nizar would play melancholy pieces as she sat at the kitchen table, the book in front of her left open on the same page, a hand placed on one cheek like an Egyptian starlet from the fifties.

Nizar possessed fingers made of silk, and a soul which roved far away from the earth-bound worlds whose cruelty he found unbearable. Laughing, he would tell my mother that he was going to live on the moon before throwing himself on the bed beside her and crying silently. No one knew why Nizar wept. He would steal my mother's underwear and dress himself up in front of the mirror, before returning it to its place. She feigned ignorance, rearranged her silken camisoles and nightshirts, and told no one about his craving for women's clothing. The two of them would spend a lot of time together in secret, having unreserved conversations about the worlds of women. Nizar would describe a desire to feel soft silk next to his body as he fingered her lace stockings with a sigh. She would hug him, full of emotion and fear, in the knowledge that his life would be wretched and sad, his manhood wasted. She pleaded with him not to accompany men to shadowy rooms in Bab al-Faraj, and he nodded and continued to search alongside her for any trace of Zuhayr.

Nine months after their first meeting, she saw him on the Jamiliya tram. She hurtled after it, ignoring the passengers' quizzical glances at this man who was reaching out of the carriage to a woman following close behind. He got off at the next stop and hurried toward her, and they met in the middle of the road in front of Farouq School. Terrified of losing him again, her body was trembling and her heart thudding, but when she looked at him her diffidence returned. In a nearby café they sat facing one another and she didn't answer when he asked if she had searched for him. He looked into her face for a long while and told her regretfully that he was engaged to his cousin in Anabiya, but my mother was the one he loved. In fact, her image had never left him. He drew from his wallet a photograph of her which had been taken secretly, in exchange for a considerable sum. She looked at her picture for a while, and felt a suffocating tightness. Her voice weakened and she asked him faintly if they could leave. They went out into the fresh air and walked through the park, and on a solitary bench he kissed her. Her whole being was transformed at that moment into a blaze that wouldn't go out. She thought about confessing how she had searched for him everywhere and had wept over him on Nizar's shoulder. She rose like a silent mummy, left him alone, and walked quickly away. The only thing she told him was that she was now studying at the Teacher Training Institute, making sure she had given him a way to find her. She thought of the revelations of love, his fleeting kiss, his scent which she inhaled quietly after going without protest to a house he borrowed from a friend especially for their trysts. Gently, he opened the buttons of her short blue dress, drowning in the splendor of her white skin, and carried her to the bed naked but for her underwear. She told him she didn't want to lose her virginity, and he kissed her unhurriedly, as if he had all the time in the world. He kissed her swelling breasts and brushed the nipples that were like cherrystones, her stomach, her toes. When she bent down to gather up her clothes, the evening shadows dressed her face with the colors of a certainty she couldn't lose. He told her in a whisper that he couldn't live without her.

Everything was concluded quietly. My aunt Ibtihal was a jealous custodian of the stately way of life she imagined the family to have enjoyed during the Ottoman Empire, and she was furious that my mother had accepted the proposal of a peasant whose family still shared a room with their livestock. Nariman couldn't believe that her best friend would live in a rundown, spider-infested house in Midan Akbas, the middle of nowhere, among Kurds and insignificant officials flung onto the Turkish border. Only Abdel-Monem was eager to get rid of her, especially after their recent battles over Nizar, who missed her. He wrote her long letters as if she were lying next to him and he was telling her how he had searched the shops of Aziziya for creams that would soften his skin, or a new perfume he liked. He was eloquent in expressing the pain that never left him, but when he reached the part about a friend who had invited him into his bed last winter, he stopped writing and crossed out the words. Instead he resumed his perpetual complaints about Abdel-Monem's insults, such as the time he described Nizar openly as a faggot who would pollute the family's honor, and tried to incite my grandfather to either kill him or throw him out.

Nizar did not send the letters he wrote. He collected them in a box and on one of my mother's visits he gave her a bundle wrapped in colored paper. She placed it in her handbag and read the letters slowly after my father left for work, and reread them, and reflected on her lot, how she had been thrown into the open country where the howling dogs reminded her of the death of her old dreams. She tried to convince my father to return to Aleppo and he reminded her that she had accepted his only condition, which was to live with him in Midan Akbas, close to his family in Anabiya. She fell silent and wandered over to the window, resuming her sewing in preparation for Suad, who would soon be born.

My mother had wanted to have her children in a clean hospital, with sheets smelling of disinfectant and nun-like nurses who walked on tiptoe and murmured in French. When she passed the Hospital Saint-Louis, she looked at the garden outside shaded by tall cacti and red, white, and violet roses, and contemplated its skillfully carved stone façade. It seemed a reassuring and awe-inspiring place. She grieved over the destiny which had led her to desolate Midan Akbas, to her cruel in-laws who blamed her for the division caused in the family ranks after Zuhayr told them that he would not marry his cousin, and flung the wedding rings in the face of his older brother in utter disregard of all warnings about this rash decision. My mother paid the price of a battle she had had no hand in. She was named the Stranger and every member of the family shunned her. We didn't see our uncles and we cared nothing for them after my father fled to America.

By the second year of their marriage, my father no longer clung to my mother at all times, he no longer courted her, and she was lonely. She would come home after teaching at the school and sit on the ground in front of her house like a village girl, and there she would meditate on the humans and the animals of the village, the children left to run naked and barefoot in the impoverished streets. She wondered how it was possible to scrape out an existence in a place she hated so much; she reflected on the reckless love which had led her to agree to my father's conditions. On her short visits to her family, she sensed Ibtihal's gratification when she ordered my mother to go the bathroom immediately, as if she had mange. She drew attention to my mother's roughened hands, mocked her clothes, which were pronounced to be those of a peasant, and spoke with disgust of her children's phlegm. My mother bore Ibtihal's scorn in silence and plunged instead into endless conversations with Nizar.

In later years she lost her desire to return to her family's house; she had stopped missing it, and no one noticed her absence apart from Nizar. She felt stifled there. Nizar told her in his letters that their father still woke up every morning, put on his striped suit, went to the train station, and sat on the platform to wait for old friends who no longer existed. He would point out every time the workers violated a regulation, reminding them of the medal hung on his chest. His comments irritated every single worker and they did not grieve when he fell beneath the wheels of a slow freight train.

Nizar sent her the news by an express telegram, that arrived two days after his burial, and she came with her four children, by freight train no less. She wept on the way as she looked back over her life unspooling chaotically over the tracks like a film reel which had been knocked over; the previous few years seemed more like a dream than real life. The imbecile Suad was in her lap, Sawsan and Rashid and I were sunk in a large wooden seat my father's colleagues had arranged for us. I felt the time to be long and the train slow; a smell of buffaloes and chemically treated animal skins wafted through the carriage and made me feel sick. We reached the house at nightfall, and everything was ordinary, banal even; only the addition of a black ribbon to my grandfather's picture made his death a reality, as if nothing had happened.

My mother sobbed and mumbled some disjointed phrases but no one approached to comfort her, apart from tender-hearted Nizar, who wept with her. He told her grimly that they would divide up the inheritance three days later. Nizar asked her not to relinquish her share to Abdel-Monem, who even before the forty-day mourning period was over expressed a wish to buy the house and divide up its contents. He produced a piece of paper, signed by their father, which deprived his daughters of any inheritance and left the house categorically to his sons Nizar and Abdel-Monem. My mother didn't care. She left everything behind her and we all went back to Midan Akbas where she received some belated words of condolence from my father.

*

Toward the end of our time in Midan Akbas, boredom had crept into my mother's life. She walked slowly, like a sick ghost. She had no wish to respond to the questions of her neighbors, mainly provincial housewives who loved her composure and her cleanliness. They tried to intrude on her world, but she had lost all desire to chat. She waited for her husband, ensnared in his depression whose source she no longer cared to know. He would come back from the train station, grumbling and criticizing everything he used to take pleasure in: her cooking, the intimate scents of her body, her elegant clothes which did not smell of onions or cooking oil. He would go out to play cards with his friends and often slept at their houses. On his days off, he would accompany Elena on trips to the River Afrin where they would catch fish and take pictures of each other crossing the pomegranate fields or olive groves, laughing.

My mother understood that she would end her life alone when she saw my father in the nearby pomegranate field, holding Elena's hand and kissing her neck while she gazed back at him in adoration. It took no more than three months for her premonition to come true.

I remember my father's worried face before he left, the last image I had of a father who soon after ceased to exist. He would get up from his bed in the middle of the night and go to the courtyard to smoke and think about how Elena was his only chance of changing his life. He felt that his life had ground to a halt the very moment he became a public official who had to proffer up eternal adoration to the Party and the President-Leader, for the sole purpose of upholding this state of misery.

My mother did not discuss his decision. She didn't follow him to the train station to plead with him not to go, as another woman, a weak woman, might have done. She read the few lines which he had placed next to her pillow before he left at dawn to catch the five o'clock train to Aleppo. He had already said goodbye to his friends. He went to the Land Registry where he ceded ownership of the small piece of land to my mother as the balance of her dowry, and in the afternoon he joined Elena at the Baron Hotel. That evening they had dinner at Restaurant Akob in Bustan Kul Ab Street, and three days after that they boarded a bus to Damascus and never returned.

Since there was no longer anything linking her to Midan Akbas, my mother begged my uncle Abdel-Monem to allow us to live in the cellar of the old family home for a few months while she finished building her house in Aleppo.

Her heart shattered, my mother rebuilt her world. Deep down she was relieved at her husband's decision and her face in the train, as we traveled back to Aleppo, shone with hope; as I looked at her I felt that everything would be all right. Gleefully, Sawsan stuck her head out of the window and her black hair streamed in the wind as she opened her hand wide to try and reach the road, or even the tiny villages of Afrin that she would return to one day with a Soviet Zenit camera and a foolish Armenian photographer who tried to teach her the basic principles of photography. Like every other man, he had been consumed with lust for Sawsan; she flirted and pretended to play along before laughing and abandoning him to his frustrated desire.

Sawsan's frivolity delivered the new house from its tedium. At that time my mother didn't believe that shadows covered her dreams. She was standing tall once more and went to her teaching job full of enthusiasm, her notebook bound with colored cardboard, her clothing trim, her hair gleaming. Her students never forgot this dreamy, romantic woman, who often guided them to topics that fascinated them: Vivaldi and Mozart, Mireille Mathieu, pictures of Paris in the sixties which she had once imagined to be the only appropriate stage for her life, before she met my father at that ill-fated party.

She thought about different destinies and in her all-engulfing fervor for life she determined that she was divorced, not abandoned; not left behind on the station platform to wait for trains that might not come for days while the workers yawned and passed the interminable time by playing cards and cursing long-vanished passengers. She was the mother of four children: Suad, the oldest, a girl mad from birth who awaited a death that wouldn't come, her body weak and her neck like a plucked chicken's; me next, my ill-omened birth having launched me into a life that ran parallel to the Party and all its doings; then Sawsan, who regarded my mother with perpetual scorn; and fourth was Rashid, whose life was spent contemplating the hardship of living it.

Suad drew me to her and bewitched me with her delicate smile. I would say to Sawsan that she wanted to die and my mother would have been sadder if it had been one of us in Suad's place. She thought of Suad as her shame which would condemn all her dreams for a family who sat quietly at a dinner table covered with a colorful tablecloth, with napkins that everyone would fasten around their necks before beginning to eat so mutely that Sawsan would compare it to the silence of the grave and drop her bowl, spoiling the sole carpet, which my mother had paid for in installments. Everyone knew to walk on tiptoe while the Vienna Philharmonic was playing throughout the house. Year by year it gradually became as gloomy as a tomb, as Comrade Fawaz boarded up every window which overlooked his house. He left us one small opening high up on the wall into which crept a smell of excrement and the noises of the livestock Comrade Fawaz raised in his house. Everything in the house gave the impression of an upper-class family gone bankrupt.

My mother reveled in the sympathy she received for the story she related so calmly, including distant memories of her father the important railway official and his friend Monsieur Henri Sourdain. She hid Suad from her colleagues at the school, who each took turns at hosting. They came to our house at fixed times and my mother never forgave any latecomer, resenting their fatuous excuses as bitterly as any Englishwoman.

She would gather us all together before her guests arrived, to dress us in our best clothes and perfume us. She taught us to smile politely and greet guests with a haughty reserve, and made us memorize a few phrases of welcome in French. She singled out Rashid for special attention; he would carry his violin to the living room reserved for guests where she would order him to play something classical, to the astonishment of her colleagues. They would applaud him in a genteel manner and Rashid would bow gravely and depart, a professional musician imparting new life to his audience, to relieve Sawsan of her guard duty of Suad. Sawsan hated my mother's guests. She would tell them about Suad and wouldn't hide her irritation at the cheap cologne and affected smiles and, worst of all, the praise for her hair ribbon. She would point to it saying, "Is this what you mean?" and when they nodded she would tear it off and drop it disdainfully in their English-style teacup. My mother would break out into elaborate explanations of these cups and speak about their origins as if she had been born there herself, and a wrong turn had brought her to this place whose backwardness she couldn't deplore enough. The next day, she couldn't rest until Nariman had told her what her guests had thought, and added how delicious the cake had been, how wonderful the tea, and how well-mannered and clean the children.

In Suad's final days my mother forgot her completely, like a puppy left alone all night in a small, cold room. Sawsan spent as much time as she could with her and tried to alleviate her suffering by stroking her and hugging her. She would tell Suad fairytales about an evil father and an indifferent mother whom the Snow Queen turned into stone. Co-conspirators, Sawsan and I would steal an apple or some grapes for Suad, or we would bring her Rashid's wooden train and whistle like steam engines. She would smile and move the train with her hand, making it fly as she had told us the train drivers did.

Sawsan stayed beside Suad on her last night. She never forgot the moment her body grew cold. Suad rested against the wall and leaned toward Sawsan's lap, her body quivered for the final time, a string of foam left her mouth, and she died so quietly that Sawsan couldn't believe it, any more than she could believe my mother's neutral reaction, as if nothing had happened. My mother returned from the cemetery and burned everything that was left of Suad—her medicines, her few clothes, her sheets, and a quilt that smelled of urine. It wasn't long before Sawsan spat on my mother, and told her that shame would follow her forever.

My mother numbly wiped Sawsan's spit away and was silent. Years later we discovered that none of us had forgotten the image of my mother wandering through her little kingdom, seeking sympathy with her perpetual complaints about a lack of oxygen. Time never erased the image of Sawsan spitting on her, aware for the first time of the feelings of shame which surrounded her on every side. She was pleased when she discovered that many people like her felt shame: her colleagues and friends, even people in the streets who ignored the pictures of the President despite the claims of his immortality.

As the years passed, Rashid grew increasingly silent. He put cotton plugs in his ears and asked where all the noise came from. He continued his lessons with Uncle Nizar, was able to gather six musicians and form a group that played in cultural centers to audiences whose members who were all known to Nizar. At night the same group performed in Cabaret Casbah, playing raucous backup for vulgar singers who serenaded drunks. Rashid saw none of the audience, and was delighted to find he could lose his vision as well as his hearing.

He imagined himself blind and deaf and added, "I may as well be mute like everyone else." He would collect his pay without enthusiasm, wave goodbye to Nizar, and walk back to a house he could no longer bear to live in. Night was the only time he could see the city as he loved it: abandoned and silent, too dark to see the signs of eternal adoration for the Party and the President. He tried to erase his memories and remembered he had no hope for the future; he could feel distress crouching on his soul. He didn't know what certainty he was looking for.

He would quietly slip into the house at dawn and open the door of the room where irrepressible Sawsan lay on her bed, half-naked. He wished he could wake her and confess that he loved her to the point of madness, but he would shut the door and continue to the room he shared with me, closing the thick curtains quietly so as not to wake me. He would put the plugs into his ears, reflecting that everything was too trivial to merit discussion, and would beg for the sleep which eluded him. Full of remorse, he would keep poring over the same questions—what was the meaning of his life in this place which oozed misery?

Daylight would flood the living room and wake my mother, who embarked on her daily rounds. Rashid would shut his eyes; he didn't want to hear her voice, having fallen asleep after exhausting, exquisite torments. He could feel his body festering from the way he kept tossing and turning. He thought that his life had been a lie; he hated himself when he remembered the admiration of his mother's friends when he played, how they would throw sweets for him to catch like a pampered dog. He revealed to me later that he never liked those moments of performance, nor the music—he would just play simple beginner exercises. "The smart ones manufacture ignorance and convince the ignorant ones of it, all to keep up appearances," he once said. He thought about the herd which destroyed everything—marches, celebrations, weddings. Even their musical harmonies were an unacceptable form of idiocy for him. He told me that the herd was the most successful invention to ensure that all ideas, philosophies, religions, candid art, would pass away into nothing.

When I saw him fast asleep, I could read in his closed eyes a wish to never wake up. He savored the image of his death. I envied his amazing ability to pass alongside the details of life without awareness or impression; he lived another life, in which he explored feelings and sensations to their utmost limits, sated with joy without having ever truly experienced it. His eyes shone with pleasure for a few moments whenever he improvised a duet with Nizar, both players harmonizing, diverging, conflicting, and then returning to sing together like two pipes with one reed.

He complained to irrepressible Sawsan about his loneliness, his fear of the light, and his wish to die, and Sawsan listened to his anxieties gravely. She smoothed his hair with her soft fingers, lit a cigarette, and suggested that he move to Canada, adding a list of places she would like to travel to, before saying desperately, "I would go anywhere." She couldn't bear to hear any more from Comrade Fawaz's relatives as they sang the praises of the Party and the Leader all night long. She couldn't bear to see the newsreaders on state television reading out the weather report as if they were announcing the outbreak of war, or announcing news of the President so solemnly that it put her in mind of committing some stealthy acts of violence— to be aimed first and foremost at the crowds that were stirred up into frenzy whenever they saw an honor guard marching, according to strict protocol, in front of the President's guests. Rashid agreed that it was like being in a vault where the mold first marked a beautiful painting, and then spread until rot saturated even the air, sullying the vocal cords and constricting the throat. He pondered that it would be a long time until the hoarse throats regained their ability to scream.

Twenty years after the never-forgotten day Sawsan spat on her, my mother was convinced that she still thought shame meant something else. She would wander through the house all day, a melancholy butterfly concealing her repeated failures. The walls were cracked and stained with moisture, the paint was peeling, and every object in the house had lost all trace of its first, more beautiful, appearance. Our house was surrounded by many others, and the alley which she had dreamed of as a haven from the city's clamor had become the haunt of impoverished, low-ranking soldiers and fellaheen escaping from the nearby villages. Its exposed drains smelled of sewage and women sat on every doorstep, cutting up rotten tomato skins to make juice and speaking eagerly, even hopefully, about their lives to come. The place was no longer surrounded with lettuce fields and cherry trees, and the smells of spring conveyed nothing to my mother any more. After the last window was closed up and the house was transformed into a tomb, nothing remained from its past apart from an old record that still played classical music no one heard.

Sawsan left in anger and was gone for days; when she came back she didn't offer any reason for her absence. She unpacked her suitcase on her bed which had started to squeak whenever she turned over (she told me that its springs were rusted) and I waited for a fearless narration of her new adventures. She came into our room and sat next to Rashid, leafed through my English textbook, then threw it to one side and lit up a Marlboro. She woke up Rashid and we drank coffee together in silence. We begged for her usual cheerfulness to save us from the chronic depression all around.

My mother gently pleaded with her to go back to university and finish her studies in French, but Sawsan shook her head and cursed the professors who tossed scraps of paper at her with their home addresses written on them. They would wait for her in their bedrooms where they would bring out her exam papers and put on it whatever mark she wanted, then she would remove her clothes and lie down without enthusiasm and they would rut on top of her until she was sick to her stomach. As the rest of the night slipped by, she would walk drunk through the streets and knock at the door of Salma, her only friend. Without a word, she would enter and close the door behind her. Salma would start to chatter about new clients, Sawsan would bathe, and then she would fall asleep on the sofa in the living room of Salma's small house.

Old pictures would surface: a cheerful student provoking gales of laughter from all around her, an affectionate friend, a good student praised by her teachers. When she was sixteen she fell passionately in love with her French teacher, Jean Abdel-Mesih, and wrote him love letters describing how desolate she felt when she was apart from him. Because of him, she loved the French language and went on to study at the Faculty of Literature. She couldn't bear being ignored and decided to go to his house; when he opened the door he showed no surprise at finding her there. He led her to the living room where she saw he was immersed in a new translation of Balzac, next to moldy cups of cold tea. No one had cleaned this house, sunk in a weird calm, for some time. Her letters, composed with such care and tied up in blue string, were on the table. She drank her coffee and spotted his mother lying on a wooden bed. The story which circulated among the students seemed to be true: he had returned to Aleppo from Geneva in expectation of the imminent death of his mother, who had been left alone after his sister Emilie married and moved to Canada.

Emilie hadn't been able to endure living alone with her mother any more. She wrote to her brothers, George who lived in America and Jean in Switzerland, that at thirty years old, she wanted to marry Boulos Hallaq and migrate to Canada. She closed her letter by writing that she would let their mother starve to death if they didn't reply.

It was a muffled scream that Jean had been expecting for some time. Quietly, he brought a few odds and ends from his house in Switzerland, resigned from his job as an interpreter at the United Nations, and limped to the house of his ex-wife Colette. He took some pictures with his son Pierre and took him out for the whole day; they went to the beach and ate ice cream.

No one came to say goodbye to him, and for the first time he realized that although he had lived in this city for fifteen years, no one was sad that he was leaving. He returned to Aleppo and waited for his mother to die. Madame Mary Abdel-Nour, the celebrated mathematics teacher, had started to have small seizures accompanied by the gradual onset of blindness. Every morning she would ask Jean when the parliamentary elections would be, so she could put on her smart black dress and give her vote to her favorite candidate, Monsieur Gabriel al-Shami. She would continue to hallucinate for a little while, and then as she resumed her silence, she would remember that it wasn't right for woman like her to chatter on so.

Sawsan asked him, "How do you like living with corpses?" Gently, he replied that he was happy he didn't have to leave the house. Sawsan picked up her letters and left. Quickly, she walked down the stairs and through Suleimaniya. She was determined never to go back. She couldn't understand how Jean could live in such a way, nor could she forget the face of his half-blind mother as she waited to die. She didn't know how a man could live in a house veiled with curtains and smelling of basterma, spices, and the incense sticks that perfumed the huge living room, in which the only thing one could see was Jean's desk illuminated by an old lamp.

Yet his silence and gentle smile captivated her. He was wary of clashing with Party members who tried to incite him on several occasions. There was no official Party branch of French teachers after most of the well-regarded professors had emigrated and the rest were dismissed on the grounds that they were "lacking devotion" during the purge of the schools and universities. They pretended not to notice him and he was soon forgotten among the hordes of pro-Party professors, some of whom boasted of tucking Russian Makarov pistols, which had been given to them to defend the regime during the Events of the eighties, into their shirts before going to class. They shouted their adoration all day long; they mastered diverse methods of outstripping and undermining one another, and claiming close personal relationships with officers from the security apparatuses. Jean felt like an alien. He could not believe this had become his day-to-day life. Emilie had written letters describing what was happening on the streets and inside the houses of his beloved city, which he had only returned to once in fifteen years. Emilie had related what her days were like and arrived, in her broad script, at the conclusion that she was living inside a cage, and she did not want to remain there a moment longer.

Sawsan's ardor turned into a deep compassion for Jean. She forgot her vow never to visit him again and without any aim in mind she brought him some hot okra that my mother had made—it was a recipe she had perfected, since it was our favorite dish. Sawsan helped Jean disinfect his mother's body and place her dirty things into an old washtub. They leafed for hours through family photo albums and Jean would tell the story behind every picture in his soft voice. He pointed out his father, Eisa Abdel-Mesih, a philosophy teacher who used to write speeches for Monsieur Gabriel al-Shami, translated Nietzsche into Arabic in the fifties, and was a dear friend of Khaireddin al-Asadi, the famous writer and historian of Aleppo. In all his pictures, Eisa Abdel-Mesih stood upright in an elegant suit with gleaming hair, and his wife (who had been lying on a white wooden bed for five years while she waited to die) stood beside him. In one picture, she held a gleaming leather handbag, a fox fur was draped over her shoulders, and she wore an open-necked black dress which showed off her large, firm breasts. In another, Jean's father and his friends, all writers from Aleppo, were gathered around Khaireddin al-Asadi in al-Qasr coffee house. This was the same coffee house Eisa Abdel-Mesih would visit every Friday morning without fail to meet his friend, the famous painter Louay Kayali. Afterward he would return on foot, taking the long way back via Baron Street so he could pause for a few moments in front of the Cinema Ramses to make a note of the new films. He would book two tickets to a showing at six and would conclude his walk to Suleimaniya through Bab al-Faraj and al-Telal Street where he would buy hot pistachios from the Sudanese seller who for forty years had relinquished neither his spot in Old Manshiya, nor his habitual silence.

For years he ate his dinner with Mary and his daughter Emilie, who would be waiting for her fiancé, Boulos Hallaq, to take her to one of the coffee shops. After Boulos migrated to Canada, he gave her a choice between joining him and breaking their engagement. He wrote her a long letter, telling her that cities die just like people. He couldn't bear the smell of the ghetto that he was supposed to have no other choice but to live in, without hope of the siege upon it ever being lifted. He added that he was not stupid enough to bring a child into the streets of this filthy city, which had been transformed into a place of murder. He was eloquent in describing his fear which grew heavier by the day: his fear of the paratroopers, of the sheikhs, of the priests and the curates who noted his absence from church. She couldn't stop him from leaving. She felt his estrangement in his final days, the frightened glances when they were sitting together, his fear whenever he saw a paratrooper walk past, his terror of the murky future which forced him to prove his devotion to the Party, and the President, and the secret police—the mukhabarat—every single day.

Eisa Abdel-Mesih would take a mid-afternoon nap, and when he woke in the early evening he would take his wife's arm in his so that they could traverse the same familiar streets together. They would watch the film showing at Cinema Ramses that he had bought tickets for earlier in the day, and afterward go to the Strand for dinner and a glass of wine, before going home to be joined at a certain time by many of their friends. When the Cinema Ramses disappeared, having been a typical family outing of the ambitious middle classes, these friends all agreed it was a bad joke. Those who were still alive in the eighties made do with sitting on a park bench and watching the ducks, in utter disbelief at what had happened to their beloved city, where they lived out the remnants of a beautiful era. Mary didn't want to see the city's present; she was determined to cling to its old image, when she used to prepare fried sausage and stuffed eggplant cooked with olive oil in the Turkish style for her friend Khaireddin al-Asadi, and listen for hours as he told her about his discoveries of the city's history.

According to Jean, the photographs formed an old world that had ceased to exist long ago. He hadn't wanted to see Aleppo again; he felt completely cut off from it. He couldn't bear the filthy streets and the Party parades he had to join so regularly, walking with a bowed head as if in submission. He moved his lips slowly when the crowds around him called out in loud voices; he felt that he would have a heart attack before reaching the end of the parade. Returning home covered in dust, he replayed the sight of his respectable colleagues holding the shoulders of the person in front of them and stamping rhythmically in time with the songs blaring from the speakers, and he felt ashamed. Exhausted, he would wash and make some strong coffee.

He went to bed much later than he had in Switzerland, and the first time he did so he felt a sense of chaos. He complained of this mixing of two contradictory worlds to some childhood friends who welcomed him on his return. They invited him to expensive restaurants and made fun of his sensitivity, and after a short time he recoiled from meeting them and their relationships were severed. He made do with the few personal connections he was obliged to maintain. He kept up these obligations with the fewest possible words, and relinquished conversations about his time in Switzerland and the genius of his son Pierre. He felt that he was entering a cocoon which would make him vulnerable.

He found nothing better to do than translate Balzac. He didn't need a publisher to offer him a risible amount to translate the previously untranslated works from French; he wanted to escape into an act of undemanding routine. He thought the existing translations of Balzac were trivial and commercial, and devoted himself to these wonderful novels as a silent protest against the desolation he described in page after page of letters sent to his ex-wife, not expecting an answer. Despite having written in French, he was still afraid and expected to be called up for questioning. He was only reassured when Colette's answer arrived by telegram, telling him serenely that his letter had arrived unopened. His only instruction if he died suddenly was to give these letters to Pierre when he reached eighteen.

He wrote long letters to Pierre, in burning, anguished words, describing with great yearning how his city used to be. He described his old, magnificent school, just like a French school with its high ceilings and gardens, its playing fields and the elegance of its acclaimed professors. Before he described the scene of his fellow teachers stamping in rhythm during the compulsory Party parades, he spoke eloquently and at length of his personal shame, because he was a witness to this moment which everyone would pretend to forget, if they were to be able to meet each other's eyes in fifty years' time.

He felt that everything was futile, thought about suicide more than once, and reread Sartre to calm his anxiety. He welcomed visits from Sawsan, who had become his friend, and although he would steal glances at her beautiful breasts, he didn't dare confess that it was her he conjured at night when he practiced his secret habit. He waited, every afternoon, for her to come with the food and pickles she had made especially for him. She would kiss his mother who, every now and then, had begun to relate the story of her marriage to Eisa Abdel-Mesih and stories from the fifties. She would wink at Sawsan as she was led by the hand, noting sardonically that despite years of illness she was still forcing her way through the odds and ends of the living room. After a silence, she would sigh that perhaps she had chosen her blindness at the right moment, so as not to see the shame that was enveloping her son. Another pause, and she added that Eisa Abdel-Mesih had chosen to die so he wouldn't see the military gagging the country's voice with their Emergency Law and exceptional courts, or changing the constitution, or impounding all powers through Article Eight, which stated explicitly that the Baath Party was the leading party of the state and society.

As they continued preparing coffee, Sawsan told her cheerfully that everything outside was fine and everything she had heard must be a lie, since it made no sense that women had acid thrown on their thighs because they were wearing short skirts; or that goatherds-cum-brigadier-generals had bought the soap factory in the middle of Jamiliya and all the shops around it in order to sell the Chinese products they imported themselves; or that army officers' sons had started snatching girls from the old families of Aleppo off the street and taking them to their own land in order to rape them. Sawsan reassured her in a tone which Mary believed automatically. Cheerfully, even passionately, she related her memories of the coffee houses in the sixties, with a passing reference to the fact that one of Aleppo's leading writers had been in love with her and written her an epic, surrealist poem. She described him as a genius whose own city hadn't given him the acclaim he deserved, and had thrown his books aside. Mary chattered without stopping as if confirming that she was still able to speak.

Jean believed that his mother deserved this time. He knew, as he observed how she spoke, that she would not die soon. He would sit by the window, its thick curtains closed so that no light could get through, and Sawsan would bring the coffee pot. She would look deeply into his eyes and, flustered, he would avoid her gaze and start talking about his translations, whereupon she would yawn with boredom and they would fall silent. Everything went back to how it was before: a half-blind woman in her seventies colliding with old furniture, afflicted with depression no one could save her from. She begged for a death which didn't come, and had to make do with the smells of the walls of her decrepit house, combining and mixing them with her memories, seeking out the lost smell of henna. She inhaled a lungful of air and asked Jean if spring was coming. Once every year she would ask him this question, heedless of the passage of the days and weeks and months, repeating lines from Orhan Misar's surrealist poem. She still had drafts of this poem written in his own hand, and she would take out the pages sometimes, running her fingers over the ink and reading the lines with a smile.

Jean would place food in front of her, and they would eat together in apprehensive silence, arising from the idea that both were thinking about her death, which they were. She was full of regret that she had ruined her children's lives. She asked her son quite seriously to put her in a nearby home for the elderly and to return to Geneva to resume his life there. Jean said quietly that he wanted to live in Aleppo even if it broke his body apart; he wanted to bear his portion of shame, and he explained quite truthfully that Geneva had offered him no opportunity to contemplate life—it was entirely dull, like living in a garden where everything was made out of plastic. Mary believed him. His kind eyes offered no foothold for Sawsan's suspicion that Jean was living out a kind of final encounter with the soul of the place before he died.

Sawsan would depart a little after sunset, leaving him alone with her scent. In all his life he had never smelled a scent like hers; she conquered him without a word. She treated him like an invalid, and he accepted both her affection and her rebuke. In class he would avoid meeting her eyes, afraid that he would lose the power of speech if he did so. Many of the girls in his class slipped letters into the pocket of his jacket hanging on the classroom door, but he was indifferent to them all. Only

Sawsan besieged him with the harmonious lines of her body. He would creep into bed and close his eyes, imagining that she was sitting next to him and taking off the shirt whose top button was always left undone. He would sink into her firm breasts and caress her nipples. He went even further when she threw aside her tight jeans and was completely naked. Images of her overlapped with those of the girls he had known in Geneva, and he performed obscenities no one saw.

He thought of how lonely and afraid he was, and it grew worse when Sawsan stopped writing him letters filled with lyrical descriptions of his eyes like the dreaming moon, and lyrics quoted from Nagat al-Saghira, Fairuz, and others. Once, he gathered his courage and read her an ode by Paul Éluard that he had translated especially for her. Sawsan understood that his inner animal had awoken at last and she was saddened by what she had done to her beloved professor. On that beautiful summer day, she kissed his cheek very gently, left, and decided not to go back.

She told me how he stumbled over the sweet words, and how his cheeks were suffused with a faint blush as he stuttered out the poem first in French and then in Arabic. He lowered his gaze when she looked at him with the insolence she reserved for those times when she wanted to scrape the marrow from the bones of someone she intended to punish; in this case, for having overlooked her in the past. She repeated sadly that when something came too late, you had to forget it once and for all.

That summer everything erupted in Sawsan: her body, her soul, her passion, her madness . . . she was a new woman, and trampled our impotence. She demanded that we climb out from death's burrow and go again into the lettuce fields. She shook Rashid bodily and urged him to play till he fell down dead; she kicked me, joking that I should tear down the wall of Comrade Fawaz's stable that blocked our view of the passing trains. Sawsan became the train which Suad used to point to in glee, but she was coming off the rails which were no longer parallel and would wreck whole cities. Coarsely she demanded that my mother stop whining and start looking after her soul and smearing herself with intoxicating creams that would reignite her craving to live. Every day, Rashid expected her to make sense of his life.

Jean waited for her for a few days. When she didn't come he felt he was strong enough to expel her from his life, but her shadow wouldn't let him sleep. He recalled her smell, the force of the temptation in her body which had awoken his own and then moved on. He thought of writing to her to beg her to come back, to confess that this was the first time he had felt such power gushing through his veins, but he changed his mind and resolved to be rid of her forever. His sudden tension affected his mother, who remained silent. She knew deep down that this girl with a voice so husky it was almost masculine, eroticism concealed within its every tone, had destroyed the silence they had lived in for years. She too waited for Sawsan, so she could lean on her arm and water her plants. Gently, she would feel each one, and knew from their rough texture and the cracking sound of their brittle leaves that they would never be green again. She wished to be plunged further into darkness. She turned back to the permanent smell of mothballs inside the long-closed wardrobes and the worn-out wooden furniture, the smell which guided Mary Abdel-Nour to that archive of memories which kept her alive. She reflected that when the past was the sole reason for living—despite the persistence of memories which passed so quickly and were repeated so often that they were reduced to nothing more than distant, faded images—it was worthless. But Mary would narrate her past again, quietly, in revenge for a present whose outrages she was determined not to see.

She sat at the dining table this time, determined to die. She demanded that Jean bring her poison and add it to the stuffed cabbage prepared by the maid he had finally agreed to hire. Unable to endure this prison, he thought for the first time of leaving the house and walking in the alleys and streets of the city to look for Sawsan. He made it clear to his mother that he wanted to remain here and asked her not to think of his destiny; it had changed, and his past no longer meant what it had.

For the first time at work he refused to repeat the Party songs in the morning meeting. He stood silently, observed by his colleagues, who were perplexed at his transformation. He looked steadily at the national flag, recalling cherished memories of his time at al-Mamoun School when he used to raise the flag and the pupils would salute it enthusiastically while singing the national anthem. There was not much delay before the reports were submitted which described Jean as an agent and a traitor, adding that he had cursed the Party and the Beloved President and had described the teachers and their dabka dance as "barbaric." They left him no time to bid his students goodbye. He picked up his bag and walked out of the school within minutes of being informed of his expulsion from the teaching profession. He spat on the door of the Teacher's Lounge, and didn't care what happened.

He went home and told his mother that he would sit with her night and day and read to her from *The Thousand and One Nights*. His mother was enthusiastic about the idea and sat in her favorite seat on the first night to hear the story of that other first night, but soon she stood up, bored. He was surprised when she asked him about Sawsan; he stammered that she had travelled to Dubai with a man who would marry her, and then both were silent.

Waiting for the investigation wasn't easy but it wasn't long before a sergeant from the military secret police knocked at his door and took him to an office branch in Seryan in an old car, where they sat him in a cold corridor and asked him to wait. He thought of using his Swiss nationality, and although his heart thudded, he wasn't afraid. The entire day was spent waiting for the interrogation, and just before midnight the same sergeant told him that he had to come back at eight the following morning. He was famished as he left the branch, and for the first time, over a huge plate of grilled meat in the square of Bab al-Faraj, he watched a life he hadn't known existed in the backstreets of Aleppo, which at the end of the night were filled with drunks, addicts, and nomads looking for whores like hungry wasps.

Jean spent seven days in the corridor of the Military Security branch, and he realized that all the things Emilie had told him about life in Aleppo were merely stories made up by a spinster lacking in imagination. She knew nothing about the political prisoners dangling from hooks like lambs in a slaughterhouse. She knew nothing about the fear of a man who pretended to be brave, and who didn't want to open the local papers and praise the editorials composed for the Party and the President. After he was sat down on an army bed, he understood that he had not been arrested or tortured because his uncle, who sold furnishings, had secretly intervened and offered three bedrooms' worth of walnut furniture to the branch commander and his officers. By a happy coincidence, they all also considered the reports about him to be fabricated. Jean signed a piece of paper to the effect that he believed completely in the wisdom of the Leader, and particularly admired his latest speech, of which he had memorized whole paragraphs. The final sentences, in phrases of great refinement, stated that it was impossible for anyone to dispute this.

He signed many pieces of paper naming his aunts and uncles on both sides, their husbands and wives, and all his relatives—a complete genealogy of a Christian family. It had been invented on the spot by a broker who carried out various trades and activities on behalf of the branch commander and his infinite sons, from the sale of visits to and news of detainees, to the confiscation of state property and its subsequent sale for building plots; this was what Comrade Fawaz had done with the land next to our house, which had originally been designated as a public park. When asked about his wife's relatives, Jean invented a veritable fairytale in order to close the file and be allowed to go home after seven days, following an improvised lecture from the branch commander about The Homeland and Directives for Respectable Citizens. Jean nodded in agreement with everything he said, and he described that moment, when he left the depressing building, as the peak of the shame which had kept him in this antiquated city. Aleppo seemed to resemble himself in its capitulation to shame, made manifest in the posters and slogans and symbols hung on its walls, and the statues of the Leader-President dispersed throughout its public squares.

He contacted his bank in Switzerland and calculated that without working he could live for five years on sixteen thousand American dollars. He was to inherit the grand old house after having agreed with George and Emilie by correspondence that he would care for their mother in return for their shares in the house. He had been uneasy about this until he acquired the signed document from their lawyers, in which they relinquished their portions of the inheritance. He felt absurd when he left the courthouse where the title deeds to the house were recorded; he supposed that its location in the middle of the city would increase its value, but he dreamt of a small house in the country, somewhere outside the city, and a new life that was hard to even imagine.

He was haunted by his moment of courage, when he looked at the flag and refused to repeat the Party slogans, and it became mingled with the hideous fear he had felt when he sat in the corridors of the secret police branch for seven days, waiting for an unknown fate. His shame never left him, but he thought for the first time that he was aware of the city, and life itself. In his attempt to regain his moment of courage and erase the fear, he felt that the tremors inside him required serious contemplation, and that vanquishing all thought of Sawsan would be the first step toward his new life.

He found and contacted a procuress, and tried to describe the girl he wanted. It came as no surprise when he found himself describing Sawsan—her breasts, her buttocks, her thighs, her stomach—and when he opened his door, he found a miserable girl with yellow-dyed hair who was astonished at his elegant appearance and large house. She hurried him through the act and felt as if things had taken a bizarre turn when she saw his half-blind mother emerge from her room, which she no longer left except to take care of her bodily functions. Jean once again gave the procuress a description of the girl he wanted. Every time she brought him another girl—although it was too dark to see their faces, he knew from their smell that each was different—until one day he heard a voice he knew. He was stunned when he realized it was Salma, his old student and a close friend of Sawsan. She tried to withdraw but he gently motioned her to sit down, and she accepted a vodka and lemon. He didn't listen to the story she concocted about taking a wrong turn the last time she failed her baccalaureate. She found his new manner of looking at her very odd, as if he were looking at someone else. She had never been crazy for his eyes like the other girls in her class.

He became one of her regular clients, and he would call her and flirt with her whenever he missed Sawsan. She would lie down, expecting a question about Sawsan, but he kept silent. She would turn off the light and walk naked through the pitch darkness, in imitation of her friend. She told him that Sawsan was deeply involved in a love affair that would lead her to the grave. Without waiting for his comments, Salma added that Sawsan worked as a hostess in the house of Habib Mawsili in Dubai. She had left everything to follow her lover Munzir, who had resigned from the army and joined the entourage of Habib, an associate of Prince Salman. Jean ignored Salma's information about Sawsan and told her curtly that she was dead as far as he was concerned, and had been from the moment she joined the paratroopers in the summer of 1982.

He added nothing else, afraid of letting slip a confession that he had had to call upon all his strength on that summer day, when after a long absence she had knocked at his door without warning. He hadn't recognized her at first, and thought someone had arrived at the wrong address. A girl wearing a paratrooper uniform with a small travel bag slung onto her shoulder reached out and shook his hand firmly, and walked inside without waiting to be invited. Without prompting, she began to chatter and told him matter-of-factly that she had no love for weaklings and that she couldn't silently endure the outrages of Fawaz's relatives and their songs praising the Party and the Leader any longer.

He thought that keeping quiet might cause him to break down, but silent he remained. He thought of all the people who were searching for the strength to destroy tyranny, and felt that he was weak, and that everything he had always believed about the power of happiness had suddenly evaporated. He let her leave. She kissed his cheek and he didn't care about her praise of his goodness. Worst of all was that he desired this new image of hers, and was questioning what it meant to be 'good.' He hated the figure of himself as a child, whom everyone had encouraged toward becoming a portly, polite man, who wore glasses and carefully pressed clothes and who laughed softly as he cajoled children and small animals. He hated his mother, and his father, and their candidate Gabriel al-Shami, and his teachers at al-Mamoun School, and the pastor who made him stand in the front row when he sang in the choir, glorying in the boy's nice clothes and family name.

The images blended together in Jean's mind. There were only a few times when he had been released from them: during his moment of rare courage; the first time he lay next to a prostitute and begged sympathy for himself, a greedy customer; and when he swore, muttering dirty words which had never been uttered in his home all his life. He felt as if he were liberating himself and his family history, liberating the silent house. He wished he could cheerfully tell his mother how nice it was outside, when in fact women and men hurled curses and gunfire like gleeful children pelting each other with water during their summer holidays.

Sawsan had laughed when Salma described in a few vulgarities what had taken place. She loved this new Jean, but had no compassion for him; she thought that a breakdown would suit him. She sent him her address in Dubai and waited for him to write to her, but he never did. She was surprised at the force of his presence in her life, and in her astonishment she rearranged her memories of him. Thoughts of him brought back thoughts of her as she used to be, and the innocence of first love. She rebuked herself for having believed for a moment that she was the one who wrote her own story, but didn't admit that his silence, which wrote the definitive version of their story, had made her realize that the destinies of herself, Salma, and Jean were tangled together like knotted threads, interwoven with her past and present and, she feared, her future.

Depressed, Sawsan wandered around the grounds of Habib al-Mawsili's palace and gazed at the nearby sea. Cars would stop in front of the palace gates, and there would emerge businessmen, elegant princes from the Gulf whose names she had overheard and who were escorted by glamorous women, arms dealers and Arabic movie stars and famous dancers, world-famous models and singers and golfers. She would welcome them and open their car doors with a practiced, welcoming smile, then drive the car to the parking lot and wait for them to come out at dawn, drunk. She was not allowed to enter the palace and had to be content with catching some details of the debaucheries from the Levantine cook, who had been employed by Habib al-Mawsili for twenty years and prepared all his favorite dishes, from sheikh al-mahshi to fasoulya bil-zeit. The cook advised Sawsan to return to Syria, adding that she would never cross the palace gates and would always remain a servant. Deep down Sawsan was furious with Munzir, who had turned her from a lady into a maid.

After her shift was over, she would go back to her room in the small apartment she shared with two friends who passed the time by biting their nails and pining for their village on Mount Lebanon. Sawsan would wait for the phone by her bed to ring, for Munzir, personal attendant to the lord of the palace, to invite her for a drink at Bar Montana. At the end of the night he would take her to his private suite adjoining the palace and spend the night with her, and then leave her alone as she raved about his love. He didn't listen, puffing and snorting like a flagging bull, when she told him he was her only hope, she couldn't live without him. He would look at her in amazement, wondering how on earth she had managed to make him keep her as a lover for three years; it wasn't enough to be good in bed for a man like Munzir to hold onto a woman for so long. He recognized that she gave him a different sensation—the smell of her, wafting between his fingers and his bedsheets after she left, always made him miss her and reminded him of her guileless laughter.

When they were in Aleppo in the early 1980s, she would slip past the guards at the Ramses Hotel, come to his room, and slink into bed beside him. After teasing him and tapping the tip of his nose, she would ask him to close his eyes like the film stars, and then she kissed him passionately on his mouth and neck. She would bare his chest and then his lower half and kiss his penis, testicles, and toes until he was on fire, then rip off her shirt and fling all her clothes into the air like a madwoman, gripping him by his shoulders and mounting him like a wild horse. When she had exhausted him, she would ring for the waiter to bring them breakfast in bed. She would go out with him in the evenings and once ordered the citadel guard to open the gates. She wandered through the dark citadel with him like a Hamdanid princess. Sawsan and Munzir stood on the citadel walls and looked out over Aleppo, stifled by the rising fumes of death, and the fear present in every street and on the face of every man and woman hurrying home in the early evening. She tried to show him our house, pointing to a quarter in the far distance and saying, "There, next to the moon." She climbed to the top of the tallest tower in the citadel and asked him to kiss her slowly. She could feel herself transforming from a dullened, wretched tortoise hiding inside its armor, into an eagle—but not like the stuffed eagles perched on her wardrobe. Her odd requests constantly surprised him, and he had to admit that she relieved his fear and made life more enjoyable whenever he was forced to stay in Aleppo for a few days.

Boredom began to trickle slowly into their relationship in Dubai. When Sawsan complained of the imminent abandonment she had begun to expect, Munzir made no comment, just picked up his jacket and walked out, like a stranger, and Sawsan heard him give an order to the maid to lock the door after she left. She lay in bed and smoked a cigarette, and reflected on a man who would purposefully raise his voice when telling the maid to lock the door behind the women he had been in bed with a few moments before, and who now meant nothing to him. In the best scenario, she was a casual lover he could buy a drink for, if they met in a bar by chance. She decided she would never go back to him, picked up her things, and left. She went back to her room and threw herself on her bed, where she went to sleep. When she woke up she opened the curtains; the evening was gradually drawing in, making her feel lonely.

Sawsan looked out of the window and got up, having forgotten her decision to leave Munzir. She went into the bathroom and stood for a long time beneath the shower, but her limbs remained tense despite the hot water that trickled over her body. Like a sleepwalker, she headed for his suite. She wasn't allowed in. She left Munzir a letter and went to

Bar Montana where the Portuguese waitress knew her order: vodka with lemon. Everyone left her alone. She gulped down her fifth glass and returned once again to hover around the palace she wasn't allowed to approach.

She never saw him again after he married a girl from his village, sent to him by his family like a parcel. He met the girl at Dubai Airport, took her to a suite at the Regency Hyatt that was kept permanently reserved for Habib al-Mawsili's men, and took her virginity.

From the first moment, he despised her village-girl ignorance. He was trying to forget Sawsan, entering once and for all into a settled family life with this woman whom he remembered as a schoolgirl with her fair complexion, taut body, and green eyes. But before they married, he went out with Sawsan one last time. When she saw a photo of the girl, she pitied Munzir. She didn't sulk or weep on his shoulder because he described the attributes of his wife-to be; she just asked him mildly to leave details out of it. He astonished her when he asked her to leave Dubai once and for all, and to forget him. She slipped out of bed, brought two empty glasses, and poured out the aged whiskey he had brought with him for their last night together. She calmly took a sip and asked if he truly wanted her to leave his life forever. He was silent and squeezed her to his chest, kissed her distractedly, and looked at his watch, which showed it was after ten o'clock. He got up from her bed like a stranger, got dressed, and hurried out before she could remember that he hadn't hugged her goodbye.

She had expected him to spend the night in her bed, and that they would have all night to talk things through. When she found herself alone in the room, her friends' voices murmuring next door, she left and went back to her seat at Bar Montana, where she drank a whole bottle of whisky at the expense of a German tourist who had asked her to join him. She told him she was Lebanese, and had made a mistake that the maids at the palace wouldn't forgive: she spent the night in his room and gave him her body in exchange for two hundred dollars. The next morning she openly went with him to a restaurant frequented by rich tourists and Arab film stars. Exhausted, she went back to her room only to find an order deporting her from Dubai at once. She felt nothing any more. The following day she stood outside the palace, pleading with the guards to see Habib al-Mawsili. They wouldn't let her in and the secretary called her a whore, and asked her to leave at once. She went back to her flat, and when her friends avoided her, she understood that it was all over.

She spent the night in Dubai Airport waiting for a flight to Paris, where she arrived exhausted. She withdrew some money from her bank account and found a room in a cheap hotel in Barbès which offered bed and breakfast in a shared room for fifty francs. She fell on her bed like a corpse and tried to recover her strength. After three days she was strong enough to seek out the house of Suheir al-Demerdash, a friend from her paratrooper days who, after sniffing out the scope of their commanding officer's influence, had wasted no time in asking him for a grant to study music in Paris.

Suheir sat in front of Sawsan, and knew from the dark color beneath her eyes that all was not well. She invited her to a café near the conservatoire, bought her an espresso, and helped her to find a tiny two-meter-square room close to the Gare du Nord. She saw her from time to time, inviting her on brief outings or to a restaurant for a hasty glass of wine. Sawsan refused to return to Aleppo defeated but thought, on cold nights, that a forsaken lover was like a train station where fleas overran the empty platforms. She lived off green beans and drank cheap wine in an attempt to overcome the difficulties of living in Paris and keep a little money in her virtually exhausted bank account. Aleppo seemed so far away, Paris so exhausting and hard, and she thought she would spend her whole life working in the Algerian restaurant being constantly rebuked by its owner.

She wrote to Jean and told him everything that had happened since the last time she saw him. She told him that she had distanced herself from him because they had asked her to write a report on him denouncing him as a spy. She asked his honest, objective advice. His letter arrived, and he told her that his mother was still doing well, that he had been dismissed from teaching, and knew why, and that now he made a living by giving private lessons to rich students in his home. In his familiar, delicate way, he made it known he wanted her to stay in Paris. A meaningless letter, Sawsan told herself, and threw it away.

She went back to the kitchen of the Algerian restaurant, washed dishes, and came home exhausted. She threw herself on her bed alone, like all other miserable girls who had no one. Her expensive clothes had lost their beauty and the expensive perfumes given to her by Munzir had run out, even though she had been economical in using them. She called Munzir's number in Dubai and hung up when she heard the harsh village accent of his wife. On another call, she left her name and the number of the restaurant and begged Munzir to call her. She waited until she heard his voice one last time before picking up her small suitcase and leaving, concluding her first year in France by returning to our house in Aleppo.

I couldn't believe that this girl, so tired, weak, and pale in the face, was irrepressible Sawsan. She hugged me and burst into tears, then hugged Rashid and finally my mother, who treated her with a coolness that Sawsan would not forgive to her dying day, as if she had finally found an opportunity to avenge herself for the time she spat in her face—the time that she would never forget. My mother, at that moment, thought that they were equal: both abandoned, both defeated.

Sawsan was summoned more than once to a State Security branch where the investigator, an old friend of Munzir's, welcomed her kindly. He offered her a cup of very frothy coffee and asked her about the details of Munzir's life. He put a white piece of paper in front of her and asked her to report everything she knew about Habib al-Mawsili, Prince Salman, and the Syrian businessmen and officials who frequented his palace. He added that it was a necessary procedure in order to obtain a presidential pardon and jump back into the fray for the Party. She observed his fear of her, the way he avoided direct eye contact. She wrote everything he asked and left calmly. At the final meeting, she asked him to close this pointless investigation; he gave her his number and offered her work as an informer, a mukhabara, which carried special privileges. She laughed in his face and walked out, with a terrible headache.

She walked toward the Strand and sat at a table by the window looking out onto the park. Everything had changed— the waiter, the tablecloths, the clientele. She felt like a stranger in this place which had witnessed some of her most enjoyable moments with Munzir. She drank her coffee slowly and watched the passersby, asking herself what had changed to make these people look so much like frightened rabbits, as they scurried past with bowed heads. At that moment, Aleppo seemed to have lost its shine, to be burdened with regret. Nothing held any meaning for her: she was an old woman looking over her shoulder at her friends, fearing an early death; she was a paper airplane in a grey sky afraid of the long journey ahead. She noticed her dragging footsteps and wanted to throw off the encumbrance of her past. For a long time she sought salvation, regretted her recklessness, hated Munzir, who had returned her as a wreck to a city that she and her paratrooper friends had helped to reduce into ruins. She wept in her room for a long time over her loneliness. She clung to me and sobbed, adding that she had lost her life to a pack of dogs. When she asked me to take her to visit Suad's grave, I understood that she wanted to regain her innocence.

We walked along roads we didn't recognize. In recent years, houses had been built hastily on the lettuce fields, and the smell of cooking which wafted from them was abhorrent. The graves, which used to be open to the sky, were now cramped between clustered buildings inhabited by fellaheen who closed off their balconies with filthy rags, for fear that strangers would steal glimpses of their women left alone all day with their children. I told Sawsan that Suad would suffocate among these crowds but she didn't answer. We sat close to the grave, pulled out the dried-up plants, and watered the ones which were left. She led me by the hand through the streets of the city as if I were a young child, then, oblivious to me, she wandered off spontaneously and peered at the engravings on the stone waterspouts like a fascinated tourist. She assured me that night that her cheerfulness would come back to her and added optimistically that she would become a great translator.

While waiting to return to university, she spent a few months reading French novels borrowed from Jean's library, which had starting growing. Certain that his residence in Aleppo would be of some duration and that his mother would not be dying in the near future, he shipped dozens of boxes from Geneva, and resolved to put his life back in order. His pupils came to his house and he welcomed them in a small room. They would try to peek at his mother as she slumbered like a queen. He would change his mother's serum and clean her up, then close the door behind him and plunge the house into silence.

Sawsan came every evening. They spoke in French and leafed through books together. She told him that she was going to have her hymen repaired and immerse herself in prayer, adding that she had no other way of saving herself and regaining her purity, contaminated as she was by the reports she had written that had ruined her school friends and their families. Jean nodded and did not comment.

She asked herself whether her remorse would have been as strong if she had married Munzir and spent the rest of her life with him. She was kept awake by the questions that sprouted in her head like a briar in a bed of sweet peas. She tossed and turned, and went into the living room choked by a fever of longing for Munzir. Her desire awoke and her body turned into a solid tongue of flame. She pleaded a sudden headache and went back to her bedroom, where she stood in front of the mirror and uncovered her entire body. She gently ran her hands over her body, closed her eyes, and lay down on the bed. She called up old sensations and images, mixing up faces as she masturbated. Fantasies came back to her, daydreams lay siege to her, and her anxiety turned into remorse and plunged her into fits of unstoppable crying. She sought salvation. She no longer enjoyed hearing Rashid play and would walk through the house as slowly as a tortoise. My mother said nothing as she watched her daughter sympathetically, trying to win her back. That was the moment Sawsan decided that her salvation lay in prayer, and the total immersion of herself in worship. She thought that the return of her virginity would win her enough self-confidence to bolster her against regret.

She went to a well-known doctor and told him plainly that she wanted her old feelings back. She didn't mention a word about honor. He explained that he could repair her hymen but she would never be a full virgin again. She restated her request to walk out of his clinic as a virgin, however imperfect. He advised her to look elsewhere to restore her self-confidence and she made him understand in no uncertain terms that she was looking for the scent of the girl she had been years before and brought the discussion to a close.

On a scorching day in late August 1987, Sawsan arrived at the appointed time at the clinic with locked doors. She rang the bell and it wasn't long before she had paid the fee and was lying on the bed provided especially for these secret operations. She sank into the anesthetic fumes and couldn't remember Munzir's face; she tried to gather up its details again but she couldn't, as if he were a stranger she had chatted with in passing. After three hours she woke up from the ether wanting to vomit. She picked up her few things and went home, spoke to no one, and fell asleep till morning. She bathed and sat on her bed, waiting to feel like a virgin, but she was assailed by absolutely no new feelings. She tried to go back to sleep, to entice her scattered daydreams, but she didn't succeed in gathering even one image.

I wouldn't leave her alone. For days, I prepared fragrant, floral tisanes for her and brought food to her room. She wrote to Jean to tell him that she couldn't visit him on the orders of the sheikh to whom she'd frankly recounted her life story, before asking gravely, "Will I go to hell if I die?"

The sheikh understood her anxiety. He saw in her extraordinary eyes that she sincerely wished for faith and to renounce her sins. He gave her a small Quran and assured her that God's mercy was far-reaching. She kissed his hand and left his house, as light as the stuffed eagles which had gathered dust while she was away. While walking, she reflected that it had been the first time in her life she had kissed anyone's hand. She had liked the sheikh's sensitivity, his pleasure at her humble veneration, and she said to herself, "Certainty and contentment can only be found in surrender." She came home wearing a dark scarf over her long hair. She opened her wardrobe and all the things which she had selected with a whore's taste—tight, stretchy trousers, low-cut blouses which showed off her stomach and navel, short skirts, knee-high leather boots, earrings in the shape of devils which she had loved after returning from her tour of duty with the paratroopers—she took them all out, threw them into the middle of the living room, and set them on fire. Furious, our moribund mother rushed to pick up the burning clothes and hurl them outside, trying to avoid the thick clouds of smoke which filled the living room and seeped into all the rooms of our house, which had become as closed as a tomb.

No one believed irrepressible Sawsan's repentance. Rashid didn't care what happened at home and my mother considered Sawsan's transformation a disaster of no lasting import.

She hated her new perfumes and long clothes, her dark head covering, the glances of Sawsan's new friends which made them seem immature and servile. When Sawsan brought them to our house, she asked me not to shake hands with them. She would bring them ginger sherbet and they would speak late into the night about the miracles of the saints and the nature of piety. They listened to and sang along with the religious songs which had spread through the city in recent years, and which consisted of simple words put to the tunes of well-known pop songs.

Sawsan tried to immerse herself in her new life. She went to college every morning wearing a long, dark coat. Her old friends from the paratroopers, absorbed in the life of the Party and the comrades, objected to her new way of living, and swore and spat at her. She was furious but kept silent. Her new friends commiserated with her, and averred that she would acquire huge rewards from God if she could bear their cruelty.

Sawsan was no longer irrepressible. She immersed herself in radicalism and fatwas day after day. She covered her face and began to avoid looking at the handsome men she used to adore watching and imagining in bed with her. She repented her daydreams, her fantasies, and her relationship with Munzir. Her paratrooper friends called her "Munzir's whore" and refused to forget her shameless behavior with him, when she would infuriate them by embracing him and kissing him on the lips after school before leaving in his car. The following day, she would tell them in graphic detail everything she had done with him the night before, not forgetting to remind everyone of his infatuation with her eyes, with her high buttocks encased in the tight military trousers like a watermelon seed in its red flesh, with her breasts which she was careful to display by leaving her shirt buttons undone so that the edge of her bra showed. She expected that this would be when they'd take their revenge on her. They wrote reports and sent them up to Comrade Jaber, my childhood friend who had become

Student Official at the university, after the previous comrade had been expelled from the Party for having allowed the students to gather and recite poetry which did not explicitly praise the President and the Party—poems which spoke about roses and butterflies in a destroyed city, now transformed (after the restoration of security and the defeat of the Muslim Brotherhood) into a city of chastisement, roamed by ravens, and divided up between secret police officers and loyal officials.

Behind Comrade Jaber, who received his instructions from branches of the secret police, Party members in the university marched with pride, swollen-chested, their steps ringing out on the cold tiles, spying even on the number of breaths taken by students, professors, and employees, who didn't dare object to their methods. They brought the students out of the lecture halls and led them to Party occasions, usually marches of support which ended with a letter written in blood and sent to the Leader, who was relaxing in his palace, having already silenced all opposing voices, destroyed the city of Hama, and arrested tens of thousands of leftist or religious university students.

Irrepressible Sawsan had a hard time breathing when she thought about what was happening around her and complained like my mother.

My mother had already begun to have fits of delirium which overwhelmed her and weighed her down with the feeling that she had committed a tremendous sin in desiring a man we had known nothing about. She imagined his warm voice telling her how he would take her on a sea journey, on a tour of the Indian Ocean, he would dance with her by moonlight, he would weave a white bed from the foam on the waves and she would lie on it like a houri. It made her regret having stamped out her sensuality; it had been some time since she watched the romance films she used to love, and she had buried her silken nightgowns in an elaborately carved wooden chest she had picked up in an antique shop whose owner had decided to emigrate.

Members of the mukhabarat had attacked the owner of this antique shop and accused him of harboring a wanted man, a member of the Muslim Brotherhood. They came into the shop, overturned the silver ornaments and antique golden swords engraved with enchanting odes to the night, the desert, and the horses. They trampled everything and took him away to their branch. He was saved from certain death three days later only because the interrogator was finally convinced that he belonged to a Christian family well known for their skills as goldsmiths, and because his older brother, a famous heart surgeon, had paid a number of large bribes.

The man went back to his shop, broken, and bearing wounds that would never heal. They had ransacked his shop but, having no idea of the value of the precious objects there, had been content with taking a few inexpensive glass vases. He sold off everything that was left in a single day and moved to Dubai. He didn't haggle with my mother over the price of the wooden chest. She paid him 1,200 lira and carried it happily back to her house, unaware that it would become both repository to and witness of our long deprivation. She placed it in her bedroom which later turned into a private kingdom, perfumed by incense and heavy fragrances which inspired lethargy and murdered desire. Into the box, she threw cherished photos of herself, smiling and optimistic, her long hair loose as she gazed serenely at the future. She was surprised to find that her wardrobe hadn't changed since my father's departure, other than for the addition of a few spartan clothes and accessories which showed that she was a respectable teacher at a school celebrated for its sobriety and severity. She didn't know why she had kept all these things for so long, just as she didn't know why she sometimes took out her expensive silk nightgowns embroidered with lace. She found that merely putting one on was arousing, and a taste for life would return to her body.

She came out of the bathroom early one morning, taking her time getting ready to play truant from school for the first time in her life. She left the house early having allowed some traces of the night to remain; she enjoyed feeling them like a weight on her body. Feeling irrepressible, she got out of the taxi in the center of town and found a café in front of the park, which had just opened. She sat down for a few minutes, suddenly struck by fear. Desolation filled her heart and her body turned cold when she saw the ruins of her city through the café window; it was as if she were seeing her city like this for the first time.

For days she would dream of regaining her relationship with her dying body; she wanted to lie next to a man who just once would embrace her so powerfully and so passionately he'd leave her in pieces. She blamed herself for the many wasted opportunities when men had tried to revive her with their strong desire; they spoke to her about their lust, about her silence which they loved. She wondered if, when a man loved a woman's silence, it meant that he loved her; she wondered, too, what it meant when a man waited for a woman in the early morning. A famous painter had proposed this to her one day; he had blocked her path as she returned from school, and told her that he would wait for her the following morning in his studio. He left her trembling. It had come too late, she told herself, convincing herself that no man could become attached to her, or would exert any effort to make her happy. They were only inviting her to bed, an offer that would be extended once. On one occasion, she was to meet a man who was waiting for her by the park gates, but then didn't dare to go. She wanted to divulge her frustrated desire to Nariman, but she was afraid.

Everything my mother had lived through involved a kind of absurdity we could never comprehend. The three of us met in a café outside the house to discuss her situation but didn't reach any conclusions. We felt that we must be too young, or too old. We walked home silently, Sawsan choked with tears. Rashid left us at the first intersection and went to Nizar's house, where he stretched out on the sofa and fell deep asleep. He didn't get up when Nizar came out of his room with his new boyfriend, Madhat. They went into the bathroom to wash and their voices rose cheerfully from below the hot shower. They pelted one another with soap and came out of the bathroom clinging to each other, wrapped in clean towels. They made breakfast and ate together before Madhat went to his job at the tax collection bureau. Nizar walked him to the door and bid him a coquettish goodbye, smoothing down the collar of the shirt he had brought him as a present from Beirut, along with other expensive clothes Madhat sold to a smuggled-clothing shop in Aziziya for a third of their price. Nizar was optimistic that Madhat would never leave him.

Nizar sat waiting for Rashid to wake up. When he did he told Nizar without preamble that my mother was delirious and would lose her mind, and there was nothing we could do other than acknowledge a fact that came as no surprise to Nizar. The two of them conducted an inconclusive conversation, with a rationality Rashid felt would choke him. He got dressed hastily and left Nizar's house. He felt the weight of my mother lying there under the influence of her sleeping pills and her hallucinations, and of her being tied up so she wouldn't escape into the street. Her old image appeared to him, when she used to sit beside the window, watching the lettuce fields and the endless cherry trees with such hope. She would nod with pleasure when Rashid was wrapped up in his difficult violin pieces and would hum along with him in the parts she knew by heart. All of sudden, other pictures assailed his memory like a downpour of rain, making him think of looking again for the person our mother used to be.

He decided to return to the family home and live with the pain. Some musical phrases occurred to him, which could be the opening of a piece about sickness and the sort of noise which caused his mother's episodes. He hummed them out loud and realized it was a phrase from Beethoven's Ninth. His frustration returned, and he went to Bar Express where he asked for a whisky and soda, ignoring the waiter who asked about Nizar and cursed his new boyfriend Madhat. The bar was sunk in silence at that time in the afternoon. Rashid tried to gather his thoughts, despite his feelings of weakness and estrangement. He ran his hands over his body for the thousandth time and the bile rose in his throat. When he left the bar he headed straight for Nizar's house, where he gathered up his few possessions and went back to the family home to quietly reassume his bed in our room.

He could sense how far apart we were. I was looking for a new meaning for my life, having graduated from the Faculty of Literature and finished my time in the service of knowledge. I spent my days translating financial statements and correspondence for a textile factory. Sawsan was dissatisfied with her hijab and heavy clothing. She would go to the living room in a flimsy nightdress, ask about my mother, and leave without waiting for an answer. On winter nights a fever of lust for Munzir came back to her. She lay down naked on her bed and feared touching her limbs which were burning with desire. She lost herself in daydreams again, and tried to remember what her new friends had to say about halal and haram. After spending two years at university trying to fit in with the veiled girls, she felt completely estranged, and longed to remove her thick clothing. After she entered the third year she spent the whole winter trying to find salvation and her lost faith. She exchanged glances with her three eagles at night and thought that she was a stuffed mummy, just like them. Without realizing it she lived a parallel life like me. She was trying to rid herself of the smells that still clung to her soul and her body: the odor of the Party, the paratroopers, and the past.

She still remembered the first time she saw Munzir. He came with the commander to inspect the ranks of the female paratroopers who cheered and shouted for him and the President until their throats gave out. Munzir was beside him, carrying an automatic rifle, and his eyes roamed the place with the caution of a wolf. The commander saluted the paratroopers and shook their hands firmly. Sawsan approached him with a firm military step and greeted him forcefully. Her eyes were drawn to Munzir's face which she felt was very familiar to her, as if she had drawn it in her daydreams. At night, she lay in her tent next to Suheir al-Demerdash and swooned over Munzir's eyes, the long glances they had exchanged. She knew that all the girls at the camp were talking with the same desire about the commander's handsome attendant. The following days saw a great deal of activity, and she was not surprised when he visited the encampment again. He sought her out and gave her his telephone number in Damascus, the badge of distinction that most of her fellow paratroopers had longed for. She was overjoyed, head over heels in love, and learned the number by heart. She told no one about their first meeting.

On her first free day she rang his number and waited. No one answered. Her camouflage uniform was covered with dust, her body desperately wanted a hot shower, and her limbs were tired after a fortnight's strenuous military training. She walked through streets of Damascus, a city she didn't know, lost herself in alleys, and wearily ordered some sandwiches and juice. She sat in cafés next to customers who ignored her, or eyed her with furtive contempt. She felt completely out of place. She rang Munzir's number a dozen times from different places, but midnight came and Sawsan was still wandering alone in the streets. She didn't know what to do in this strange city and thought of going back to the military base near Damascus. She went into a cheap restaurant in Kiraj where troops would idly pass the time while waiting for the buses to convey them to their faraway cities. After midnight, his voice reached her from the other end of the line and she told him she had lost all hope of tracking him down. He asked her not to leave, and he drove her to his house without protest from her. She bathed and put on a set of his pajamas while he ordered a superb dinner to be delivered, and they spoke about their childhoods until dawn—she would always love hearing about his childhood, his endless stories about his poverty-stricken family in the mountains of Masyaf—when he went to his bedroom alone. She refused to have sex during the early months of their relationship; she had decided she would not be like some cheap girl he picked up in a bar or off the street.

He continued pursuing her, and six months later she traveled to Damascus and sprung on him a request to make her a woman. They weaved an insane love story. He confessed to her that for the first time he found himself missing a woman. He slipped her the answers during the exam which all paratroopers had to take, and no one dared complain. She went as his guest to a private dinner with the commander, who looked into her eyes and praised the taste of his personal attendant. He gave Sawsan a silver-plated pistol which, in her eyes, was glorious. She put it on her hip and went to Comrade Fawaz's house, where she commanded him and his relatives to shut up, in revenge for all their insults to her mother. Comrade Fawaz's relatives fell silent and tried to appease her. For a few moments, my mother was pleased. Sawsan and her friends walked around Aleppo, proud of their camouflage uniforms and their immunity from the law; they went to school and patrolled the corridors, stamping their feet in time when Party songs were played over the loudspeakers. They elevated punishment of their enemies into an art form. The day they graduated, the commander ordered them to remove the head coverings of all the girls in Damascus. They spread through the roads like ants, stopping cars, removing head coverings from the women and harassing the men, spitting on anyone who opposed them. Terror crawled through the city, and over the following days the capital was half-deserted.

Her desires drove her wild. She asked Munzir to come to Aleppo at once and he burned to meet her. He asked the commander to send him on a mission to Aleppo; the commander understood why, and charged him with supervision of the affairs of the paratroopers there. At that time, Munzir needed her madness. Her boldness astonished him. He immersed himself in the perfumes he had given her, which he had received as gifts from the big traders in exchange for promoting their interests with the state. Money gushed over Munzir, who was well known in Aleppo. He took Sawsan to the best restaurants, where he kissed her in front of everyone while the other patrons averted their eyes. Life was endlessly carefree for the lovers. Silver necklaces, golden bracelets, luxury clothes: Sawsan piled them all up in her wardrobe under the envious gaze of her friends who had tried to seduce Munzir, believing that he was only in love with Sawsan's taut brown body that was like a field of ripe wheat rippling beneath the burning sun. At night she writhed in his hands like a fish, sighing and offering him an unforgettable taste again and again. For a few months, the two of them lived in total surrender to their violent love.

Sawsan felt that her body was weighed down by these heavy clothes, by her estrangement from the city and her university classmates. She sought out her reclaimed virginity, and she told me that the smell of carrion came out of every pore whenever she sweated. She prayed for winter to depart. Her daydreams appeared again, she felt a sudden joy when she sat in the classroom, watching her classmates who had avoided speaking to her in the past for fear of her gun and her camouflage uniform, and who now swore in French about her body odor. Daydreaming, she summoned up girls wearing elegant clothes as if they were on a catwalk straight to her bed. She would undress them and exchange kisses with them, and she would assemble them in orgies like the ones she had been addicted to watching in Dubai with her friends. She admitted to herself that she missed her old daydream of being a porn star, her naked pictures hoarded by men all over the world as they masturbated over the scenes she composed in her fantasies.

Her daydreams returned to her with force, and with absolute, inescapable clarity. She told me that daydreams were the hell which followed us, and I nodded in agreement. Her salvation became impossible. She plunged into the rot of our house, which was beginning to be invaded by humidity. My mother, walking slowly like an old tortoise, complained of a lack of oxygen in the air. I bought dehumidifiers from the shops on al-Khandaq but after a few weeks even they wore a veil of algae. There was no escape from the mold which had started to develop in the corners of the living room and the bedrooms.

Sawsan no longer cared. She stood in front of the mirror, looking at her body. She felt that her salvation would come after she left this hell, as she termed it. She hated the university and its canteens and its corridors. She hated the students and the professors who harassed her, and treated her like a reformed prostitute. She wished at times that she could reclaim her gun, the commander's gift, and go into the hall and open fire on Nadal Ahmed, the professor of modern French literature, who was a Party comrade and nephew of a high-ranking secret police officer known for boasting about his role in the Hama massacre. The state had sent Nadal Ahmed to France for six years, and he still couldn't distinguish between Molière and Robbe-Grillet and spoke French like a lazy high-school student.

On one occasion, he blocked Sawsan's path and asked to see her in his office. She came at the appointed time and he spoke to her about her past, which he knew all about. He expressed his sorrow at her transformation into a woman of shaky confidence, and asked her kindly to remove her hijab and heavy black cloak and relax over a cup of coffee. He locked the door and confidently took his member out of the zipper on his trousers. She ignored him and stood up to leave, when suddenly she found him behind her, holding onto her breasts and rubbing himself against her buttocks, cursing Munzir who had snatched her away from them all, the traitor. Sawsan didn't move. He ejaculated over her clothes and his own trousers. She lodged an official complaint against him with the university authorities, and Comrade Jaber summoned her and told her that she was accused of seducing Comrade Nadal Ahmed, citing her dubious and immoral history as evidence against her. He asked her to apologize to Professor Nadal; if she refused, he would take up legal proceedings against her. Sawsan swore at Comrade Jaber and left his office.

She looked at my mother, laid out silently on her bed like a corpse. She looked at her eyelashes, at her lips which never stopped moving. She remembered the words of Comrade Jaber, who used to come to our house as a shy child and share the toys my mother was determined to provide for us: tanks and wooden horses, and clockwork trains which whistled. Sawsan had never been afraid of him in her life, and she remained that way; whenever she saw him, she cursed him. She despised him for his family, which used to sell grilled corn in the streets of Ashrafiya, and now smuggled iron from Lebanon and pimped for officers of the secret police both great and small, sharing the profits with sons of the ruling sheikhs. Jaber was afraid of Sawsan's mania and her hidden connections.

Sawsan felt a great compassion for my mother's body when it was quiet like a stagnant pool, but returned to her hatred when my mother woke, for a few hours at a time, from her episodes. She would ask about the plants and about Nariman, who no longer came to visit my mother, now that she was well; she had taken pleasure in the downfall of her friend who had been so imperious all her life. Everything went back to its true nature in the house, a reminder that odors brought in from the streets were all that was needed to corrupt the clean air. She polished the bed posts and dusted the furniture, but her lucidity didn't last long, and soon she slipped back into her delirium.

I thought of how, when my mother was restored to health, her longing for old things would revive. She blamed irrepressible Sawsan for neglecting the plants in the living room and walked heedlessly around the darkened house, complaining of how parched her throat was and how dry her hands were. She called on us to save her from her burning lungs. She spoke at length about the air of a corrupt country but no one listened to her; Sawsan just looked at her and left, as if there had been some mistake. My mother mourned her terrible fortune and stood in front of old pictures which no longer meant anything to anyone. Sawsan told me, pointing to my mother, that she wanted to die, but wouldn't.

Sawsan's prophecy came true. My mother used to say that she would die alone, because a proud woman didn't want anyone to see her last breath. I didn't think, then, of what Sawsan had said of burial and its rituals some months before. It was the first time we were burying someone so close to us.

A Regal Neck and Red Shoes

I DIDN'T ASK HOW SHE had died. I knew that it had occurred in the early evening—an inappropriate time, as most people die before dawn or in the dead of night—in a manner which revealed that sleep, if not our dreams, is a rehearsal for death, which in our family usually occurred somewhat unexpectedly.

My mother's father, Jalal al-Nabulsi, lived till he was eighty-seven years old. On the twentieth anniversary of Independence he put on his new suit, and with all the tranquility of someone who loved ritual, carefully pinned on his medals and his Railway Institute badge, before leaving for the annual celebration he attended with his friends when they recalled the struggles of their generation and enjoyed a magnificent meal at Restaurant Andalus after placing a wreath of roses on the grave of the great mujahid fighter Ibrahim Hananu. In his official clothing, decked out in all of his medals, Jalal hobbled to Baghdad Station to offer a casual greeting to the workers, who all detested him. No one reached out a hand to steady him when he lost his balance on Platform 1 and was crushed beneath the wheels of a slow freight train.

My mother's mother, Bahiya al-Katibi, before she was fifty, died of laughter—her body remained on her broad sofa for hours, smiling, because no one dared to verify that she was dead. They had expected that her endless laughing would stop, but it didn't. When the features of her face slackened, my mother, who was no more than thirteen, stood in front of the heavy corpse of her mother and thought about how difficult it would be to bury her. She also reflected that she hadn't told her mother that she had entered puberty, although she doubted whether she would have shown much interest in this. My mother grew to be a woman and still remembered a recurrent dream from her childhood in which she was a swan, and she was flying. She clung to her dream and considered her mother's death from an unrepentant fit of laughter to be a message from fate. She guessed that the error which kept my dreamy grandmother stuck in her place had also led to her joyful death. She decided that she would keep it to herself that she was a swan, and she would not allow rot that came from staying put to set in and work its way under her soft skin.

She told Nizar, during the long nights they spent talking in her later years, of her dream of turning into a swan, and concluded that their mother had been careless. Marrying my grandfather, Jalal al-Nabulsi, was not that different from choosing death, as he never raised his eyes to look at her and had never made any effort to claim his lawful right of khalwa to see her alone before the marriage. From the first moment, she thought of him as a heedless sheep; his family had shepherded him to fulfill a duty which had to be undertaken quickly and without fuss, so that he could turn back to his work with Monsieur Henri Sourdain who had poisoned his mind with old sketches of trains and designs for fabulously decorated stations containing marble statues of the Greek gods. My grandfather would recount the conversations about the long research paper published in a famous journal of architecture in which Monsieur Henri criticized the new theories on building stations using iron and glass. In his books and the funding appeals which he sent to officials in Paris, he called for a stance against this new culture which would destroy the public taste. He described the train station as 'the city's welcome,' and demanded a stop to the wanton recklessness perpetrated by young engineers who could not distinguish between, on the one hand, the magnificence required to preserve these places for eternity, like the Acropolis, and the temporary lavatories for military encampments, on the other.

Monsieur Henri Sourdain laid out his maps, and with a small cane he pointed out the sketches of the stations he dreamed of building throughout Syria after the network of iron rails had been completed, which he wished to see reaching from Paris to Baghdad. Aleppo would form the focal point from which every line had to branch out, so that this city could become the heart of the world, as it deserved. He bitterly resented the officials of the Hejaz Railway in Damascus, the pilgrimage route, who commanded all attention for the southern portion of the line leading to Medina, to the detriment of the line crossing Aleppo en route to Baghdad from Istanbul.

My grandfather's eyes would fill with tears as he gazed reverently upon Monsieur Henri Sourdain. My grandmother secretly hated this man who, with his lofty height and self-assurance, and the way he spoke quietly while his eyes wandered elsewhere, looked so much like her ideal man, ever-present in her daydreams. She was afraid of being tempted, and did not want her tender feelings to be wakened by this tedious real-life version, this counterfeit daydream who never laughed, even if he was more gentle and alluring when discoursing on train stations in all their varieties. Despite my grandfather's repeated pleas, she never allowed him to invite Monsieur Henri Sourdain to her house which, from her first days, she felt was an ideal breeding ground for hatred, with its metallic smell of oil and train rivets.

My grandmother grew distracted, despite the noise made by the lodgers in her friend Thérèse's house whenever she visited. Her laughter and irrepressible spirits ceased, and she strewed her suffering all around her. Her depression grew whenever the time came for her to return to the house she neglected, and she left the task of running it to her eldest daughter, my aunt Ibtihal, who had inherited from her aunts

an unpleasantly long nose like a crow's beak, and endless pleasure in the details of traditional Ottoman life.

Ibtihal went to great lengths to run the household. She
sank deep into the mode of this Ottoman way of life whose
vocabulary she used with a veneration which bothered my
grandmother at first, before she utterly relinquished any idea
of protesting or returning things to how they had been, as
if she had severed the relationship which bound her to the
house forever. She admitted to herself that she didn't like
anything which my grandfather had favored or collected.
She didn't even defend her bed when Ibtihal swapped it for
a high iron bed girdled with Quranic verses, and then placed
an embroidered cloth for covering the Quran next to it and a
copper finger bowl and high-necked water jug on top of the
Bombay chest. My grandmother thought of her house as an
enclosure where she slept and bore children. Uncaring, she
remained sullen and discontented all her life; she was cold
in bed as if punishing my grandfather, who had never asked
her if she wanted to live with him and was content with conversations revolving around trains and types of engines. He
spoke gravely and ardently about Henschel trains, enumerat-
ing their various specifications, and triumphantly he told her
how they were able to run nineteen carriages carrying iron at
forty kilometers an hour. He waited for her to be amazed, but
she only looked at him in bewilderment.

As if he were in another world, one far removed from
the details which might convey meaning to another man, he
would come home and put an arm around his wife, who all
her life kept wondering how this had all happened. From the
first day, my inattentive grandmother hated it all: the small
balcony overlooking bustling Jamiliya Street, and the large,
interconnecting rooms. My grandmother told my mother that
Jalal al-Nabulsi had never really looked at her in his life, to
the point that he didn't know if her mole lay on her left ear
or on her nose. She scorned the photo where they had been

gathered as a family for the first time after my mother was born. My grandmother tried to summon up some enthusiasm for the baby's long neck and delicate fingers, but her overpowering estrangement had brought her to the point of no return.

This estrangement caused her to wander through the house all day, carelessly leaving full pans to burn on the stove, cursing men, traitors all, who never defended their beloveds, who kidnapped them on horseback, as she had dreamed of ever since she had first seen a Western. She became devoted to the cinema, which she discovered at forty years of age when she was fat and slow. She didn't listen to Thérèse's advice to avoid eating grease, retorting that they had nothing left anyway, except memories of the laughter they had shared with Thérèse's tenants, or the card games with Ibtihal that had continued late into the night, according to an invented Ottoman ritual. Ibtihal would prepare a pitcher of tea in the Turkish fashion, some nuts, and a heavy scoreboard. She would cover the table with an embroidered cloth, not forgetting to play the songs of a group whose music was steeped in olden times. Quietly they would begin to play, and quietly they would speak about the family lineage, grumbling about the marriages made by scions of the great Aleppan families to village girls.

Thérèse was content with a few secrets she never told anyone but Nizar, who always visited her and spent some time with the girls who lodged with her at the end of her life. Just as he had done when he was a child, and then a teenager and a young man, he would wander from room to room, entering each without knocking. He would play Syriac songs for them on his violin, and nudge them gently like their girlfriends, and try on their lipstick. This behavior had terrified my grandmother, who would observe him and then yield to his tears to tie his hair with colored ribbons like a little girl. She couldn't refuse his request to accompany her to Sitt Thérèse's house, who by now had only Nizar as a friend. He would visit her at all hours, bringing her turkey breasts and basterma he had bought specially from Sirop. Sometimes he would press a few coins into her hand. Each new inhabitant of the house knew Nizar well; they asked him about new brands of face creams and unrolled their underwear for him, and listened to his sharp criticism of their insistence upon cheap lace which couldn't absorb their fluids when they were excited, and which added nothing to the fragrance left with their lovers after their departure from their bed.

I would see Sitt Thérèse when I was young. Uncle Nizar brought her to visit my mother, and she heard Rashid play and ate lunch with us. We didn't understand at the time why my mother so warmly welcomed this old woman who smoked ravenously, so that her teeth were dark yellow and her voice as rugged as a man's. She needed Nizar's arm to walk even a few steps. Another time I saw her in Nizar's house. She put my brother Rashid in her lap and stroked his hair, and Nizar played her a piece which she found very moving. Her eyes welled with tears when he told her that it was written for cello and violin and its title was "Sitt Thérèse with the Regal Neck and Red Shoes," to remind her of the red high heels she no longer wore after she stopped attending soirées in rich houses, having lost her social standing and become an old woman nobody cared about. Nizar teased her that the piece was a nod to the memory of her silent love; he didn't realize that this old woman had never had a silent love story. Nizar added that it was included in his collection "Shadows of Regret" and he fell silent so as not to tell her the rest of the story, which Rashid alone knew. Nevertheless, she understood everything when she saw Uncle Nizar weeping bitterly as he listened to the pieces on the radio being played by the Berlin Concert Orchestra, especially "Shadows of Regret."

The last time I saw Sitt Thérèse's house was the day my mother took me by the hand and we stopped in front of Mar Asya Church with a few other people, to join the funeral procession of a poor old woman. I heard children repeating that Sitt Thérèse had died last night, leaving her house to the church, which had promptly evicted her lodgers. I still remember Mary threatening the pastor with a lawsuit, asking him where she would go after having lived in this place for thirty years. My mother sobbed as she accompanied the coffin and its few mourners to a tomb in Ashrafiya to bury Thérèse in a grave my mother couldn't recognize years later when she wanted to visit it, any more than she recognized its new guard.

When the shadows were settling and evening was slinking in through the window, my mother used to wander through the house on tiptoe. Everything within gave the impression of an eternal serenity: restored sofas and high ceilings, fragrant perfumes, landscapes in oils hung uniformly on the huge living room wall, a Phillips radio now so outdated that Nizar was able to convince his brother Abdel-Monem to omit it from the list of objects they divided up after my grandfather died under the wheels of the slow freight train.

My mother loved the clean streets and tranquil evenings of Aleppo. With my grandfather she would dust off the family tree hanging on the wall in the living room, proud of being from a family which had been in Aleppo for a thousand years. She sought out her relatives but only saw them on fleeting occasions. They were not there in their spotless suits to receive condolences at her father's funeral reception, to which she arrived late; they had hated him on account of his eccentricity, and his attachment to the trains whose wheels he had insisted on expiring beneath. They left the house unmoved, shaking hands firmly with Abdel-Monem who approved when they cursed Nizar; he shook his head disapprovingly at Nizar's request to receive condolences in the women's chambers. Abdel-Monem was furious at Nizar's candor in feeling that he was a woman who had been born as a man at a crucial moment by some divine mistake. Ibtihal, who believed that the family tree hanging on the wall went all the way back to the Prophet, regularly demanded in a superior tone that he be locked up or killed. She would boast of her ancestors' yellowing tomes, kept carefully in the zawiya of Sheikh Abdel-Salam close to the hammam at Bab al-Nasr.

After the funeral everything slowly fell apart. Nizar, Ibtihal, and Abdel-Monem divided up the house's contents, leaving my mother only the remains of broken chairs, rusty copper pans in need of polishing, some flimsy old bedding, and a ridiculous painting of water fountains that she couldn't sell for fifty lira. She left it all, asking Nizar only for an old copper coffee grinder my grandmother used to boast of having bought during her only trip to Istanbul in the late 1930s. Nizar didn't keep anything other than the radio, his companion from childhood. He would tune in to the different stations, looking eagerly for Vivaldi, Mozart, Schubert, or the foreign musicians whose works had moved him and led him to the classes of Ahmed al-Mabid, who taught him to listen closely to himself. In just two months, Nizar could play complicated pieces and various instruments. Music ran in his blood, his teacher told him. Ahmed al-Mabid had returned from Berlin after the outbreak of the Second World War and waited every day for the war to end so he could go back to play in the orchestra of the city he loved, and revel in his adoration of its magnificent daughters. He would look miserably at the pictures of its destruction in the French newspapers he read regularly, even though they were a month old by the time they reached Aleppo. He swapped them with a few friends who would gather every evening in a small café at the end of al-Telal Street, sipping wine and speaking in foreign languages with French officers who held parties every Thursday night and never stopped talking about their love for Aleppan cuisine.

As a child Nizar was included in these Thursday parties. He received praise and sweets and records from the French officers' wives, who adored seeing his fingers moving over violin, cello, and flute with such ease. He would play for hours with a passion that never waned, and leave at the end of the night with his teacher Ahmed al-Mabid. He would hand some francs to Nizar, who spent them on silk hair ribbons. Nizar would walk cheerfully into the living room, showing off the precocious femininity which was so shocking for his family, who liked to sit at the dinner table and discuss their superior morals.

After he reached puberty he felt an apparition dazzle him; sensations of lust turned him into a woman whose secret no one wanted to know. He would wait for Ibtihal to leave her room, and then he would open her wardrobe and take out her short skirts, put them on, and sit for hours in front of the mirror. He tried on her lipstick and lay on her bed, feeling his body, recalling photos of the men he cut out of the Egyptian magazines his father bought on a regular basis. One particularly exciting photo remained with him, of President Nasser making his famous speech nationalizing the Suez Canal. For a long while he imagined himself the lover of the dark-skinned president whose photos he adored. He would swap them with his friend Michel and together they would walk the empty lanes of Aziziya, continuing a conversation that lasted fifteen years before Michel left to live in Paris. He sent Nizar a photo which showed him kissing his French lover, hugging him publicly in one of the city's famous squares.

Nizar wept as he looked through a secret album only my mother had seen, which held pictures of Nizar in the bars of Beirut in the sixties, where he had lived for a whole year. Nizar described it to Rashid, his friend as well as his nephew, as 'the days of honey and bliss.' He would tell and retell the story of how he left his family's house one night with a small bag of clothes, leaving a long letter addressed to each member of the family in turn. His father didn't read it out at the dinner table, as Nizar had begged. In the letter Nizar also cursed his eminent grandfather, His Excellency Sheikh Abdel-Salam, to whom women came from all over the country to be blessed. Nizar said that he stole money from the poor and spied on the ulema on behalf of the Sublime Porte, and that he would patrol at night with the Janissary troops, disguised in a niqab and woman's clothes, to guide them to the homes of those wanted for the draft in the raid on the Suez Canal in 1915. He called Abdel-Monem a rodent who spied on his sister Ibtihal and masturbated over the smell of her clothes in the bathroom. This was the same Ibtihal who left the window of her room ajar so that the son of their neighbor could spy on her as she slowly undressed before reciting Surat al-Baqara and slipping into bed, weighed down by her heavy Ottoman nightclothes.

He wrote that he hated them all and loved only my mother, whom he described as a waft of perfume; she didn't curse him when he lay close to her on the bed wearing silk underclothes. He would tell her about his daydreams and the kisses he longed for from men with thick moustaches. In the course of ten pages, Nizar wrote his life story, hiding nothing. He declared confidently that he loved his femininity, and described the family home as a place which reeked of hatred in every corner; he cursed their lavish spending on religious holidays and how they connived with each other to affect grandeur in front of strangers. He spoke of his father for the first time and called him a silly man who cared more about his picture with Monsieur Henri Sourdain than his own life. He advised him to acknowledge, truly, that they were a fragmented family, like all families who only cared how they appeared to the outside world.

He spoke bitterly, painfully, about their collusion, all of them, in turning him in to the police. He had been detained for six months on charges of sodomy after being seen by a medical examiner who handled his rear with disgust and confirmed the charge. The following morning two policemen led him in chains to the Court of Justice and laid his file in front of a judge who piously called on God to deliver him from his sight, and ordered he be locked up in Aleppo Central Prison. In the letter, Nizar dwelled at length on how he suffered when an elderly guard threw two filthy blankets and a pillow stuffed with straw at him and led him to the quarters reserved for sodomites and others accused of moral crimes. Nizar went in and sat beside the door, the sharp smell of excrement wafting from the barracks built in the style of an old domed shrine. He felt humiliated, and his tears choked him silently.

The first night he slept on the doorstep and didn't respond to the other prisoners' provocations. On the second day Sheikh Jumaa, the imam who gave the Friday sermon and who was in prison accused of raping seven children, of whom the oldest was no more than eight years old, told him to wash the floor of the barracks, and that night he took Nizar to the toilet where he violently raped him and asked him to moan like a woman. He kept Nizar as a servant who washed his socks and handled his member every morning during his ablutions. Nizar cried in desolation, but never said a word. He wrote on paper bags, music which spoke of separation, suffering, and silence and which he kept after he left prison on bail, which had been paid by Ahmed al-Mabid. He went back to the family that had left him in the hands of Sheikh Jumaa, whose trial continued for three years, after which he emerged innocent. Sheikh Jumaa later sought out Nizar to disclose his desire for his soft body so like an ostrich, and to invite him to live with him in his grand house in Muhafiza. Nizar spat in his face, remembering the cruelty of the months he had spent among the collection of perverts who didn't know the meaning of love—not the kind Nizar sought with all his strength.

He entered his family's house after six months, wide-eyed and emaciated, a collection of music under his arm. He sat at the dinner table next to his father and summoned up the long monologue he had many times imagined himself stand-ing up and delivering to his family, accusing them of wishing to murder him. He couldn't reply to his father's question as to whether prison had made him grow up and put him back on the true path, to being an honorable man who didn't grope men's bodies in dark alleys.

He got up quietly and left the house. He walked through Aleppo feeling nothing but hatred for it. He returned at night to my mother's room and didn't leave it for ten consecutive days. She would come back from school and bring him food on tin plates, which they would share. She conveyed their father's regret for his cruelty and for having been swept along by Abdel-Monem, who wanted to kill him and be rid of the family shame.

Nizar slipped into bed next to my mother and told her about the death he had passionately longed for all the time he was in prison. When it got to be evening in the prison and the lights were turned off in the cells, when darkness fell and the prisoners' murmurs rose, Sheikh Jumaa would come to him. He had made it known that Nizar was his lover and thus under his protection, and had turned him into a servant who washed his underwear and mopped the floors. He added that prison was like a jungle where the beasts screamed eternally. Having no money and no family asking after him had made him an easy target. The guards spat on him every morning, the prisoners harassed him during their outside breaks, and when they were inside the barracks they demanded that he imitate the Egyptian actresses who placed candelabras on their heads and jiggled their hips and their wide thighs. He had no choice but to accept Sheikh Jumaa's offer of protection and payment. He smeared Nizar's body with the perfumes of the sheikhs and led him to a nearby corner of the bathroom. He bared Nizar's rear and forced himself inside like a mangy dog, and Nizar didn't dare to cry out.

My mother listened to Nizar's grief as he cried gently into her chest. He got up and spread out his pieces written on paper bags, avoiding responding to his father's pleas. He would look with bitter hatred at Ibtihal whenever he heard her demanding their father kill him and throw his body to the dogs, or ardently seconding Abdel-Monem's suggestion to throw him out. Nizar said that he couldn't bear to live amid this hatred any longer. He packed a few clothes in a small bag and left for Beirut where he arrived broke and hungry. He hated the way he smelled, and felt that Sheikh Jumaa's odor clung to him. Nizar thought that our lives were a collection of brutal smells we spent our entire lives ridding ourselves of. Sheikh Jumaa would make him perform his ablutions, before forcing him to go to the Friday prayer where he led the prisoners seeking forgiveness for their sins.

He sat in Café Modka, waiting to accost Nadim al-Aghwani, the famous Lebanese musician who was never late. Nizar introduced himself briefly as the favorite pupil of Ustadh Ahmed al-Mabid and said that he was looking for work. Nadim al-Aghwani contemplated him and asked him to come to his house in Ras Beirut that evening. Nizar passed the time watching the passersby and the shops, clutching the music he had composed in prison. He glanced at it once more before entering the office of Nadim al-Aghwani, who knew as soon as Nizar started playing that he couldn't endure the presence of this talent, this genius, in his band.

Nizar lost no time. He took out one of the pieces and offered to sell twenty more like it, and their distribution rights, to Nadim's group The Conservatoire for three thousand dollars. A whiff of conspiracy arose in the stylish room. Nadim al-Aghwani drew the curtains and dismissed his servant after he had brought the two of them a light dinner. He looked over the short pieces. Nizar played one of them, called "Shadows of Regret," on the violin, and then played it again on the flute. Nadim al-Aghwani didn't require much time to settle a deal, pursuant to which Nadim al-Aghwani would pay three thousand American dollars in return for Nizar's surrender of all the original copies of the music and full distribution rights to The Conservatoire and a written statement that he was sole arbiter over Nizar's brilliant ideas, and that the latter would absent himself from Beirut's music scene for a year.

In the eighties, Nadim al-Aghwani was famous for songs which were played on the radio and on Syrian television constantly. He was praised by the Syrian president, who ordered the doors of television and radio be flung open to this hireling, and relaxed for years in the permanently reserved suite of the Sheraton Hotel in Damascus, composing stirring songs in praise of the Party and its onward march, bringing girls from Beirut for the security officials who constantly saw to his needs, until he was found dead in his grand house in Beirut at the age of seventy. Every artists' guild in the Arab world lamented him and a great critic wrote a lengthy study on him, dusting off the album called "Shadows of Regret." The Berlin Concert Orchestra made a recording of it in the studios of Berlin; Nizar would listen to it and criticize the entrance of the violins in such a blunt way, without the accompaniment of the cellos.

Nizar left al-Aghwani's office determined to make a success of his new life. He clutched the money in his pocket and looked for a cheap hotel. He went alone to the places he had frequented with Michel in frivolous moments during their few and fleeting visits to Beirut, and it didn't take him long to find new places. He settled in Old House Bar, and felt liberated in this place where gay people gathered every night and freely exchanged drinks without being disturbed. He bought some delicate women's nightwear from expensive boutiques, and perfumes, and leather trousers and linen trousers and tight silk shirts that showed off his soft body. He rented a small flat on the sixteenth floor with a view of the sea, close to Hotel Saint George, for three hundred dollars a month. At last, he found in Beirut what he had been so desperately seeking. He wrote to Michel telling him how happy he felt and cursing Aleppo, which he called a fortress of regret. He sealed his letter with a kiss printed in red lipstick and invited him to come for a visit.

Michel wasted no time accepting his old friend's invitation, but was forced to return to Aleppo to complete more of the country's endless bureaucratic procedures. They agreed on a time for him to come to Beirut; Nizar wanted to express to Michel how grateful he was to have him in his life. He sent a private car to transport Michel from Aleppo to Beirut and they spent a week 'living in Paradise' as both called it. Nizar didn't leave him for a minute. They drank their morning coffee in Hotel Saint George, ate dinner in expensive restaurants, and closed out the night in bars where Nizar was welcomed as a wealthy profligate with exquisite tastes. They had fleeting adventures, and then Michel said goodbye and wished his friend a new life filled with happiness. He went back to Paris and waited to see the pictures they had taken as incontrovertible proof that they had realized a dream that had haunted them for a long time—to indulge themselves in a city far from Aleppo, without any restrictions.

Nizar felt himself to be light, caressing the earth when he walked. He made new, wonderful friends and spoke with them about his desire for love. He ignored the string of offers for casual encounters, not wanting to ruin his mood or come off as cheap, and was invited to his friends' private parties. He was taken up by Hussein, a player for Nejmeh FC who was proud of his athletic body. He became Nizar's favorite, and he opened up to Nizar all the remaining secret doors of the city. He drove him in his Mercedes to an apartment in the heart of Hamra, to secret parties at which Nizar would play all his instruments and set his friends ablaze with excitement, while he looked for Hussein, who he could feel was close by. After they had swapped burning glances at more than one location and party, Nizar had declared his love and Hussein had taken him to his apartment. They had been at a birthday party where the wine and champagne flowed freely. Hussein's friend Caro displayed his amateur and somewhat obscene belly dancing, in a show of hostility to Hussein for having begun to ignore him. In honor of his friends, Nizar played from Umm Kulthoum's "Love Story." Dawn was breaking as they headed home, and Nizar had felt the nearness of Hussein's breath. He placed his hand gently on Hussein's and confessed that he loved him. Soon they were kissing, and Hussein moved into Nizar's apartment shortly after that, to the bitter envy of Caro, who accused Nizar of stealing his lover. Nizar no longer went to Old House Bar, tired of hearing Caro's threats to tear him limb from limb and feed him to the dogs.

Hussein and Nizar shared the deep devotion that Nizar had been waiting for all this time. He felt purified, rescued from the traces of Sheikh Jumaa and his filthy night sprees, which he told Hussein about in between sobs. Hussein sympathetically stroked the hair which Nizar no longer cut, at his lover's wish. For three months he felt complete happiness, which he would never forget all his life, before Hussein, accusing him of being frigid, left him and moved to the apartment of a German journalist who had seduced him with offers of cash and weekend trips to Cyprus where they would lie on sandy beaches and dine on grilled fish. He bought Hussein the presents which Nizar was unable to, after his money had run out. He left his apartment and moved to a room in Basta Tahta, and looked for work after pleading with Nadim al-Aghwani to let him work in a remote bar in Bint Jbeil. Nadim gave him a non-renewable permit from the syndicate to work there for three months, no longer. Nizar remained unemployed over the winter of 1959 and wandered through gay bars, looking for Hussein in order to express the desire that never left him. Weeping bitterly, he begged Hussein for just one night to return the warmth to a body that felt as if it were decaying beneath his fingers, while his German lover stayed silent, ignoring Nizar, who couldn't make Hussein hear his pleas.

Nizar returned to his vagrant lifestyle. He tried to write music like "Shadows of Regret" but it just didn't have the same emotional power. He regretted selling his music so cheaply—and was distressed whenever he heard his pieces on the radio. Hands in his pocket, carrying his small bag, he wandered around the rain-drenched streets, looking for a taxi driver or a porter in the Port of Beirut. They would take him to their squalid rooms and sleep with him, and ask him to leave in the morning without offering him breakfast. He was mired in the darkness of desire, alone, thrown out of the bars and unwanted at the private orgies held by his old friends. Everyone agreed that he was cheap, unsuitable for the secret congregations of Beirut's gay aristocracy which had welcomed him at first when they saw his elegance and his haughtiness and the way his silken fingers glided along the strings of his violin, then turned him out and ignored him when he began to curse Hussein and glean clients from the street.

Hunger and cold tore at him and he could no longer pay the rent even of his poor little room. He thought he saw Hussein on the falling autumn leaves, on the glass windows where he stood and looked at the low-cut silk evening gowns. He was lost in the details of lingerie shops for hours.

He went back to Aleppo and arrived, exhausted, only to find my father Zuheir al-Anabi and his family sitting gloomily in the living room. My grandfather was engrossed in the details of my mother's wedding and Nizar was introduced to my father's family as a dutiful son and a great musician who had played in Fairuz's band. He withdrew from the meeting, pleading tiredness from his journey, and went into my mother's room. He blessed her and then proceeded to vent his yearnings all night, telling her about Hussein's kisses which he would never forget. Everyone in the house desperately hoped that the groom's family would not discover the truth about the prodigal son, whom Abdel-Monem kicked under the table, demanding once again that their father kill him if he didn't leave their respectable home.

Nizar wandered around the house in frustration after his father left for the train station as usual to boast of his medals and annoy the rail workers. He could do nothing but return to his friends, who accepted his contrition after Michel mediated by letter and he burst into tears before them, promising that he wouldn't betray them again.

I thought of my Uncle Nizar, who seemed to me at the end of one particular visit to be an old man with no time for regret. He avoided speaking with people and came home from working at the cabaret loaded with vegetables and meats. He would spend hours cooking complicated Aleppan dishes in his own particular style and hoarded supplies of pickles and cheeses in anticipation of his casual lovers, the latest of which was Madhat, the public official he had picked up at a party at Cabaret Casbah. He liked the desire and the impetuosity of this thirty-year-old, although Nizar no longer fell in love. He remembered Michel, who sent him photos from various European cities showing himself with an arm around his lover (later his husband) as they stood together in front of museums and theaters, or pictures taken outside the hammam while they wore floaty, floral nightclothes.

Most galling of all for Nizar was the wedding picture Michel sent him. On the back was written *Darling Nizar, I wish the same for you. Pray for me, I am so in love with my new family.* And a last word: *Damn Aleppo, which I miss so much. Come and visit.* Nizar threw the picture in the bin and wallowed in grief and loneliness. He spent hours looking through the photo album of Beirut, and in later years he would Google old pictures of Nejmeh FC and Hussein's bio; forty years later Hussein seemed to him to be a cheerful man who befitted all that love—and the pain Nizar had suffered in order to forget him. Now he disbelieved men's flirtations and avoided their insults, wishing only to keep his position as a famous violinist. Everyone still remembered his silken fingers and the praise of his teacher Ahmed al-Mabid, who left him over a thousand records. He distributed them among his casual lovers without regret.

He lured Madhat to Café Mawhid and there the two of them seemed like friends having a quiet coffee and chatting about life. Madhat told him about his family in a village called Biyanon, about his dreams of a large house and a wife chosen for him from among his relatives. Nizar sensed his intense repression and liked his powerful peasant body. They continued meeting, but Nizar held himself back from expressing his desire; he felt they were soul mates even though they had just met. He used his long experience in seduction, and they eventually embraced after a couple of joints which Nizar had brought specially. He discovered a hunger for many things. He wrote to Michel that he was trying to recapture his taste for vigorous sex, and he mocked their old group whose genitals had started to dangle like bunches of withered grapes. He kept a distance between himself and Madhat so as not to fall in love, although love somehow crept into his heart nevertheless. It turned him into a madman who couldn't be apart from Madhat, who in Nizar's house relaxed as comfortably as if he were a king, stretching out his feet for Nizar to wash with warm water and the laurel soap Madhat insisted on using to perfume the large living room. He would order Nizar to bring him lunch and sent him to collect bribes from merchants on his behalf. Nizar gave Madhat the keys to the city and its merchants, the city whose secrets Nizar knew. Nizar thought the finest kind of love was that in which you were turned into a servant and ended your life a lord.

In Madhat's hands Nizar became servant, lover, and a wife called Maha, although Nizar had begged to be named Nahla, Hussein's name for him in Beirut forty years earlier. Madhat would lash out if he made a mistake, and Nizar accepted the blow like an obedient wife before lying down next to him in their imposing bedroom. He wandered through the large house on Faisal Street which looked out onto narrow streets shaded by quinine trees, waiting to hear Madhat's footsteps at any moment and vowing that he would be the last lover. He ignored the cheap prostitutes Madhat brought home from time to time, explaining Nizar away as an old uncle just returned from Brazil who intended to leave all his money to his nephew. Nizar would weep as he heard Madhat's moaning from the bedroom over women he described as 'vile' and, unable to bear it, would leave the house. He called Rashid at home and asked if he would meet him at Bar Express. He would wait for Rashid, but he didn't appear. Rashid could sense everything from his uncle's voice. He hated Madhat and considered him shameful and unworthy of his beloved uncle. He thought several times of killing him but didn't dare. Reflecting on his weakness, he explained to my mother in the midst of her hallucinations that the family she wished to hold onto was nothing more than a mirage, a delusion that had to end.

Rotting Corpses

MY MOTHER, WHO DIED IN the early evening, used to believe
that everything would be all right as long as she could open
the window and watch the sun set over the lettuce fields and
distant mulberry tree. She asked the headmaster for our marks
and was reassured that the days to come would be filled with
joy. The odor of the alleys in Midan Akbas was behind us,
the smell of oil and metallic grease and train screws we would
of course forget. As long as she surrounded herself with perfumes and cleaning agents, she was content with her decision
to build our home in the gardens close to downtown. She
would be enveloped in the silence she loved and which she
considered proof of refinement.

My father was finished for us. We no longer remembered
him or waited for the letters he never sent. When asked, we
bragged that he lived in the United States; not only that, he
would send for us as soon as we finished our baccalaureate. My classmates would look at me in suspicion, trying to
imagine how far away America was. My mother had stopped
caring about the remnants of my Midan Akbas accent; she
left me to my fate in desperation, repeating that the city would
invade me and defeat my inner peasant. She didn't know how
much I loved the power of words spoken in a village accent,
or my passion for the vast fields of wheat and the groves of
olives and pomegranate. I never forgot what it was to walk
in their shade when I was running amok with the railroad

workers' children, or watching the trains crossing the beautiful stone bridge amid the fields. We waved to the Turkish border guards in their huts and flung bunches of grapes and pomegranates at them, trying to make them understand in Kurdish (which I knew a little) that we lived at the station. When we grew older we would wear military-style outfits and stand on the other side of the border, where the guards would make do with pointing their rifles at us when they saw our group, augmented by this time by the leadership of Azad, the young goatherd. He would tell us legends about how he crossed the border daily while distributing smuggled hazelnuts among us so that we believed that he lived a double life: one life here, and another one there. He would tell us seriously that when he grew up he would marry his Turkish sweetheart Barihane who waited for him every Thursday behind the Turkish station. He added proudly that her father was a rail engineer who was expected to become the director of the Turkish railways.

The goatherd always had something which amazed us: his feet (which were lacerated from walking barefoot), his body (which was colossal for his eleven years), or his sweet voice when he sang Kurdish songs. We would repeat a pale echo of his songs after him in an attempt to grasp their meaning.

I saw my childhood friend who smelled of goats more than a decade later by chance at Restaurant Kilikya, close to our house. He was swigging arak and telling an old man with thick eyebrows about how great it was, smuggling tobacco from Turkey. I approached him and greeted him. Although he didn't remember me at first, I could sense how proud he was to be greeted by this young man with a stylish shirt and fashionably cut hair. I reminded him of the day he had led us over the border by accident and we got lost in Turkish fields of green beans and okra. Turkish soldiers had surrounded us with guns but let us off with a pinch of the ear and hauled us back to the other side of the border. They beat Azad with their rifle butts when he tried to stop them, and he let out a string of threats and abuse in Kurdish. When we reached Midan Akbas that night we hurried away, leaving Azad alone. We still believed his stories and his obstacle-ridden love for Barihane, daughter of the Turkish train engineer.

Azad roared with laughter and I saw his yellow teeth. He kissed me warmly on both cheeks as you would an old friend and introduced me to the old man, saying with great showmanship, "Poet of the Kurds, Uncle Hamid Badrkhan," adding proudly, "He's a friend of Nadhim Hikmat, in prison."

He was a man in his sixties, and as shy as a caged bird in the face of Azad's excitement. Azad brought me a chair and suggested that I sit by the window looking out onto the street. Our conversation was brief but I gave him our telephone number and I was pleased when he folded up the piece of paper I had written on and placed it in the pocket of his flared trousers. He kissed me demonstratively once again and passed on his greetings to my family, promising to visit me when he came to Aleppo.

Azad had not changed at all since childhood. I still remembered every detail of his face—all the children of the railroad employees in Midan Akbas remembered him, along with their wives who had bought fresh cheese from him. Its sharp taste still remained on my tongue, bringing with it the smell of his flock.

My mother craved that cheese but she didn't want a villager, a Kurd at that, to be included within the ranks of my friends. She consigned to oblivion everything that characterized Midan Akbas and the time spent there. I remember how she avoided welcoming her friends from the village when they tried to come to our house; they had enjoyed chatting to her on the doorstep about the best way to preserve pickles. She escaped nimbly, as if throwing a maggot-ridden cat's head out of the window, or cutting off a finger so as not to remember when it had hurt in the past. She threw away the ten years of her life spent in that border village that smelled of poverty, the dark fate of its inhabitants perpetually besieged by border guards and their mines, and the trains that moved so infrequently spiders nested in their cars. It seemed a perfect place to exile the employees of the Railroads.

Everything seemed quiet. Sawsan was sitting in her room, Rashid was languidly playing his violin, and my mother was anxiously reassuring herself that the new houses surrounding ours had all the hallmarks of being temporary and would eventually disappear, and that everything would go back to how it was. When she went for a walk in the lettuce fields she loved, she couldn't believe what had happened. Those dwelling on the land had been surprised by how quickly the city had expanded and had started encroaching on their fields. Land prices doubled hundreds of times and overnight the landowners had become so rich they didn't know what to spend their money on. They left the lettuce seedlings to die and the peach trees to wither. The beautiful meadows were transformed into tightly packed houses smelling of cheap bleach. When the narrow lanes became swamps in the winter, the sound of grasshoppers rose at night. My mother had to put a handkerchief over her nose to cross the street, enduring stares from the new neighbors who didn't know she was a respected teacher.

Her increasing frenzy for cleaning turned our life into hell. In her eyes we became filthy vehicles for microbes, brimming with bacteria, and she had to cleanse us before we came into the house. She didn't notice how the stones outside grew filthier, so that the charming engraving of the Quranic verse on our house was gradually hidden.

Gathering for dinner was no longer a fun occasion for swapping jokes and laughter and commenting on Rashid's shyness as he ducked his head coyly in Sawsan's embrace. He had started avoiding my mother now, and pretended not to hear whenever she asked him to play that piece again whose name she had forgotten, the one he used to play at the Armenian Cultural Center; coldly, he would say that he didn't remember playing

it, or what it was called. He was ashamed of my mother's ignorance and described her to Sawsan as a snob with no grasp
of music, who should stick to singing at home in the morning
and dancing at weddings to bridal songs. Sawsan laughed; she
enjoyed disparaging my mother, although she didn't know if
she truly hated her or only pitied her.

With some trepidation, Sawsan remembered classmates
of hers who had joined the Party seeking revenge for their
own ugliness and to teach her old friends a lesson—those
pretty girls with whom Sawsan used to go to Aziziya. There,
they would loiter in front of the shops and steal glances at
the handsome young men wearing colognes which battled to
dominate the air above the pavement.

The day after a meeting with one of the leaders from
Damascus, the girls decided the time had come to get back
at Hiba. Intoning the leader's name reverently, they barred
her way and presented her with a Party badge that she was
supposed to gratefully accept and pin onto her front, but she
curled her lip and kept on walking. They lay in wait for her at
the end of the day; they ripped her headscarf and bloodied
her body with their gun barrels, all the while calling her a reactionary bitch. They tore at her clothes until she was naked in
the street. A woman hurried over to wrap Hiba in her abaya,
and the other passersby bowed their heads and walked on as
if they couldn't see anything.

Hiba didn't go back to school. Sawsan always remembered
her delicacy and her wit. When she met her some years later,
in Hiba's boutique, she couldn't believe that the girl she had
dawdled and laughed with in Aziziya was this elegant woman
who sold gorgeous clothing for veiled women. She was the
proprietor of one of the most luxurious shops in Aleppo that
men were forbidden from entering. Hiba was astounded when
she saw Sawsan in a veil, and realized from her cheap coat that
things were not going well. Taking her affectionately by the
hand, Hiba led Sawsan to a small, stylish office containing a

grand walnut desk and ordered her a coffee, strong as Sawsan had always liked it. Hiba asked if Sawsan still liked everything strong, listing, with a glee she had not lost, her previous loves: the smell of men, armpits, sperm, roses, and coffee. She opened up a drawer in her desk and showed Sawsan a small photograph album with a lock. Inside were photos of the comrades who had torn Hiba's headscarf on April 9, 1982. She said, "I am waiting for these bitches right here in my shop." From her other desk drawer she took out a gold-plated gun and said, "This will do for my revenge." She opened the back door of the shop leading to a large garden and concluded, "I'll bury them here." Then she was silent.

Ten years hadn't been long enough for Hiba to forget that shame. She told Sawsan that afterward her family had forced her to marry Ziyad al-Hiyani, the son of her father's business partner in the old textile factory.

When Sawsan left Hiba's shop her burden was stronger than ever. She thought that the past, which had never left us, simply had to die. She recalled Hiba's innocent face, and how she always used to flee from Ziyad al-Hiyani when he waited for her after school, staring at her from his Mercedes window with a tortured romantic look pleading she accept him.

Depressed, Sawsan remembered that the comrades whom Hiba was waiting for in order to take her revenge had been sitting in the cold People's Hall of the Party a few weeks earlier, listening in boredom to a man whose words stank of desperation. He recited a statement composed of phrases they had heard a thousand times. The comrade waited for questions that didn't come, gathered up his pages, and left the hall. Seen from behind, he looked like a beggar in his old, faded suit.

These comrades, former paratroopers who had terrorized the city and torn Hiba's headscarf, were now so poor they wouldn't refuse charity. Their clothes smelled of fried potatoes, and they swapped news about their search for elementary pupils who might want lessons in exchange for a small handful of coins. Others were looking for additional work for their husbands, so they could settle some of the installments they'd missed for their fridge or washing machine.

Sawsan had left the meeting and decided that she would never go back to that depressing building. Her frustration increased, as most of the comrades hadn't recognized her. She had become nameless. She could feel their torments, and remembered their cruel faces as they screamed Party slogans, or as they watched girls who were divided in their loyalties and didn't raise their voices loud enough while singing Party anthems, or as they wrote reports to the security branches with a zealousness whose origin she wondered about even now.

I thought a lot about the pain of my life, connected as it was to the Party's coup d'état and assumption of power. The Party and I were living parallel lives which never met. I could feel Sawsan's frustration and her unwillingness to speak about it, but she did say that the vast majority of Syrians lived a life parallel to the Party and the regime, which ruled with such tyranny, and these lives never intersected. She divided the country into two camps; in the first were the freeloaders who knew nothing about the other camp, the one where life was propagated, where it ran quietly and slowly and knew everything about the camp of the regime's people. She didn't complete her theory. She was silent, as if she had made a mistake by wanting to come back to our camp. I looked into her eyes and for the first time they were dulled. I felt her defeat and dreaded her reaction; I knew her, and she would not accept living like a mouse in a hole. She was so weak now that a light breeze could shatter her, but her speech about the two camps and her parallel life had returned lost meaning to her existence

She threw her degree into a drawer in her wardrobe. When she saw it had spotted with the mold that invaded our house from all sides, she didn't care and just wrapped it in a cheap plastic bag and put it back where it was. I told Rashid that his beloved Sawsan had lost her irrepressible cheer and might kill herself, describing how I had seen her dusting the three stuffed eagles and repeating that everything was lost. Rashid nodded indifferently as he put on the same black suit he wore every evening to go to work. He was repeating the same actions, wearing the same clothes, leaving every night at a specific time to go to the same place, where he played the same music, and walked along the same roads on his way back to the same house.

We avoided each other at home. My mother ate her dinner alone, desperate for some warmth to return to her table. She stared at the television, waiting for each program to come on in turn. She never raised her eyes from the news broadcast, which might last three hours, in which the presenter would review each activity and affecting speech of the President. Even more emphatically, he would review the plethora of sacred directives made to governors and ministers and, of course, His gifts to His people—everything was a gift, and a mark of beneficence from He whom God may hallow. My mother was suddenly aware that the opposition she used to feel to it all was missing. She observed the fear that was growing inside her every day, and she identified with the pictures of the President. She convinced herself that she loved him, she had never hated him in her life, and she overlooked having ever described him and his friends as a group whose eyes did not exactly inspire confidence, or as thugs who wouldn't be able to smell the difference between Sawsan and pickled turnip.

Nothing in her life had been as expected. Nariman told her the same thing; the day after her monthly flow had stopped, she revealed that she was still a virgin and had never been touched by a man. My mother was the only person she had left to visit. An old woman not yet fifty, Nariman would come to our house with tangled hair and an old coat she had inherited from her mother. She sat with my mother and mumbled distractedly about performing the Hajj next year with her nephews, the sons of her brother, Hajj Abdel-Latif. While Nariman and my mother waited for the cycle of daily soap operas to start they would swap recipes for chamomile tisanes, and they only realized it was midnight when the television stopped broadcasting and they were left with the sound of white noise.

I came out of my room, switched off the television, and accompanied Nariman to the door of her family house in Jamiliya. As I passed it, I glanced furtively at my grandfather's house, sunk in silence even though Uncle Abdel-Monem wailed endlessly within; the place meant so little to us we heard nothing. I thought about time on my way to Uncle Nizar's house—I guessed that at that late hour he would be preparing to go and play with Rashid at the cabaret. The streets of Jamiliya had changed, and held abandoned houses alongside new, makeshift buildings. The narrow streets were missing the quinine trees which had made our noses run as children on the few occasions we came to visit my grandfather, when we would have to bear contemptuous looks from Ibtihal for being the offspring of a peasant.

Ibtihal left for Saudi Arabia as the second wife of a Syrian man in his sixties after her husband, Haitham Sabbagh, a wool trader, fell in love with an actress playing Ophelia and divorced her. Haitham was exhausted by my aunt's snobbishness and angrily concluded that her beaky nose brought bad luck. He sent her the divorce papers, which she signed nonchalantly and disdainfully, unaware of the chattering at family councils. Haitham complained of Ibtihal's devotion to praising her lineage, her constant invocation of ridiculous stories about the forebears he termed "venal minions in the pay of the sultan." He scorned the pictures of them she had hung in their home in Seif al-Dawla, while she looked down on everything that was not related to Aleppo and its Ottoman era. She would curse those from the villages for no reason, and over and over again she would tell the story of her ancestors which was somewhat dubious in its facts.

Haitham Sabbagh was a unique man. He loved to laugh, and memorized every simile, aphorism, and joke that could raise a smile. In his youth he had acted small roles in comedies, happy to play the idiot manservant slapped about by the hero, and he was engulfed with joy when he saw the auditorium crammed with people laughing as they watched avidly, shelling seeds and embroiling each other in discussions with an anarchy that delighted him. He sought enjoyment in every minute, and believed that one lifespan was too short to drink in the whole cup of bliss. From the earliest weeks of his marriage to Ibtihal he felt the dilemma of living with such a prickly woman. Aunt Ibtihal loved everything to do with Aleppo and the Ottomans. She was perpetually dropping Turkish phrases into her speech and her kitchen was crammed with embellished copper pots and platters, each one weighted with ridiculous ornamentation, chrome-plated, and appropriate for an eternity in rich, ancestral dining rooms. She wore long dresses ornamented with heavy, traditional jewelry. She surrounded her bed with multiple filigree teapots that Haitham Sabbagh felt were a burden on his very soul. When she came to his bed on Thursday nights, she would walk over weighted down by a nightdress in the style of centuries past, which she would remove imperiously, and then stand for so long that his desire would disappear and he would be repulsed by the strips of heavy chiffon. He missed his reckless youth spent in the company of the city's greatest wits, the clowns who were the heroes of comic theater. He missed the simple mode of living which he had inherited from his mother, the first woman to stand onstage in Aleppo. Undaunted, she would smile broadly in the face of the abuse from sheikhs who used whole sermons to single her out for criticism and incite their adherents to burn down the town's only theater, which one of the city's richest men had built in his house overlooking Hatab Square.

However many zealots threw rotten tomatoes at her and ruined her white dress, she was not swayed from her love for the theater. She learned French and read Molière, and her young son Haitham inherited her passion for joy and the theater. She had thought that Ibtihal took after her mother Bahiya al-Katibi, my grandmother, who had been her friend and had shared her love of telling dirty jokes. They would meet frequently at Sitt Thérèse's house and the three of them used to spend whole evenings eating fried seeds and marmalade, and rocking with laughter.

Haitham Sabbagh couldn't bear living with my aunt, who hated us and called us "summer bugs." She cursed our mother for having accepted a peasant's proposal, and abused her when my father abandoned her. She prevented Nizar from visiting Uncle Abdel-Monem to offer his condolences at the secret funeral reception his friends had put together after Abdel-Monem buried his son Yehya.

Haitham Sabbagh fell in love with an actress from the City Lights theater company, which was touring Syrian cities at the time. It produced plays in the cultural centers which had largely been abandoned by their founders after the eighties.

Haitham Sabbagh sympathized with Nizar, although he felt ashamed that he was uncle to his only son Najib. After Najib died of an asthma attack, Haitham Sabbagh no longer felt any need to stay with Aunt Ibtihal, who returned to her house from a short visit and found the locks changed. Haitham dispatched his brother to reach an arrangement with Uncle Abdel-Monem so that the divorce proceedings could be finished quickly.

Aunt Ibtihal was dazed at suddenly finding herself without home, child, or house, whose many objects she had bragged about and which had choked Haitham Sabbagh's spirit. She understood his resistance against trying for another child as his escape plan. In their last year together he hadn't entered her room once, content to lie on a mattress thrown down in a small room among the piles of French books he had inherited from his mother, along with some old costumes from small roles she had played in the early sixties. My aunt packed up her many possessions and did not cry, believing that she would find another husband, someone richer and sterner who would share her interest in the splendor of Ottoman life.

Year followed year and she remained alone in Abdel-Monem's house. He no longer loved her haughtiness and remembered her harsh orders when she was younger and used to control the house down to the colors worn by my grandfather, who surrendered to her every wish after my grandmother's death. He used to be afraid of Ibtihal's strict tone when she ordered him to wear a woolen robe when he sat on the balcony of his own house, where he liked to have breakfast and bask in the springtime sun as he watched the trains from his seat. He knew their timetables by heart, as well as each one of the drivers, whom he called his pupils, and he would wave as they passed by the house.

I had only been to my grandfather's house on a few occasions, the latest being the day my mother took me to offer my condolences to Uncle Abdel-Monem on the death of his son. We sat in the secret funeral reception, where a muffled tape recorder played verses from the Quran and a few mourners conversed about the price of vegetables. Most of them were illustrious teachers and former colleagues of my uncle, who from one day to another had turned from a lauded physics professor to a criminal's father, arbitrarily dismissed from his teaching post and prevented from traveling abroad. He contented himself with sitting for hours in his bookshop, where he had previously spent only a short time, giving private lessons to a few students selected from the many who wished to learn from him. He placed a large table in the middle and a few chairs which were occupied by students from six until nine. The place seemed more like an office than a bookshop and contained dusty papers, a few summaries of study courses which he would sell to his pupils, and a few reams of the paper my mother used to buy to write the letters we never read.

My mother sobbed for her brilliant nephew. She didn't stay at the reception for long, afraid that if my aunt Ibtihal made any misstep regarding her children, she wouldn't be able to control herself and the secret reception might turn into the sort of uproar that my uncle's bewildered family couldn't endure. Everyone felt that everything they had achieved, any comfort they had found in their small successes, had vanished in a puff of wind. Staying alive became a primary aim, and it would cost the two remaining sons of Abdel-Monem all the money they could gather from their small businesses after it was discovered that their brother Yehya, the dreamer who had loved watering the parsley planted in pots on the balcony, was a member of the armed wing of the Muslim Brotherhood.

My mother did not take the bait when Ibtihal resumed her unprovoked abuse of Uncle Nizar. She picked up her bag and left, grieving for Yehya whose large picture had a black ribbon in the corner, as if he had died in a car accident and not been murdered in a house known to belong to the Brotherhood. His picture had been published the following day in the faded pages of the local newspaper, along with his full name and six forged identity cards which all bore his picture and different names. One of the names was that of an outstanding physicist Yehya had met one day lost in the souk, and had invited him back to the family home. Yehya put on a lavish welcome for his guest, who was astonished that such a young man knew of and followed his research. Yehya left the professor to wander freely about the house while he went into the kitchen to make some mulberry syrup, and then engaged him in an enjoyable conversation about his interest in physics, in which he skillfully discussed theories of light and the limits of measuring it.

No one understood how this idealistic young son had slipped into this trap, this physics student who was outstripping even Uncle Abdel-Monem and was competent enough to criticize long-established classical theory. He read fluently in English and followed a reputable American academic journal which reached him by registered mail. He sometimes wrote his objections to the research it published in long, well-argued letters. He even received a reply signed by the editor, Professor Mike Hamilton, a leading researcher at NASA. Abdel-Monem dreamed that his son would be a pioneer, his name recorded in letters of gold; the greatest physicists and academics in the world would host him, and he went as far as dreaming of a Nobel nomination for his son, even a win.

When I crossed Bab al-Nasr Street, I lingered for a few moments to look at Uncle Abdel-Monem's shriveled-up face. He seemed to me like a wretch waiting to die. He had spent twenty years speaking to Yehya's picture, and lost the fierce vigor which I remembered as overwhelming and which my mother described as oppressive. Everything was a punishment for his cruelty and his alliance with Aunt Ibtihal in arranging family affairs just as they liked, without reference to peasants or perverts. Even so he didn't apologize or allow Nizar to weep for the young man who, he believed, would have been a genius if he had learned music. Nizar remembered Yehya as a dreamy child who displayed certain eccentricities which his family recounted with pride. Nizar interpreted the same behavior as the first signs of genius in a youth who would suffer for every one of his twenty-three years on account of his inability to conform either with his family or with society; he discovered one day that physics was no more than apostasy and only combat could bring him closer to God.

Yehya was not surprised that his companions in the secret training camp had so much in common with him. In their breaks during the day they would pelt each other with comments about sport or biology and generally fool about, but at night they would search for meaning, and sought the inimitability of the Quran with the sheikhs who came especially to bless them and lead them in prayer. These sheikhs dreamed of a nation of Islamic certitude, and were terrified that the ignorant public was turning to physics, chemistry, and biology, which would inevitably lead them to deny the existence of God. These discussions never ended without going back to the idea of forming a nation in which power would be the exclusive preserve of those who were close to God, those who had been urged by Him to bear arms and assume control over this life and the one to come.

Uncle Nizar did not enjoy his family history. My mother was enough family for him; he called her his beloved sister and his wonderful mother, and showered her with presents on Mother's Day. He would kiss her hand with a sweetness that overjoyed us, and with a cheerful mimicry of Ibtihal pointing at him to get out. He wasn't moved when he heard my mother's describing Uncle Abdel-Monem sitting silently in a corner, or Aunt Ibtihal as she begged to be married off to anyone to escape feeling so suffocated in her brother's house. Abdel-Monem arranged her marriage to a widower in his sixties who worked as a caretaker in Saudi Arabia and who was very respectful of Ottoman tradition, even though his knowledge of it went no further than a picture of a group of men standing with brocaded robes in front of the barber's shop he inherited from his grandmother. He pointed to the oldest man in the center of the group and said it was his grandfather, Nazmi Effendi, holding the keys to the Sultan Ahmed Mosque. She didn't hesitate in accepting him. Over the previous year she had been afraid of dying in an old people's home after the decline in Abdel-Monem's circumstances, and after his sons Hussein and Hassan emigrated to Dubai to work as apprentice chefs at an Aleppan restaurant owned by one of their old friends. She thought bitterly of how the municipal authorities would bury her, a woman who had dreamed many times that she would be wife to a sultan, or to one of his commanders at the very least.

She had to be content with a photograph of her husband's imaginary grandfather as proof of his ancient and unspoiled lineage. She packed her bags and traveled with him to Saudi

Arabia. Sawsan was astonished when she learned from Hiba that my aunt, whom we had sarcastically named the Haramain Temptress, was maid to a Jordanian family in order to support her husband.

One day, Sawsan shyly turned over a gift from her friend and took out a large, elegantly wrapped bag, suitable for the clientele of Hiba's shop, who were drawn from the rich, conservative classes. She was taken aback by its contents: an abaya embroidered with gold thread, a silk dress, small diamond earrings, a magnificent coat, a black headscarf, and a small card on which Hiba had written, in the handwriting Sawsan knew so well, *The princess remains a princess even if, on December 18, 1995, she turns thirty. Warmest kisses.*

Sawsan was moved by our celebration of her thirtieth birthday. Uncle Nizar gave her his golden bracelets, and I brought her a beautiful woolen cap instead of the thick hijab she usually wound around her head and which turned her into a woman I could never have imagined. She opened Rashid's gift amid our screams of pleasure—it was a brand new Canon camera. She kissed us and cried when she saw my mother had regained her vigor and suggested that we invite our friends over.

We were struck, however, by the realization that we had no friends. My mother prepared two types of vine leaves (stuffed with rice and with meat) in the Aleppan way, and tabbouleh, and many other dishes. We were surprised that she hadn't forgotten our favorites. She didn't protest when Rashid poured a glass of Johnny Walker Black Label and toasted Sawsan, "Princess of the world," as he called her.

We were content with our half-celebration. Sawsan was no longer our madwoman who inflamed our few occasions with a display of belly dancing; we sufficed with cutting the cake my mother brought from Salloura in Jamiliya, in an attempt to resume the old family warmth. Sawsan heard the first part of "Love Story," which Nizar played in a dozen different ways in honor of the birthday girl, who used to love it. She asked us if we would mind if she went to bed, and after going to her room, she thought about Hiba's message. She remembered when she used to visit Hiba at her family's house in Shahba. The two of them would go to her large room and the maid would bring the china patterned with birds, some sweets and petit fours, and a large plate with fruit in season, then Hiba would lock the lock and she and Sawsan would lie on the broad bed. Hiba would dangle a ripe berry to Sawsan's lips, who would catch it gleefully, her lips stained with the delicious taste of berries. Hiba would wipe Sawsan's lips with her own finger and they would carry on gazing at the ceiling, talking about the girls in their class. Sawsan recalled the touch of Hiba's soft hands when she brushed them gently over her lips, letting the locks of her long hair fall like a delicate waterfall. Sawsan would play with them, and Hiba would close her eyes, remembering the sensation of Bassam al-Deiri's body. Bassam had tried to guide her to Marxism but had been arrested in 1984; by then he was languishing in Sednaya Prison playing chess with his comrades. Hiba could still quietly describe the fruit of his body and the taste of the milk which he spilled over her breast.

Looking back to those visits, Sawsan thought that Hiba had loved her, and more than once had tried to tempt her into kissing her like a lover. Sawsan's innocence at that time meant she hadn't thought for a moment that Hiba, the veiled daughter of a conservative family, was attracted to women. She recalled old details, sorted through pictures; such as the way Hiba remained close whenever they danced to their favorite group Baccara, all by themselves in the large room with the curtains closed. She urged her to try leather trousers whose touch excited Sawsan, making her almost swoon, and when they danced Hiba would insist on hugging her from behind, clinging to her tightly.

At the time she had enjoyed Hiba's eccentric ideas, and her odd taste in lingerie which she brought from Beirut, or which her sister Mona, wife of the son of a Saudi diplomat, sent her from Paris. Sawsan missed the innocence of those days before she had the idea, one scorching day in September 1981, of entering the room of the female Party members and asking for a membership card. She quickly wrote all the necessary information, signed it, then left without a glance at the 'seals,' as she and her clique used to sneer when they sent perfumed letters to Radio Monte Carlo with false names, asking for songs they would dedicate to the Party members in mockery. They would turn up the voice of Hikmat Wehbe as he broadcast their requests: *From Sisi bint Hayy al-Sabil to the Enchantress of Mahabba School, Dalal al-Samra. Also from Sisi to her loyal friend with the most beautiful eyes in the world, Suad al-Shaqara, on her birthday.*

Soon Sawsan was invited to the first Party meeting. She wore her short skirt and a tight, stretchy blouse, and aroused the interest of the comrade who had come from Damascus to welcome the new female Party members and warn of the danger threatening the country. Hiba ignored Sawsan's Party membership, and didn't stop inviting her to her family's house, or to birthday parties attended by Hiba's female cousins and family friends. Sawsan would observe the bourgeois pomp and was taken aback by the demure clothes of the girls who entered in veils, long coats, and pitch-black head coverings. Once inside they removed them all and nothing was left to the imagination; it was like a monstrous fashion show at a cabaret. Sawsan hated the girls who nipped her chest from time to time, looking licentiously at her taut body in its tight jeans. In their eyes, she could see they longed to violate her. Hiba mocked them and shared Sawsan's cheeriness, which no one else in the room contributed to. She mocked her mother, who removed her golden bracelets when she read the Quran in the emphatic voice learned from female reciters who descended on her frequent receptions. She described her father as a gentle rabbit, but then backpedaled and spoke about him as a wonderful man who never refused her a request, a truly pious man who spent all night in prayer before leaving at dawn to see to his factories. He managed all their affairs himself, all the while repeating that material things would pass away.

Fourteen years later, Hiba concisely conveyed to Sawsan her wish to have her as a lover, forever. Sawsan hated her at that moment. She picked up her gifts, rewrapped them and threw them in her wardrobe, which by now contained only the rags of a poor woman; no perfumes, no creams, no preposterous lingerie, no sunglasses, no sleeveless leather jackets which she remembered Hiba used to love wearing in imitation of foreign pop stars. She would open the buttons one by one to reveal her bare breast to Sawsan, who would laugh naively and applaud like the hysterical hordes Hiba dreamed of every night. She told Sawsan once about a fantasy she had where Bassam and his friends all ravished her at the same time on her broad bed.

Our voices were still raised in the living room, when Sawsan heard my mother laughing. She realized that she was laughing too, with her; she asked God to forgive her hatred for her mother, who had never hidden her from anyone. She heard Nizar's music, which hadn't stopped.

Sawsan closely reviewed each of her thirty years. She now considered herself the daughter of a poor family living in a slum settled by impoverished soldiers, mukhabarat, Kurdish fellaheen, and day laborers in the textile factories. It was ruled over by Comrade Fawaz, whom she saw on television speaking about the state of the nation, and his family who shot their guns in the air in delight at his success in the elections for the People's Council on the Party's ballot. They now lived in well-heeled districts of the city and used their old houses as warehouses for iron and other goods brought by trucks which crossed the Lebanese border without enquiry as to their cargo. The noise from these trucks and the voices of the men carrying their contents kept us awake for days at a time.

She reconciled with herself and admitted that the operation to repair her virginity had not given her the certainty she was looking for. It wasn't right that her lot would be to look for a man who would buy a small house in installments and furnish it with a fridge and a small oven from cooperatives and an iron given as a gift by impecunious friends and family. She took off all her clothes and lit her candle. She stood in front of her mirror for the first time in a long time and discovered that the mirror had rusted, like her body. She touched the small amount of flabbiness between her legs, alarmed by the thought of the rusty mirror. She ran her fingers through her hair, which had coarsened since she started neglecting it. In recent years she bathed hastily without any additional creams or conditioners to soften the hair she had never neglected when she was Munzir's lover. She used to celebrate her body with long baths fragranced with perfumes and soaps and concoctions of fresh herbs. She would linger when putting on her bra, imagining his delicate fingers unhooking the clasp. She thought now that the acid in her throat was the same she used to feel from her mother when she would look with hatred at her slender body and swelling chest.

She thought that we created fear to make others afraid of us, only to discover that it clung to us as well and made us equally afraid. It was like the delusions of glory Sawsan had dreamed of when she was arm in arm with Munzir on the streets of Aleppo. Then, she saw people's fear when they met them and she shivered. She would feel her body heat rising, as they transferred their fear to her. She had tried to rid herself of this idea, and believed that she would be the mistress of Munzir's large house in Damascus. She would wander through it freely, ordering the privates working as servants to bring breakfast, cursing the drivers for being late in bringing the boys back from school, retreating into her own private bathroom. She immersed herself in fantasies and perfumes and it didn't occur to her for one moment, as she wandered around in a light nightshirt bringing Munzir's breakfast, that she would become the woman on the edge of the bed, overlooked. Everything had indicated that she would be mistress of the future.

Zealously, she attacked the opposition shown by other girls; she wrote reports on her classmates, on every whispered word about the Party, or the paratroopers, or God, or the Leader. She used to think that she was defending her Party, her country, and her lover who yearned for the highlands of his village in the mountains of Masyaf. When he spoke of it he was transformed into a child who wanted to leave the army and return to the fields of prickly pear and run headlong through the meadows of blue sweet peas. He raved about the images of the dead, the images of their faces. She felt his fear but didn't catch the references to the executioner's fear of his victim. She was proud when she left her house and saw Comrade Fawaz and his relatives lowering their eyes; before that they used to give her obscene looks, wishing to rape her. She thought when you lived in a jungle you had to be a beast.

The idea of being wife to a great officer never left her. She was nauseated by the wives of Munzir's colleagues who were content to rattle their gold bracelets and converse with their drivers in village accents. They bragged of their huge diamond bracelets, while their clothes reeked of their bad taste and the remnants of their provincial upbringing. She felt proud when Munzir's colleagues praised her taste in perfume and her simple clothes. She was happy when Munzir whispered in her ear that he loved her, and when he embraced her forcefully and tore off her nice clothes. She learned that he was aroused by visualizing other women in bed with her, so she brought him Hiba, whom he liked at first glance. Sawsan fumbled at Hiba's stomach to see what her body was like, and it was soft as a feather. For a while she had the idea that Munzir could never leave a woman who infused his nights with the scent of women drawn from the city the two of them ruled. She was proud when she saw cars of the mukhabarat circling the city to detain a student for questioning on the basis of her report. For hours, the student would sit in the interrogation rooms, trembling with fear while the troops' eyes snapped at her like dogs and the interrogators showed her accusations she could only defend herself against by weeping. She returned to school another girl, if she was not lost in the prison gloom. Afraid and obsequious, her old friends avoided her. She scrutinized every voice surrounding her for all of its possible meanings.

After Hiba stopped going to school, Sawsan avoided everyone except for the Party members she used to view suspiciously. She mocked their haircuts and walked through the school corridors wearing spotted military trousers, tight against her body, imitating the female American soldiers she saw in films.

She was mortified when she arrived in Dubai and discovered that she was a servant outside the castle, and the lover of a servant who could enter the palace just to receive instructions. Everything changed. Munzir was no longer the ambitious and cheerful man in his thirties. Sawsan would wake him every morning and, on the condition that he shave and use a napkin, made him a breakfast which made him forget the sour taste of the fried egg and jam he used to be served in the barracks.

After their first year in Dubai, his irritation increased daily. He hit her for the first time when he came back from the palace drunk. He took off his leather belt, swore at her, and rained violent blows on her face and body, repeating that he wasn't created to be a servant or to marry a fallen woman. She didn't understand why he was so incensed. She didn't enjoy his brutal blows, although she used to be aroused at the thought of being beaten gently with a leather whip. She burst into tears, fled, and wouldn't leave her room. Her Lebanese friend brought her bandages and some antibiotics, and advised her not to go to the hospital. The Emirati police wouldn't release her until she told them it was Munzir who beat her almost to death, and Habib al-Mawsili, the owner of the palace, was not in need of problems with the royal family or the government. Sawsan sat on her bed and made do with the few medicines she had. Three nights later Munzir came in and sat next to her, head bowed. He apologized in a few words and unpacked some food which the cook at the palace had made for her, after Munzir told her that Sawsan was suffering from a severe case of flu.

She felt desolate, and didn't respond to Munzir's blandishments. For the first time in years his jokes met no response. He had sex with her and she felt repulsed by his body. In the morning she got up and walked through the small apartment, enjoying her solitude. She thought of everything she had done in the last five years. She remembered her mother and Rashid and Uncle Nizar; she wrote a long letter to me and for the first time she felt unnecessary. She was like the palace maids who ate table scraps, went to the bank every month to augment their account balances by a few dirhams, and spent their weekends in cheap bars where they accepted the invitations of men just like themselves, who also waited for Happy Hour to make their few coins go further.

Her cheerful tone was missing from the letters in which she used to draw faces and cheery captions for them. She would also include a handful of hundred-dollar bills, and urged me not to mind if the postman stole it.

She asked how love could turn to hatred, and didn't linger long over the answer. She thought that she had to forget the image of the lady who would order servants to bring in roses from the garden, and to take the children to their riding lessons. She regained her strength and walked through the apartment half-naked, made some strong coffee, and went back to bed. She thought that she didn't need anything that was end. Endings terrified her. She thought of death, an ending there was no time to protest, and believed in its justice.

She imagined the lord of the palace would never die, and the victims of her reports would look at her with eyes full of vengeance deferred. She imagined a world where no one died, and wisdom ripened on everyone's lips.

She no longer desired the impossible from Munzir's infatuation with her. He deeply regretted resigning from the army to work as a servant to a man in a palace who seemed so weak himself, beleaguered by a history of dubious dealings. Munzir wrote to his friends in the mukhabarat and the army to cajole them into interceding with the leadership so he could return to the army. No one replied. After urgent and endless calls, his friend Abbas told him that his work in Dubai was preferable to selling cigarettes on the pavements of Damascus, or working as a taxi driver, or as a servant taking his master's children to birthday parties. Munzir resigned himself to his choice and started to look at everything in a new light.

Like every fellaheen's son beset with dreams of buying land in his village, and subjugating the sons of the feudal lord who had humiliated his father before the series of military coups, Munzir began to hoard money. He sent it to his brother Jaafar and urged him to buy land. It wasn't much at first, but over time it accumulated into enough money to buy farmland whose crop of tomatoes and citrus fruits could make a him living.

Munzir looked at Sawsan as she sat next to him in silence at Bar Montana. He violently missed their days in Aleppo and sympathized with her pain. For the thousandth time he thought about asking her to marry him, but the fear which had built up in him over the previous months made him reassess where his loyalties lay and he only felt safe within his own sect. Jaafar recommended the books of certain sheikhs, and he piled them up in his apartment and spent much of his free time with their yellowed pages. He thought about his fearful childhood in the bleak mountains, of walking to school barefoot. He felt greatly comforted by the hope of walking barefoot to visit Sheikh Khadr's shrine and spending an entire year in its sanctuary. He didn't appreciate Sawsan's remark that a shrine was the only place they hadn't had wild sex.

Freed from his burdens, he decided to marry whichever girl his brother Jaafar picked from their sect. He inspected the pictures of his female friends from school, and the face of Sahar's sister jumped out at him. He had seen her before he left his village on his last visit; she had been wearing the uniform of the seventh year and her books were tucked under her arm. He was aroused by her resemblance to Sahar with her green eyes, her large breasts, and her sharp voice. He remembered his only adventure with Sahar, when he took her by the hand to the fig orchards. There, he lifted up her sweater, which smelled of hay, and buried his head in her breasts. She moaned with such a strong Damascene accent it made him laugh, and Sahar explained with some asperity that village boys like him loved women from Damascus, so she had decided to become one. Her younger sister was now eighteen, and her poverty-stricken family wouldn't turn down an offer to marry her to the officer they were all so proud of. When he sealed the envelope containing a long letter to his brother and put it in the mail, he felt a chill in his fingers and toes. Sawsan had remolded him in the shape of a man; a woman like her would never consent to live with a servant.

Munzir's transformations irritated Sawsan and made her think of turtles who pass other creatures without noticing them. She decided she would be like a turtle and take no notice of Munzir. For the first time, she experienced what happened to love when it grew old.

She sorted through her memories and piled up old family photos on the small chest of drawers in her room. She felt an irresistible longing for Rashid, for when he used to lie next to her on the bed, hugging her and drawing strength from her. Of the pictures of her school friends, only the image of Hiba was clean and unstained; the others were distorted now, the victims of her reports who never left her dreams. For the first time she pitied her Party friends when she imagined them as she would later witness them: poor, hankering after the power they had dreamed of abusing for fun; widows without the right to mourn their dead men. Sawsan convinced herself that she was happier than this. She been living an untrue image of herself for all these years as Munzir's shadow, just as Munzir was shadow to a man more important than himself. She imagined the image of everyone who felt strong and terrorized the country; they were just shadows of the President and his family, the rulers of all. She decided that she would not remain the shadow of a servant who could only feel safe within his own sect.

In Bar Montana one night, Sawsan returned the flirtations of a Danish man who had been drinking heavily since early evening and was joking with the Portuguese barmaid, who smiled and winked at Sawsan. She thought of what he would be like naked in her arms. She wanted to regain the power of her body, she needed a man to kiss her feet to get her to hold him, to cry on her shoulder. She spoke to him in French and asked straight out if he was German; he replied smugly that he was Danish and clinked his glass against hers. He chattered for over an hour about his views on The East. She wasn't listening; she was watching his tall frame and white skin and thinking that she wouldn't leave Dubai without having tasted a European. She told him she was a drama student visiting her sister who lived in Dubai, and he launched straight onto the topic of Henrik Ibsen without taking a breath. She agreed with him on all points and continued to seduce him. Abruptly, he stopped chattering and invited her for a drink in his room. She nodded, picked up her bag, and left with him.

When Sawsan arrived at his hotel room she found a woman in her forties whose insolent nose reminded her of her mother, and she was somewhat disconcerted when the man introduced her as his wife Susanna. She greeted Sawsan warmly and poured her a vodka and lemon, and the three of them spoke dully about boredom in Dubai. Sawsan relaxed when she caught Susanna's glance at her husband, and laughed inwardly. She was surprised at an adventure she hadn't expected. She immediately unfastened her top button and brushed a finger along the edge of Susanna's nightdress; she could tell it was expensive. She stood up, wanting to leave, but was taken aback when the man suggested that she stay and watch them while they had sex. She asked him to kiss her toes, and Susanna hurriedly bent down and kissed them, her enquiring hands running all over Sawsan's body and stroking her soft stockings. She poured Sawsan another glass of vodka and her husband watched Sawsan from behind as he undressed. She saw his penis was large and flaccid. Wanting to take charge, she took hold of it and was pleased when it leapt up from its torpor. She ordered the woman in a harsh voice to undress and lie on the bed.

Excited by Sawsan's orders, the woman lay down and begged her like a servile maid to touch her husband's penis again. Sawsan went along with the game, but all of a sudden her head grew heavy and her enthusiasm waned. She gave the woman a long kiss on the lips and left without a word.

The failure of this affair gave Munzir a new luster. She waited for him again like a maid begging for a master. She asked him in as many words if he would marry her, and in fewer words he told her simply why it wasn't possible. She listened to his justifications with composure and was not annoyed, but she begged him not to leave her. She was astounded when she found herself repeating the words the Danish woman had used: she was a slave and he was her master, and she wouldn't stand in his way.

But in the end, she found herself repulsed by Munzir's new beard and discomfited by his new loyalties; it was the utter destruction of the old image of her lover that reconciled her to leaving him.

We didn't recognize Sawsan when she stood at the door to our house carrying a small, battered suitcase. My mother looked into her eyes for some time and despite her sympathy Sawsan could sense that she hated her for having done what my mother had only dreamed of: traveling and wandering the world. Sawsan bore her tepid embrace because she could see that I was crying from emotion as I kissed her, and behind me, Rashid was crying silently as he waited for his hug. She felt like a mother who had left on a whim and was returning to ask forgiveness and to be allowed back into our life, which was now entering a tunnel of infinite isolation.

Each of us walked through the house as strangers to one another, indifferent to the furniture, which had begun to disintegrate. At forty-six, my mother was so decrepit that Sawsan couldn't hate her. She went to her room and found Rashid's violin and cello there, next to the saxophone on which he had begun to play jazz pieces which reminded us of the faces of the women fellaheen and the railroad workers of Midan Akbas. My mother adamantly insisted he play "Death and the Maiden" by Schubert again, and Rashid commented sarcastically that our mother must have been born on the steps of the Viennese State Opera. Sawsan begged Rashid to keep his instruments in her room, and he played her a French song by Jacques Brel which she translated for him and enthusiastically explained.

As if she hadn't left us three years earlier, she apologized for being too poor to buy us the presents she used to look at in the shops of Paris and Dubai. As we recovered our cheerfulness my mother became more depressed, and we were deflated by her severity and her constant complaints about a lack of oxygen. She no longer wanted to invite her colleagues to her house, as most of them had joined the Party. She was anxious and afraid she would be too frank with them, and instead wrote letters which she left out for us to read on the dinner table, on top of the embroidered cloth which had grown faded. Nothing in them aroused our interest though.

I was in my last year of university at that time and Rashid was working with Uncle Nizar as a professional musician. He would distribute his scant earnings among us all and only kept the small amount needed by a young man who never went outside during the day. He was absent from our house for months at a time and slept in his room at Uncle Nizar's well-appointed house.

It was Uncle Nizar who remembered that it was Sawsan's twenty-second birthday a week after her return from Paris, and he invited us and the families of his band members to a sumptuous dinner at Restaurant al-Shalal. He took great care of his guests and ordered up the best dishes for them: plates of meat seasoned with mint, mushrooms stuffed with meat, fatty kibbeh. He tasted everything, gave animated instructions to the waiters so that they impressed upon the chef to hold back on the spices. We saw him in a new light: someone universally respected, who gave orders and pressed generous tips into the waiter's hands to get better service. The wives of the other musicians exchanged pleasantries with my mother and we felt it was possible to once more be a family who didn't fear the future, a family of irrepressible spirits who shared tender secrets. That night, we hoped. Sawsan stood up and blew out the candles on her large cake, where frosting spelled out *Long Live Sawsan, Princess of Hearts*. My mother asked Nizar to invite us out again so as to improve our family's image. Nizar didn't waver in obeying his beloved sister's simple request. Every week he took us to a new restaurant, and astonished us with his knowledge of the city's secret corners.

These invitations, which continued all through the winter of 1987, couldn't save my mother from feeling abandoned though. They couldn't make her forget the smell of her own body, that smell of cellars, and they brought Sawsan no closer to her. At the last moment and for no apparent reason, Sawsan would always refuse to come with us and would stay alone in the house. She was restoring the sense of self which had been shattered, so she told Rashid, who insisted that she tell him the details of her travels.

On her thirtieth birthday, we had tried to revive the remnants of warmth between us all. By that time, we were surrounded by hastily thrown-up buildings, constructed using corrupt funds and then sold for enormous sums to poverty-stricken fellaheen. For them, Aleppo still embodied a dream of wealth and urbanity even though three-quarters of it had turned into slums unfit for human habitation. Crime was rampant. Bearded men would trail menacingly in broad daylight after any woman wearing short sleeves or a skirt; if they got arrested, they'd use their appearances in court to speechify at every opportunity about honor and moral decay, and their right to hold to account anyone who recklessly ignored the teachings of the true religion. A festival of veritable insanity and strange odors, Aleppo became a city given over to ceaseless fear, a city of retribution, whimpering under the appetites of the mukhabarat and the corrupt officials who were proficient only in loyalty, or dancing dabka in circles during presidential referendums.

Sawsan expressed her anger and worry at the new Aleppo. The fear that she and her friends had helped to spread now began to lay siege to her. She no longer dared to wear short skirts, and in order to protect herself from harassment she put a large, sharp knife in her handbag; she had had to surrender her gun to the local security branch.

She wanted to erase her old image from her memory. Her reports weighted with slander had destroyed dozens in the interrogation rooms and wrecked the futures of many of her classmates. She thought that she and her friends had sold themselves for nothing, for no more than a few coins every month which couldn't even buy a pair of shoes, or a trifling job whose salary couldn't feed three people for a fortnight. She thought about the scale of the turmoil that would be required to kill the source of the influence enjoyed by Jaber, Fawaz, and his relatives, and all the other city officials. She regretted her brief faith in the Nationalist Party whose pamphlets were compilations of various laughably constructed formulations by Party intellectuals who themselves had been dismissed by the President and placed under surveillance after his ascent to power. It was made clear that the demands to "reform Party thought" were no more than words, just like the "liberation of Palestine."

Jaber had been part of a delegation sent to Romania at the state's expense for seven years. He spent this time trading currency and writing reports on Syrian students and expatriates and returned bearing a doctorate in town planning. To him, this meant destroying everything beautiful within the ancient walls, every place which held the city's memory, and partnering with building contractors who didn't leave a single one of the old buildings in Jamiliya or Manshiya untouched, ruining the character of these neighborhoods. They easily obtained permits to tear down buildings and expel their inhabitants from their warm, welcoming homes, slapping together cheap buildings whose rooms resembled mouse holes. Dr. Jaber defended this modernization in Party conferences, which had become ideal places for anyone in need of a nap. These conferences occurred unnoticed by ordinary Syrians, wrapped up as they were in their parallel lives. One after the other, Jaber would repeat Party slogans or the President's statements and recommendations. Then the rambling would stop and he'd simply call for the dismissal of any professors who criticized the sad state of the city, or who averred that the souls of great cities will haunt their destroyers to the grave. For those idealists opposed to Dr. Jaber, their only option was to pack their belongings and leave the city they loved. Most spent the rest of their lives in the United States, Dubai, or Paris, cooking their city's unique cuisine on the weekends and telling their foreign colleagues about the history of each dish in tedious detail, before resuming their silence, mortally homesick strangers in these cities.

After Jaber devoted himself totally to the Party, Sawsan had been summoned to the branch. She stood in front of Comrade Jaber, who contemplated the miserable girl before him wearing long clothes and an excessively thick headscarf. He offered her coffee and conversed with her as any friend might, reminiscing about the distant childhood he had spent with us and with my mother, for whom, he said, he had nothing but the greatest respect. In fact, he had intervened with the leadership more than once so that she would not be dismissed from her school after she refused outright to join the Party. He brought out a dozen sheets of white paper and a pen with dried-up ink, and asked her to take her time and write everything she knew about Munzir and his activities, adding that it was the wish of the Party to reconsider her current status. She wished she could take the gun she had surrendered to the interrogator at the security branch and fire all its bullets into him. The soul of the city and its victims might forgive her, if she did. She felt like throwing up. She picked up her bag and left the office without a word.

She walked for a long time, searching her city for the soul she feared would be crushed one day. She imagined herself standing in a long row with her friends while the city's soul questioned them about what they had done. She went into the Umayyad mosque and chose a distant corner where she prayed, bowing in dozens of prostrations and reciting all the prayers she could remember. Flooded with tears, she asked for mercy on her soul, and to be forgiven by the victims of her reports.

The cold December breeze brushed her as she left the mosque. She wondered why she hadn't finished university yet, and why she still worked as an assistant teacher at a school in Biyanon, where her clothes were dirtied with mud in winter, and dust in summer, traveling in buses jammed with villagers who stepped on her feet without noticing or apologizing.

∗

While we were celebrating Sawsan's thirtieth birthday, Munzir lay next to his wife and sought out the fragrances of other women in her apathetic body. He searched for the sharp acidic scent which reminded him of the breasts of her sister Sahar; from the first week he had despaired of trying to find anything of Sawsan in this cold cadaver who did nothing but pile up clothes in her wardrobe. He became more immersed in the books Jaafar sent him by mail every three months without fail: readings on the Iranian experiment, interpretations of Shi'ite thought, and lives of the martyrs. He wept when he reread the story of Hassan and Hussein and memorized whole passages of Imam Ali ibn Abi Talib, may God bless him. In his new marital home he designated a small corner for himself where he placed a prayer mat from Isfahan which he had requested as a gift from one of his Iranian friends, along with a clay water jug, and a large bookcase. He was pleased with his corner, which seemed to be the ideal place to contemplate the destiny of Man and Being.

Sawsan no longer caused him sleepless nights, apart from when he lay in the bath of the luxurious bathroom. He plunged his body into the hot water, which loosened his muscles and restored the blood to his veins. He became aroused when he remembered Sawsan. He had been wrong in not placing her beside him; he was confident she wouldn't have refused him and he imagined his life with her again. His isolation required a secret sexual life that placed him at a distance from the relapses of lust which he tried hard to stifle, although he was surprised by how they transformed and insisted on staying in his blood. He preferred to masturbate over his conjured images of Sawsan than to sleep with his wife. He left his room weighted with sin and plunged further into his hermit's life, content with the few duties the lord of the palace had charged him with. He didn't protest when most of the sensitive tasks were assigned to Guillaume, a French graduate of the Institute of Eastern Studies in Damascus.

*

When the noise from her thirtieth birthday celebrations had died away, Sawsan got up before the dawn prayer and went to the bathroom, whose heater had been lit for hours; she could hear the water bubbling in the boiler. She sat in the bath, which had turned yellow over the years, paint peeling off the sides like the walls of every room. She felt how defeated her mother was when she remembered how it used to look, how the bathroom used to gleam and the fragrance of scented soap wafted everywhere.

She soaked in the hot water for three hours, relaxing as every pore in her body opened up, and when she came out wrapped in a towel she saw my mother sitting on a wobbly wooden chair. She didn't look at Sawsan's body, she just offered her a coffee. She was wearing her usual drab clothes. Sawsan thanked her shortly and before going to her room she opened our door. Rashid was fast asleep and Nizar had placed a cotton blanket on the floor and was lying on top of it. She nursed a deep love for the three of us in that room. Sawsan closed the door quietly and performed the dawn prayer for the last time. After she woke up I was astonished to see her throwing her heavy clothes in the garden where most of the trees had died. She threw out her long coat, her head covering, her long gloves, and her prayer mat. She set them all on fire, smiled, and said to Rashid, "Irrepressible Sawsan is back. She won't be defeated so easily." Her resolution lacked conviction, and I read fear in the candid face, thrown slightly into shadow by the fire as it turned into ash. Dozens of faces looked out from the roof terraces and balconies surrounding us, watching the flames subside quietly. They didn't realize that she had turned the last seven years into cinders, whose dispersing motes scorched my face and restored me once more to the anxiety which beset me whenever I saw Sawsan lose her certainty.

She spent a lot of time at home with Rashid, discussing how to be emancipated from the past, which was a weight on his soul as well. He spoke in disjointed phrases about Suad while pointing to the urn containing her ashes which he had placed on top of the wardrobe like an icon. He went on to tell us how much he missed our father and longed to see his face once before he died. Rashid spoke ardently and seriously about death, and cursed Madhat who had thrown him out of Nizar's house. Nizar was powerless in the face of Madhat's tyranny and ignored all the obscene abuse he heaped on our mother. Madhat had thrown the shards of Rashid's violin on the steps and emptied his wardrobe of the clothes and trea-sured possessions which were kept in his uncle's house. Sawsan didn't respond to Rashid's ramblings. She gazed at Suad's ashes and realized that we needed a miracle to be saved from our fear and our restless dread of everything.

"When anything can destroy you, you have to beg for death," said Rashid, pointing with disgust at the new violin my uncle had bought for the beloved nephew he'd raised. Rashid had recently lost his eagle-eyed stare when he took hold of his violin and began his solos. Nizar still backed him, repeating in front of the musicians of Aleppo, "Try him, you'll see he's a genius." Everyone waited for the compositions which remained unwritten. Rashid kept silent and ignored my mother who, by then, had begun to write letters every day, sending them to wrong addresses. I started looking for work. A friend of Nizar's interceded on my behalf and found me piecemeal work translating textile ads. I would go to the textile factory in Safira and wait for hours to be given the leaflets, passing the time by peeking furtively at the men and women working in the huge factory. I struck up an innocent friendship with a girl who would say to me that you can't befriend those on the other side. I didn't pay much attention to her suspi-ciousness of people. It was a natural state of affairs; everyone was afraid of absently letting slip a word about the state of the country, or inflation, or the violence which was becoming more overt. If you mentioned that parsley was expensive, as far as the spies were concerned you were complaining about the Party's policies. If you said that you were thinking about death, then you didn't love life, an offense punishable under Party rules. Everything was connected to the Party, which liked to see Comrade Jaber and his friends hauling people into the streets in endless, million-strong marches of support.

Jean was consumed with shame as he watched his colleagues from his house; they still locked hands and rhythmically stamped their feet as they had done for ten years, only their backs were bowed even further.

I would sit in the corridor of the textile factory and wait for the public relations official. As he handed me the leaflets he would give me a look as if I had just arrived, and I would leave without heeding his repeated comments about the precise usages of textile terminology. I would stay awake all night translating, to make myself feel that I was doing important work. I reformulated the sentences, opened my dictionaries, and for the fifth time searched for the most appropriate meaning. I thought that working on these leaflets was preferable to standing for hours in front of a blackboard teaching morons who would write reports to the mukhabarat when they grew up; I valued my freedom. But I didn't know what I would do for the rest of my days, and considered retranslating T.S. Eliot's "The Wasteland," for no other reason than a feeling of sympathy with those great verses which spoke of ruin. Sawsan told me she had seen Jean after all these years, and regretted having tempted him; when the passion she had baited for two years came to full ripeness, she had fled as if she were punishing her lover for being late to an assignation she had arranged.

I was afraid of large crowds that might become hysterical, like a group of young men and women gathering to sing in one voice after watching a rousing film. My mother told me that spies lived in the trees, and advised us to keep silent and nod in agreement, as she had begun to do some years earlier after a colleague of hers, a geography teacher, had disappeared.

Everyone was so silent they bored the security officers who had nothing to do but play backgammon and reopen buried files, although most of their subjects had anticipated the summons and fled abroad.

Sawsan observed the city silently from the citadel at sunset, with the Armenian photographer who had followed her for years in order to photograph her naked and premiere his first exhibition about the body in Paris. The silence seemed oppressive to her. She held her breath and for the first time she felt afraid of the dark. Qurh Bayt looked at her and took a picture. When he hung it on the wall, he saw the difference between the face whose sharp, lascivious lineaments he never forgot, and this one which was too tranquil for a photographer who aspired to world fame. He also surmised that her body was no longer that of a model worth paying to remove her clothes.

His intuition turned out to be true the following evening when Sawsan knocked on his door and went into the room he had prepared as a studio, with lights and shades and a sofa and a white Persian carpet bought in Calcutta especially for this experiment. While Sawsan undressed and asked him where he wanted her to lie, he looked at her, and saw creases on her legs and some puffiness in her stomach. He gestured for her to curl up on the sofa, took some quick shots, and gave her her fee. She felt that he was disappointed and returned the money, and stipulated that he could exhibit the pictures provided he not show her face. He apologized, saying he had been seeking her old body, which he had adored, and which he had kept away from out of fear of Munzir. Humiliated and miserable, she asked for a vodka and lemon.

Everyone wanted her past. She resolved not to lose her battle against these eunuchs and demanded to have the negatives with a determination that alarmed him. She took the film and walked out, leaving the money on the little table. Sawsan developed the ten pictures with the help of an eccentric Kurd-ish photographer who never stopped justifying why he had accepted the request that he join the Baath Party, and spoke to his fellow patrons at Bar al-Shabab about his mother who knew no Arabic but dreamed in nine languages. He looked at the photograph of Sawsan's face buried in the sofa, and asked her for a copy as his fee for developing and printing the pictures, which he had done at his own expense. He sent the picture to the journal *Photo* with the help of an American girl who studied Arabic in Damascus and was visiting Aleppo to meet this crazed photographer.

Sawsan's photograph was published in the famous French journal *Photo* under the name of Rasho Dawoud next to pic-tures taken by the greatest photographers in the world. The magazine sent him 1,000 francs and six copies of the jour-nal. He showed the picture in coffee houses, claiming that it was his American girlfriend who had bought him a leather jacket for a thousand dollars, and waved the letter signed by the chief editor inviting him to send other photographs, and promising to invite him to Paris if their collaboration contin-ued in the future.

The published pictures restored Sawsan's confidence in her body. She contemplated the ten photographs stuck onto the walls of her room and asked Rashid the meaning behind the curled-up body, and he replied simply, "You have to become a mother."

Rashid no longer slipped into Sawsan's bed and dozed on her chest. She no longer stroked his hair as if he were her son. When she left her room on the third day of her fourth decade wearing a short skirt underneath an old raincoat, and old but chic leather shoes which she had repainted and pol-ished, it didn't provoke the surprise which she had hoped to see in our eyes; we merely admired her taste and were silent. She went out and returned a few minutes later with disheveled hair and a torn shirt. She looked for a large kitchen knife to take revenge on the group of farmhands who never left the streetlamp on the corner. They had been excited by the sight of her breasts bound in a pink silk bra which was left visible, and had attacked her and groped her chest. She took hold of one of them and slammed his face into the wall, and fled from the hands that wanted to violate her in the early evening. She picked up the knife and went out to look for them, and instead found various mothers opening their doors, cursing her and calling her a whore.

Sawsan never forgot that day. She could no longer appear in the alley unless she was modestly dressed and had wrapped her hair in a scarf that she removed as soon as she left the alley. She saw our weakness and fear, and felt that she was alone. There was nothing she could do but go to Comrade Jaber and write the reports he wanted and reclaim her gun, but this she wouldn't do.

Jean allowed Sawsan to read his last letter, signed February 26, 1998, in which he told Pierre about his grandmother who no longer left her room, content as she was with stroking the lines written by Orhan Misar. She didn't want to hear the sound of his prostitutes, whom he still invited over although he had stopped seeking a resemblance between them and Sawsan after he saw her in her old clothes. He let them wander at will around the large house, through the dust which covered the Turkish furniture. The family portraits seemed as if they were from an earlier century, bound to an era no one believed in any more and which my own mother was no longer proud of having lived through. She had grown forgetful of the picture of her colleagues strutting in their elegant clothes, their hair smoothed and held in place with scented oils.

Jean wrote to his son Pierre and elaborated on his theory of historical shame. He sketched out the inhabitants of a city, who shared the air of that city but were afraid of each other: Christians afraid of Muslims, minority sects afraid of majorities, and the many afraid of the despotism of the few; races and religions and sects afraid of the President and his mukhabarat; the President afraid of his aides and his own guard. His aides constantly sought creative ways to slander each other and to present their own undying loyalty, breaking promises and denouncing each other, elevating the President to the rank of holiness, of deification, and even so he remained in his palace, afraid of his guards. He didn't dare walk ten meters on the street without hundreds of guards, despite the regular and repeated television broadcasts showing millions of people calling his name in marches of support.

Jean resumed writing about his seductive female students who kept singing the songs of a Party which had no connection with most of them. Like him, they lived a life parallel to the Party, never meeting it, like strangers dividing up the road and pavements of the city. In ambiguous phrases and mocking her for her lack of knowledge about his magnificent city, he hinted at his happiness at being away from his ignorant wife Colette, who had left no method untested of making him ashamed of a country whose inhabitants, as she said, still rode camels.

On winter nights he would spend hours writing letters, savoring the taste of the dried beans his prostitutes cooked. They would move about the kitchen as they wanted and used the same pans his mother had boasted of, engraved with scenes of Diana, bare-breasted goddess of the hunt, the most resplendent garb for a woman. He always sealed his letters with a line of French poetry and an Eastern proverb, wanting his son, a mixture of both, to become half Eastern and half Western. He concluded his advice with his description of a citizen of the world, who battled shame wherever he found it, like the great saviors his city needed so much in her most difficult years.

Sawsan was pleased by Jean's transformations and drew strength from him. Repetition and his immersion in the works of Balzac made him realize that time, which never alters its pace, has no real substance. It just marches on indifferently, leaving scars on our souls. He would wipe his mother's body with cologne and tell her that her time had not passed and her candidate Gabriel al-Shami had returned to the People's Council. She smiled incredulously, just grateful he was nearby. She refused any suggestion of leaving the house, not wanting anyone to see her as a blind, clumsy old woman. She urged him to ensure that George Hanoush, the coffin-maker, would remake her coffin, widening it on both sides so she could lie down comfortably, having already decided on walnut wood and gold handles.

At night, Jean listened to her regular breathing, closed the door, then went out into the empty streets and headed to Bar al-Shabab. He avoided the rowdier drinkers and addicts, choosing instead a remote corner, and he left immediately after drinking his arak. He followed the path which his father would take while returning from Cinema Ramses, and recalled how, when he was a child, his father would take him by the hand and detail the history of each building and the family who lived in the rooms with high ceilings and rose-strewn balconies. He reflected on the stagnation which sank his feet in the mud. He hadn't dreamed for a long time, and his passivity stirred up uncomfortable thoughts about his resemblance to his mother. Like her, he was waiting for death, and he imagined his son Pierre sitting beside him, waiting for him to die. He resolved to commit suicide and finish everything; he wouldn't be torn apart piece by piece. Alarmed at the thought of suicide, he inhaled the fragrance of the trees in the park, relinquished the chaotic ideas snapping at his tranquility, and calmly returned to his house sunk in silence. He told Sawsan the following day that death wasn't as bad as we imagined.

Sawsan no longer came every day. To ensure that his living room wasn't jammed with prostitutes, she would call in advance to ask if she could come over and they would agree on a time. Jean liked the fact that he didn't miss her or resent her if she was a few minutes late. He poured her coffee and waited for her to tell him about her life. She sensed that he was bored, that she couldn't attract him, especially when she recalled the heat of his former words and his joy at her former visits. She was horrified to think that fifteen years had passed since then; he had aged a little but seemed to have halted time. He told her cheerfully that he had written to Pierre after his twenty-eighth birthday the previous spring, but she felt his torment at Pierre's disinclination to correspond with him, making do with a few hastily written cards and some brief, indifferent phrases at Christmas. Jean was content with these few words for now, and thought that there would be time enough in the future to watch a film together or to wander through Aleppo's souks. Pierre too would age, and would no doubt be glad when he reflected on the belated wisdom which came from belonging once more to those who supposed that they were out of your life.

Sawsan found it disturbing to think about our father. What if she found his address and wrote to him about the shame she had felt when she left the gynecology clinic with a repaired hymen and hadn't succeeded in restoring innocence to her body? Or she could write to him about Munzir, whose latest incarnation as a confirmed man of religion, content to draw his salary from the aloof lord of the palace, she had learned from a letter from her Lebanese friend. She was pleased that Munzir had weakened so much. He waited for petitioners, displayed his learning, and recounted his life story. He would speak of his beginnings as a village boy kissing the hands of his sheikhs, ambitious like most boys in his class to graduate from the Military College; of the stroke of luck when the commander chose him as an aide; his transferal to Deir al-Zour desert without any duties after he requested permission to leave the country; and his subsequent resignation, hoping his friends would intercede with the President to allow him to emigrate so he could work for Habib al-Mawsili, who had left Syria in dubious circumstances that were still shrouded in mystery. It was rumored that he had gotten mixed up in the old mistake of selling weapons to the Muslim Brotherhood which they used in their struggle against the regime.

What Sawsan thought of as weakness was not quite true of Munzir. He was peaceful, and immersed in a comfort whose tranquility was disturbed by nothing, apart from the image of Sawsan wearing his pajamas. He couldn't forget the sensation of her body, which could still physically arouse him. His greatest lapse would have been turned into his greatest spiritual triumph if only he had been endowed with patience and had married her, then converted her from her own sect to his. She had often expressed a feeling that unfamiliar blood flowed through her body, and she felt more connected to those mountains than to the smell of cellars in the plains of Anabiya. He counseled himself to patience once again, so as not to do something that he would regret, like divorcing his long-suffering, if stupid, wife. He would have already done so were it not for her tolerance at being left alone for nights on end. It was still too soon to return to his village, even though his properties now brought in enough to live on as a powerful sheikh, a founder of a dynasty of sheikhs. The idea of a warrior sheikh glittered in his eyes and wouldn't leave him after he saw Sayyid Nasrallah's sermon at a political gathering in which he threatened to burn Israel to the ground. Munzir hung up a large photograph of him lifting his fist into the air like a great revolutionary. He knew that the feeling of battle would not leave him. Sawsan replied to her friend with a short, courteous letter. She didn't want anything which reminded her of Munzir, although she liked to think of him as a peaceful man, a dervish, a far cry from when he had aspired to command a battalion of paratroopers.

Sawsan felt mediocrity all around her, in the looks of her neighbors who feared her depravity, and the desire to assault her which gleamed in the eyes of most men she came across, such as the slovenly taxi driver who, when she removed her headscarf and put it in her handbag, suggested without preamble that she move to the front seat so she could see the size of his penis. For a minute she thought she would commit a crime against this man, but instead she asked him to stop the taxi, got out calmly, took off her shoe and began bashing it against his head, cornering him behind the wheel with his penis still hanging out of his zip. She swore at him in front of all the passersby who congregated within seconds and spat at him. She suddenly realized she was in the middle of a large crowd of repressed men who might all want to rape her, and she forced her way out through their rancid smell of sweat and filthy clothing.

She sought refuge at Uncle Nizar's house and arrived at his door in tears. Madhat opened it and leered at her, and suggested she come in and wait for her uncle, who was sulking at his family home. He spoke with the insolent familiarity of someone referring to his wife, and went on to say that he had been waiting for a visit from Sawsan for some time and had in fact asked Nizar to bring her here to share his bed. She spat in his face and rushed down the stairs, afraid of his violent eyes and the powerful hand which was reaching out to drag her inside.

Sawsan sobbed when she saw Uncle Nizar's bloodied face, and his body covered in purple welts from the cane which Madhat had used to beat him savagely while cursing his mother, his sister, and all of his line. It wasn't the first time Madhat had hit him; he believed that several slaps and a kick every week were inviolable among his rights as Maha's husband. But this time, there was in Madhat's fury a desire for murder that was equal to his state of arousal. Madhat had returned from work furious at being turned over to an investigative committee and questioned about certain reports presented to the Minister of Finance. These reports had complained of an imbecile who no longer merely accepted gifts, but had turned into a thug who stipulated sisters as his price like some kind of highwayman, and whose family contained no high-ranking officer to protect his thuggery.

When Madhat received the memo summoning him for questioning he was enraged. He picked up his papers and walked out of his office. Nizar tried to mitigate things and went to a trader he knew who liked his band. Nizar wept and pleaded with him to intervene to withdraw the complaints against his beloved. From his tone, Nizar knew that his friend would do nothing for Madhat, and was trying to reassure Nizar that everything would be all right.

That night Madhat promised him a festival of debauchery that would go down in history if the investigation file was closed. The following day the security patrol was waiting for him. He went into the branch and was kept there for seven hours. He swore on a small Quran he brought with him that he was innocent of all charges, and the reports were a malicious plot, and hinted that he would refute everything resulting from it. Briefly and dryly, he was given to understand that the investigation had been opened on the order of the President, who had received over 1,400 reports about violence, street harassment, and corruption that was so endemic it was practically regulated. Additionally, close associates of the President had visited Aleppo and were astonished at the total neglect of the city, which was beginning to drown in its own filth, and at the news that more than a thousand instances of murder, robbery, and armed attacks were all reported as "perpetrated by persons unknown." The investigation would comprise over five hundred employees both great and small, and all the intercessions in existence couldn't spare them. Madhat felt a cold sweat break out over his body. The investigator asked him to come back the following day and without another word he gestured to an officer to take him outside.

Madhat felt himself falling into the trap he had avoided so far. He would pay the price which even great men had to pay. He had nothing left but Nizar's body, which was in the kitchen wearing a robe, as he prepared sheikh al-mahshi according to his own recipe, a dish which Madhat had tasted for the first time when Nizar made it for him. He had been languid with happiness that Madhat hadn't left his house for a week, that his old body was recompensed at the end of his life with a man he had trained in the art of good dressing and (somewhat amateurish) music appreciation, who would be there in his old age and would never leave him to scour the backstreets for mercenary men. But Madhat opened the door and charged like an enraged bull, raining blows on Nizar. He didn't calm down and in his eyes Nizar could see a lust for the kill that he knew more about than most, having experienced the violence of many men in his life. He pushed him away with all his strength and was able to reach the door. He fled and it was only when he was in the street that he noticed his torn clothing, the robe stained with blood.

Nizar moaned all night, and Rashid and Sawsan stayed beside him weeping silently. They washed his wounds with a clean white cloth, and I brought strong medicines. Nizar was incoherent, mumbling the names of strangers as well as his father and mother, his brother Abdel-Monem, and Michel, his friend who sent endless pictures of the child he had adopted with his French husband.

My mother looked at him steadily but did no more than complain of a lack of oxygen, exhausted from her own fits in which she hurled vulgar abuse at everything that came to her mind: Comrade Fawaz and his relatives, her colleagues at school, the Party. She walked through the house in utter disbelief that the smell of rot hadn't killed us yet, wondering out loud what we were doing there, in her house. Suddenly she would fall totally silent and look stupidly at the yellowed landscapes on the walls, or at her beautiful sofas whose colors had faded and whose springs had drooped so much that it was hazardous to sit on them. Everything she had worked so hard to create had become so worn out that, were it thrown onto the street, it would be scorned by beggars. She regretted having never traveled, even if it had been to hell. Her mother's death had been a warning that stagnation would turn roses into straw.

Signs of my mother's hysteria had accompanied her to school. Her colleagues complained of her rambling sentences, and her high-pitched voice mocking the Party members who tried to reinvigorate the songs they were so bored of that they stopped punishing students for sounding drowsy when they repeated them. She hushed the students, neglected her appearance. Once she left in the middle of a class and walked out of the school to wander through the cafés, looking first for my father, and then for the famous artist who had invited her to his studio. She went to his building and knocked on the door and an old woman opened it. My mother asked insistently about the painter who used to live here, and asked to come in and meet his gaze, to look for the red sofa where she had dreamed of making love. She searched in her bag for the short dress from Allilaki which she had bought especially to wear at her tête-à-tête, and wept when she saw that mice had chewed it up and smeared it with filth. The old woman who lived alone in the studio hoarded old clothes which she cut into strips and made into rugs to sell in the souk at Bab Jnein. She was surprised at my mother's visit and repeated the same answer she gave to everyone who asked her about her nephew—that he had left years ago for Paris. She took pity on my mother and offered her some tea, trying to imagine the past of this woman whose refined background still shone from her face. My mother went on to Bar al-Shabab and summoned the waiter to ask about the artist; the waiter told her, as usual, that that was all before his time. He didn't know the artist she always talked about, and the old waiter he had drawn in a famous painting was dead, drowned in the Midanki Waterfalls years before.

My mother was like one of those women who never stopped chattering, even while yawning. It wasn't long before she was dismissed from the teaching profession she had been so proud of. She insisted on a hairstyle which had been popular in the sixties, persisting on living in the past, yet she prepared classes every day which were known for their vitality and vast scope. Unique and beloved, the calm and aristocratic impression she gave, and which she was very careful to keep up, allowed many people to respect her. Even her bitterest enemies forgave her lapses and spoke neutrally to the informers paid to produce annual reports on all the teachers, but after six months the headmaster could no longer take responsibility for her. He requested a consultation with the school doctor, who recommended retirement on account of her excellent record and great service to the teaching profession.

She was lucid when we left the school clinic. She asked to go to the school one last time and spat on its wall. Sawsan and I held her by her arms and we walked through the poverty-stricken houses that had swallowed the lettuce fields. The smell of uncovered sewers made us sick and she reassured us that everything would be fine, but we didn't believe her when we saw her swearing at our neighbor who had murdered his wife after catching her in the arms of the gas vendor. Every evening he would stand in his doorway surrounded by his six children and curse all women, offering up a whore's children for sale and pressing moral instruction on passersby who paid him no attention. His aspect was pitiful and his cotton vest stank from the filth that dripped from cold-ridden noses.

We couldn't prevent her from leaving the house. She felt suffocated and wouldn't use the tranquilizers I brought her after consulting doctors and which my friends, fellow chess players in the cafés, had secured for me at no charge. She would leave the door open behind her; a house containing nothing but misery doesn't need a door to protect it from petty thieves. She would wander the streets and return at the end of the night looking like a beggar. She would toss and turn in her bed, anxiety never leaving her. She would then fall quiet for days at a time and sleep for hours, and then afterward would walk slowly, recovering her health. She would make coffee and sit at the dinner table, and tell us that in her dreams she saw the Arab heads of state praying in Jerusalem. She jumped ahead of our comments by saying that dreams are never wrong. She seemed like an old woman, and only lacked grandchildren to complete the picture.

She walked into our room and saw Nizar lying on Rashid's bed, and Sawsan feeding him hot lentil soup. Nizar was flung on the bed, sadder than he had ever been. He was thinking of killing and burying his sexuality, to save us all and to shield us from the shame which we had endured as a family for years. He no longer wanted anything but comfort. Sawsan helped him to get up and take off his clothes, maneuvered him into a hot bath, and prepared a rich dinner of fried meat and slices of tomato. She behaved as if she were mistress of the house, and we relied on her strength in these moments.

We hovered around the dinner table and spoke quietly on topics which were removed from anything that might remind Nizar of his tragedy. He surprised us with his determination to rid his life of Madhat and all other men, saying, "Memories are enough for me." He turned to Rashid and begged him to devote himself to composing the music the world was waiting for so it could know the meaning of pain. He recounted the story of "Shadows of Regret," which was played by the greatest orchestras in the world while all that remained to him was regret and shadows. He admitted that he had ruined his life here and should have gone to Paris with Michel, but he was incapable of staying away from my mother or Aleppo. Despite his lively speech and graceful movements he seemed like an old man for the first time to us. Like my mother, all he lacked was grandchildren to round off the image.

He asked Rashid to take him home, and on the way he stopped by a locksmith. He opened his wardrobe, took out all of Madhat's possessions, and put them in a black plastic bag. He waited with Rashid for the suitable moment to take his revenge. He seemed like his old self, the one Rashid loved: leader of an orchestra, accepting no mistakes, unsparing of public rebukes to his musicians. He had only needed a more public life to be counted as a genius in a city whose rulers had been punished throughout history, who went on to punish its genius sons in a cycle of unconcealed, unremitting violence.

Madhat was astounded when he tried to open the door and realized the lock had been changed. He rang the bell and Nizar opened it and calmly invited him to come in and sit down on a plastic chair. Nizar informed Madhat that he had decided to rid him from his life forever, and pointed to the bag left by the door. Rashid was gripping a large knife, ready to commit murder if there was any attempt to threaten his beloved uncle. Madhat couldn't believe that Nizar was capable of throwing him out, or of this cold, sober tone. He attempted a half-apology and patted Nizar's hand, but he was surprised further still when Nizar placed a bill in front of him for the 650,000 lira Madhat had borrowed from him over five years. The bill was accompanied by an accounts book in which details of all the payments were recorded. Nizar added that he would overlook all the expensive presents, such as the gold watch Madhat was currently wearing, which Nizar bought from a famous jeweler in Aleppo.

Revolted, Rashid observed Madhat's face as he quickly realized the catastrophe that would follow if Nizar talked about everything he knew. He felt weak, ridiculous, a fugitive in need of purification. He knew all of Nizar's faces, apart from this terrifying one which was fully capable of avenging the honor Madhat had trampled dozens of times. Nizar repeated that he had been mistaken in allowing a hungry man to enter his house. Madhat tried to apologize using words he had never imagined he would use, trying to placate this insect which had brought him to the brink of a disgrace that would shadow him all his life. He knew, with absolute clarity, that

Nizar was not Maha whose backside he had rent apart hundreds of times. He knew Nizar had strong relationships with the greatest families, who despite knowing of his perversion still venerated him. Daughters of these families consulted him on the colors of their dresses, and wives of important men sipped goblets of champagne with him. Madhat used to prevent him from attending these gatherings, and he remembered, now, that he had been the lover, not the beloved.

Madhat faltered for a few moments, thinking that Nizar was playing some sort of game to provoke him. He tried to bluster and go on the attack but Nizar warned that he could send Madhat to the gallows, adding, "This is a house of love, not of hatred." Madhat resumed his apologetic tone, and suggested that Nizar think about his final decision for a few days. If Nizar wanted to get married, in any country in the world, Madhat promised to give him a happy life, to be his slave in his old age. But all his sweet words couldn't divert Nizar from his purpose. Madhat bent over to take hold of Nizar's feet and kissed them fervently. Nizar coldly grabbed him by his hair and kicked him in the face, hard. It was then that Madhat knew that Nizar was serious. He took a few steps toward the rubbish bag containing his filthy things which Nizar had kept just for this moment, and was reminded of the bill left on the dining table, with a pen next to it. He read the due date: April 21, 2000. He picked up the pen, then realized he wouldn't be able to guarantee the amount in that time. He asked Nizar to defer the due date until August. Nizar did so and Madhat signed and left, after hearing's Nizar parting shot that he would kill him if he got in his way, or if Madhat even mentioned his name.

Madhat left, dripping with sweat. He opened the bag and was taken aback at seeing his old striped shirt, which smelled of a squalor he couldn't bear after having lived with Nizar all these years, although he smiled sadly when he saw his cheap, beaded key ring. He threw everything in a trash can and couldn't hold back his tears. Alone and burdened with his problems, the March chill bored into him. He found himself walking to a cheap hotel in Bab al-Faraj where he took a room for two days and ate his dinner alone. He watched the other patrons late at night, and knew beyond doubt that he was expelled from Nizar's paradise. The following day he rented a small apartment in the square, trying to convince himself that everything would be fine, that Nizar would forget everything and he would go back to his normal life.

In the first week he felt an irresistible longing for Nizar, who only a few days earlier had been his lover, Maha. He wanted to resemble Nizar, to swap roles so he would know the source of the bliss which Nizar used to provide in such abundance. He thought of the happiness of his previous life, his deprivation of it now, and his body which Nizar would constantly rediscover over the years. In recent months he realized he had no desire to sleep with women. He was shocked at wanting Nizar's life.

He couldn't close the investigation at the security branch. He paid back all the money he had amassed over five years so they would be lenient in charging him, and to his great relief they were: now he went to that terrifying place every week instead of every day, to wait for hours in the gloomy passages. He remembered it had been months since he visited his family, but he had no wish to return to his village where rumors of his secret life had started to circulate: that he was a corrupt official, how he was a deviant who wandered the streets looking for lovers. He wanted to seek out some pleasure. For a few days he observed potential customers in the cafés and places where gay men gathered late at night, but he didn't possess the necessary courage to embark on his new life.

One night, he dreamed that Nizar was leading him like a lamb in a silk halter to an orgy of gang rape. He sat up in bed, convinced that dawn was the best time to make life-changing decisions. He was very different from the youth he had been before he met Nizar. The desires of a woman crescendoed inside him and he dared to enter into conversations with impoverished gay men, all looking for customers beside the abandoned cinema, or among the drink sellers in Bustan Kul Ab. The image of Nizar never left him: the happy woman who had filled his entire life.

He left the house in the afternoon and sat for hours in a cafe in Bab al-Faraj. In the early evening he picked up a young man carrying a suitcase, a soldier killing time on his way to the infantry training school. He reminded Madhat a little of his old self. He inhaled the young man's odor as he came close, and was not surprised at being penetrated by desire for a man such as this. Many times, he remembered daydreams in which he had wanted to become Maha, but he had looked at Nizar's small, flaccid member and supposed that it wouldn't be enough to take his virginity. The soldier told him simply that his name was Jasim, and he came from one of the villages near Mayadin. In civilian life he worked as a builder. Madhat invited him to Bar al-Shabab; he needed a strong drink to take the edge off in order to surrender to him. Jasim caught the desire in the invitation and told himself that this elegant man was preferable to donkeys and cattle. Madhat borrowed Nizar's life story and told Jasim that he was a musician with a band that played classical music and toured the world from north to south. In the morning he thought that he had turned into Nizar. He chose the name Maha again so that he would be caught by the same sweet delusions he had felt in the last months of his relationship with Nizar. He no longer wanted to sleep with women, and thought that he had learned the difference between right and wrong, between love and lust.

He would never forget how he sobbed when Jasim left him the following week. Before he left, Madhat pressed a thousand-lira note into his hand, and Jasim put it in his pocket and refused to kiss him before he left as a married couple might have done. Madhat thought of the ache in his guts, and felt that if he was going to imitate Nizar he had to take his time in picking up a lover with more taste and experience.

He felt flooded with happiness at taking the first step on a path that would turn him into a woman.

Nizar couldn't restore the vitality to Rashid's face. He watched Rashid when he played, when he couldn't catch the rhythm, or struck off by himself in an unsanctioned solo which featured ugly, dull improvisations borrowed from popular songs that Nizar didn't like. He was like an amateur. He would finish working as usual at two in the morning but wouldn't wait for his uncle so they could come back together to our house, where Nizar had moved while his house was being repainted and his bed restored.

Rashid walked in the empty streets and reflected on his loneliness. He wondered how people could bear all this noise, all this flattery and hypocrisy; what it meant to live to a hundred, to become a father, to stay alone. He wondered if he was capable of composing a piece that could surpass "Shadows of Regret" in its existential complexity, or the questions it yielded when the violins hid, leaving space for the drums and the mizamir, which had been replaced with four saxophones in the recording made by the Berlin Concert Orchestra. He liked the idea and sounds began to invade him. Finding it impossible to sleep, he went to a café at the bus depot which never closed. He sat alone in a corner, away from the shouts of the drivers and their standbys. He asked for a large, strong coffee, took out some paper, ruled some staves, and started to write, unaware of the waiter who hovered next to him to peer at the notes. Rashid crossed out what he had written and started again. He didn't notice the noise and movement in the morning until he felt that he was ensnared by the crowds rushing to catch their buses. He hastily gathered his papers, folded them up, and hurried away like a fugitive, avoiding the stares of the crowds who seemed to him like beasts waiting to attack. He put himself in the closest taxi. He didn't know why he wanted to go back to a house whose rot and damp smell he hated, where he felt that he was inhaling curdled lime, and where every morning he felt his nose full of the stink of distant corpses. The air was stagnant and the wintry cold bored into his bones, but he had nowhere else to go.

Rashid was possessed by a fever of composition but didn't tell Nizar where he went every night, dreading his uncle's exaggerated encouragement. He liked to live and get to know himself, by himself. Every night he sat in the same café at his own table which the waiter kept reserved for him; he had told Rashid that he sang at weddings, but was unlucky. Rashid avoided commenting, sipped his strong coffee indifferently, and began to write. He knew the fever would engulf him so that he would be isolated from the world, alone as he always wanted. He gave one piece a name which came to him unexpectedly: "Lonely Man at a Station Waiting for His Body to Take Flight." It wasn't long until he scratched out the title and rewrote the piece, which was about a lonely man who didn't like low ceilings.

He felt a great comfort when he saw the pile of more than a hundred pages tucked into a drawer in his wardrobe, which he was careful to keep locked, although he was just about the only one in the family who possessed no secrets. He was afraid that he would read one of the poems he had written when he was a teenager which described the pain of living. For three years he had recorded every detail of the family, and particularly of Sawsan: her movements, her gestures, the colors of her shoes, her dresses, her words. In fact, he recorded Sawsan in all her details. Perhaps he was afraid that this record, which he knew by heart, would fall into the hands of our mother, who resented his attachment to Sawsan. He threw the papers which held his compositions in next to his well-loved diaries and placed the key under his bed. He considered recomposing his piece about irrepressible Sawsan who resembled the trains moving over the lovely springtime plains, where expanse had no limits; it was the only place he wished he could spirit Sawsan away to, where they could both live on the fruits of the earth, as their primitive ancestors had done.

As if he had thrown his burdens aside and gone back to being a normal young man, he played with the zeal required for working in nightclubs every night. Nizar would insist that every night they locate something they loved in the room—a woman, a chair, a table, a lightshade—and play to it, adding, "So you don't all commit suicide before you're forty." Rashid put his arm around his uncle as they left the club together, proud of the elegance of this man who was entering his seventies, sad as he had been born and cheerful as he had lived, like all his passions.

Sawsan knew about her record. When she was away, it often occurred to her to write to Rashid and plead with him to send what he had written that day in his flowery notebooks. She wanted to read about her past, when she had been certain of her future. She had thought that she would possess a large garden and a grand house and lovely children; it never popped into her mind for a moment that all her power was a dream that would pass, never to return. After her thirtieth birthday she tried to mix with a small group of foreigners who lived in Aleppo, who spent their time together happily talking about how amazing Aleppan cuisine was and never feeling homesick. They were looking for young musicians who could play qudud for them and translate maqamat for their women.

She accompanied Nizar twice to these exclusive parties. She felt rusty, and despite her proficiency in speaking French she could sense their skeptical glances. Through a contact of Jean, she provided maternity cover for an employee in the library of the French Institute, which hosted European researchers on temporary secondments. She thought it was wonderful to sit amid all this silence, engaged with books and manuscripts. She even loved the place itself, surrounded by cypress trees and cacti that were over a hundred years old.

Her soul was healing; she dreamed of working like this forever, and going to a small, warm house at the end of the day where she would lie on her bed leafing through French magazines, stroking a pet cat. Trivial details perhaps, but enough for happiness, Sawsan thought.

She couldn't secure another job after the employee came back and thanked her kindly for having accepted a few months of temporary work for a pittance. When she left she accepted a dinner invitation from a German researcher and didn't protest at going to his house although she hated his greed and his avidity. She remembered that she was a virgin, and was determined she would never give her forged hymen to this snob, until she realized that he was waiting for her to leave so he could close the door.

She had no one to turn to but Jean, whose excuses began to proliferate. He didn't tell Sawsan that he was occupied with a prostitute who spun him a story like they all did—she had escaped from a cruel stepmother or a husband who wanted to appropriate the price of her body, or she was working in order to pay for her mother's medicines. Jean believed them all and did not examine these stories too closely, as in the case of Riham, whose tale was filled with contradictory details: a wrecked marriage; a father with cancer (at one time he lived in Beirut and another time in the Sukkari district); a mother who had left her as a child to her aunts who, on another occasion, also died when she was young, along with her father, in a car accident. Jean loved Riham's body, which he afterward discovered bore some resemblance to Sawsan's when she had been a delectable student. He felt desperate when he realized that more than twenty years had passed while he waited for two events in his life to pass: his mother, who still hadn't died, and the sensation of Sawsan's body, which he had neither tasted nor forgotten as he had believed he would. He was overjoyed when he saw Riham undress piece by piece as if she were performing a striptease and lie down next to him.

Her body was taut and brown and he smelled Sawsan's old fragrance for the first time in a long time.

Jean suggested that Riham come to his house when she couldn't find shelter. She liked his quiet nature, and hadn't believed that Christian bedrooms also smelled of mucus, and Christian bodies also rotted. When she saw his mother she felt great pity for this honorable man who spoke to her all night about an imaginary life. He enjoyed composing a new life story for himself and found an opportunity in her that wouldn't offer itself again. Trying to diminish his standing, he told Riham about his oppressed childhood, and his faithless wife, and his drug-addict fugitive son who hung out with gang members in Beirut. He tried to enjoy living with a woman who belonged to him, as well as to any man who paid a few lira to take her home and would button his trousers in the cars after the first turning in the road. Boredom set in after a few weeks, even more odious and powerful than before. He thought that the bliss of living with prostitutes lay in freedom from duties and the lack of regret.

He no longer wished his mother would die. He felt the sweetness of waiting for death with a being who wouldn't die. He guessed that Riham was his only opportunity to be saved from Sawsan forever, and he proceeded to sleep with her in every position and in every corner of the house.

Before three months had elapsed, he began to lose his desire for Riham. He asked her to consider him a client and not a friend, and she did her utmost to make him erect but couldn't succeed for more than a few minutes. She hadn't known what it meant to love before and was overwhelmed when she left him, but she knew that the clients who returned to her again and again, even those who requested her by name from her madame, Umm Hassan, didn't so much love her as tried to delude her. She felt something missing in her breast, and considered returning to Jean and offering to repent and marry him despite the thirty-year difference in their age. She also enjoyed the illusion she created when she added a new story to her repertoire for her richer clients, who had more time to spend with her and luxurious houses which weren't raided by the police. She told them she was in love with a great translator who lived in Suleimaniya, but the vicissitudes of fate (which she recounted in gruesome detail) had made him blind and impotent and no one supported him but herself. She added that she worshipped him, arousing jealousy in the men who dreamed of being this blind translator who lived off Riham.

Jean wanted to win back Sawsan, who felt sick when she heard him speaking like any vulgar man. His eyes had lost the goodness she had once adored. He was coming to resemble all the men she hated, approaching sixty and fearing that his desire would cease. He was entranced with the stories his prostitutes made up, and didn't think it strange to recount parts of them as if they were facts about friends of his who expected his help. She vowed not to go back to Jean's house; she didn't like losing the images of those she loved in such a cheap way.

She clung to Nizar's image, which was returning in full resplendence. This elegant man had salvaged his relationship with his old tailor Rahmu al-Haritani, who still crouched inside his small shop at the top of Nadi al-Ittihad Street in Jamiliya. He received a limited number of his old customers, and kept silent when he heard that some of them had turned and now wore suits by the famous brands which had invaded the city. Nizar was his favorite customer, and the two spent hours discussing colors and inventing their own styles. Nizar distributed four new suits between me and Rashid and gave Sawsan a beautiful fur coat for the coming winter along with a collection of real leather shoes. To my mother he gave the caps she used to love wearing in photographs, but she ignored them as if they were of no more interest to her than my uncle's three-month residence in our house. During this time he took us to dinners at upmarket restaurants; we seemed like any carefree family.

The most enthusiastic about Nizar's new image was Rashid. The two of them reignited their long, cheerful debates about eighteenth-century music and Sufi songs which used to fascinate Rashid with their profound rhythms. He didn't tell us of the rapture he felt when he walked alone in the streets at dawn and was halted by the muezzin of the Rahman Mosque. He listened to the entire call to prayer and was entranced at hearing it every morning from a new location. Rashid disassembled each line of the prayer and whispered along with the muezzin, who never made a single error of pronunciation. A new sensation flooded him; he remembered the compositions he had thrown into a drawer and was afraid to look at. He felt the uneasiness of a beginner, but remembered the lovely moments when he had sat in that dirty café amid the snorts of the bus drivers sleeping in the corners on foul-smelling sponge mattresses. He had needed that filth and that strange world of the city at night in order to write a single note. He replayed and rearranged his compositions in his head dozens of times, remembering each note exactly as it occurred, and carefully recorded some comments in a small notebook to add one symbol here or to delete another there.

The pages piled up chaotically in the wardrobe drawer, where order was discernible only to Rashid. He planned to move definitively to live with Uncle Nizar and picked out a bed, a new wardrobe, and two cheerful little sofas, which Nizar paid for, declaring that he had more savings than he was able to spend. Sawsan was dubious about the pride Rashid had affected recently, and guessed that it wouldn't suit him to go back to living like a poor tramp in a back alley.

The day after Rashid moved in was the day that Madhat's bill was due, and Nizar didn't hesitate to entrust his lawyers with obtaining the money. Madhat was ambushed by a police patrol, who led him to a judge, who gave him the choice between paying in full at once or going to prison. Madhat didn't have enough time to arrange his affairs; he had consumed most of his savings, which he had once dreamed would be sufficient for him to join the ranks of the nouveau riche. There wasn't much left now, and he hadn't expected Nizar to be so severe that his lawyers were instructed to refuse any kind of negotiation.

Prison was an opportunity for Madhat. He had been saved from the Public Investigation Committee and the interrogators of the security branch, who wanted to question him for the thousandth time about bribes paid to him and other high-ranking managers, raking over every detail of the past ten years. He thought about his past life. His few experiences with casual lovers hadn't brought him the happiness he had shared with Nizar. He considered giving up life as a gay man and requested to see his elder brother, who informed him from behind the visitor's window that he had been dismissed from his job, along with seven other employees whose names had been published in full in the state newspapers. Madhat begged his brother to somehow procure the sum and settle his debt to Nizar to get him out of prison, which would ruin him forever if he didn't leave soon. He didn't clarify that he lusted after the men who surrounded him night and day, and his resistance was beginning to erode. He barely held out another fortnight before he began to compete with Susu, as they called a skinny man who walked like a woman and offered his services for a paltry fee. Madhat offered himself under the name of Maha and tried to sneak into the wing which housed the murderers and drug dealers, who paid more. In the prison for years at a time, they constituted an uninterrupted source of delight and income as they lacked the daily comings and goings of the other detainees.

He particularly enjoyed being the lover of Abu Fahad, sentenced to life imprisonment and the longest-serving prisoner there despite being no older than forty. He was accused of raping sixteen children, the oldest a girl of barely seven years old. Abu Fahad bribed the guards to allow Madhat to pass into his own wing in the dead of night so he could vent his lust on him. Madhat was determined to relive Nizar's life as it had been told him during long winter nights.

News reached his family in the countryside, and they were dumbstruck at discovering the calamity which their neighbors secretly circulated. Despite their poverty, they collected the money for Nizar and the proceedings were dropped. They met Madhat at the prison gate and ordered him to legally change his name, claiming that he was a foundling and his use of their family name had been a thirty-two-year-long mistake. They paid large bribes to be delivered from their misfortune like any respectable family would, and maintained their innocence of any connection to him. They would repeat a peculiar story, believed by few, that he had renounced Islam through a Dutch preacher who had been turned out of the country after converting thirteen families to Christianity, and as bad luck would have it these families had also been forced to flee to Holland after their conversion had been revealed.

With a sense of relief, Madhat took Nour as his new name. He chose it for its ambiguity, suitable for man or woman, and looked for certain locations in Aleppo, ones that Nizar no longer frequented. Nizar placed the repaid money on the dinner table in our living room and suggested that we divide it up to make life easier for ourselves. He went back to his beautiful apartment, and told Rashid he wanted to be broke again, to regain his motivation to compose great music. He repeated that it wasn't right for artists to hoard money in banks; they should always teeter on the brink of peril and starvation.

The first night he slept in his new house, Nizar waited for Rashid to come and help him copy out the old music he had written on his return from Beirut all those years before. The sheets had been left neglected in the old suitcase where he also kept his photos with Hussein and his old friends in Beirut.

Rashid shared his enthusiasm for recording the pieces again, and understood his wish to recover the flavor and power of "Shadows of Regret." He was moving between

Nizar's house and ours, which was like a putrid cave both he and Sawsan wanted to escape. She packed up her clothes and all her possessions after an escalation in the harassment she faced from the men who waited for her at our door. She couldn't withstand their aggression any more and suggested to my mother that they abandon the house and rent one elsewhere—anywhere in fact, as long as there were no gangs of murderers roaming the streets. With the collusion of the police, the mukhabarat, the hash sellers, and the judges, these gangs snatched young children and took them to nearby gardens, raped them, and dumped them by the sewer drains.

Sawsan couldn't endure it when the neighbors' houses were wakened by the sound of women howling. Everyone gathered to observe the howls of Huda, a maid in an old Armenian refuge, after four men raped her four-year-old daughter. Sawsan wept and hugged her stricken neighbor, who used to visit us and help my mother prepare makdous, tomato paste, and pickles, weeping for the fate of the little girl and the destitution of her family. She couldn't bear it when she saw the four criminals released after an investigation in name only. She knew that one of them was brother to Comrade Fawaz, who was forced to intervene and contain the scandal. He had done his best to nip it in the bud, but the courage of a young journalist kept the story alive. He was able to convince his chief editor to publish every detail of the scandal, along with a picture of the little girl, and the medical reports which Sawsan had encouraged her neighbor to give to the newspaper. There were stirrings from the silent intellectuals and charitable organizations. Echoes of the crime reached every house in the city, forcing the public prosecutor to follow up and put the criminals behind bars.

Sawsan could no longer bear the violence which increased day after day. She packed her bags after my mother refused to leave and rented a room in Salma's small house in an alley near Station Baghdad, within walking distance of Jean's house.

She set up her life again and took a job in an office of legal translation where the pay was low but enough to live independently, if frugally. She was wary and wanted to succeed in her new life. Salma invited her out with men who asked her to their parties. Sawsan declined politely and spent her time staring at the wall and the television screen she was addicted to, although she was starting to feel like an idiot from following so many Arab soap operas and Lebanese talk shows. She suspended her brain from thought, deeply afraid of a late-arriving wave of madness whenever she recalled our recent disjointed conversations, as if we had lost our minds. We no longer expected reasons for anything that happened, and just tried to avoid misfortune. We were like many families who moved slowly and heavily and considered violence a part of normal life. Weak people didn't have the strength to defend themselves, and plunged ever deeper into a cocoon of fear. The city circulated stories about the sons of tribesmen who fired on each other for no reason; sons of officials and high-ranking officers who divided up the city without fear of the law; new partnerships which put Aleppo outside the passage of time, as if it were a fragment independent of all other cities.

My childhood came back forcefully in those days. I suggested to Sawsan that we visit Midan Akbas, knowing she wouldn't refuse. For some time she had urged me to take the long journey so we could reexamine the places of our childhood. I had thought she wanted to go to Anabiya—she had often invoked the family name she had felt in need of in the past three years, and blamed my mother for distancing us from our father's family despite their cruelty to us in our childhood.

Going back to search for family meant we had all failed in our search for ourselves, longing to belong to this group we had spent years priding ourselves on being able to avoid. "How afraid we are!" I said to Sawsan on our way to Midan Akbas on the same ancient train which had carried us time after time on our few visits to our grandfather's house.

Sawsan's gaiety and her joking with the child sitting next to her gave me a rare opportunity to immerse myself in the villages and the olive groves we were passing through. When the train entered the German tunnel, thousands of memories came back to me. I inhaled the clean air and felt it was possible to accept Azad's invitation of ten years ago, and to visit the places of our childhood. I hadn't believed I was still so attached to them.

We had to shatter our memory in order to scrub out the rot; this was what I attempted to do when we arrived at the station. I was taken aback at how decrepit it looked. I had thought that everywhere had grown unbearably squalid with age: there were the same streets, looking as if we had just left, with open doors and narrow alleys. There were still children in ragged, dusty clothes, but there were more of them; everyone had multiplied in our absence. Without thinking Sawsan took out her Canon camera and took dozens of photos, while the Kurdish women fellaheen sat in front of their houses, chopping tomatoes and chewing the fat, as they had done thirty years before. I pointed to Azad's family home, and saw his mother, old and stiff now, feeding the only goat that remained of the flock of thirty. We went over and Sawsan tried to help her, and asked permission to go inside for some water. A woman in her forties came outside carrying a small child, who I guessed was Azad's sister, Sherine. She looked at us neutrally, unaccustomed to visits from strangers who wanted to cast a rapacious eye over their home, and invited us to take shelter from the afternoon sun. She brought us cold water and tea and Sawsan introduced herself, and Sherine remembered our mother and said, laughing diffidently, that we were the children of the respected teacher.

It had been the right decision to accompany Sawsan, confirmed when hordes of children started to congregate around us, asking Sawsan to take their picture. Sherine told us that her brother had left the house five years ago, escaping from the mukhabarat for the last time with his friend Juan al-Hajji Ibn Fani, the mechanic, and they hadn't returned yet. She added that he was living in Diyar Bakr now.

I was assailed by old memories and wanted to cry. The faces of childhood friends came back to me, even our desks in the classroom. My mother hadn't wanted us to follow Azad the goatherd, who wandered the streets of Midan Akbas in the dead of night like a worried ghost, releasing his heavenly voice in Kurdish songs before returning to the goat pen to make sure they were chewing their fodder—he loved the smell of his goats, and teased them affectionately and gave them girls' names. He would then slip into the bed a half-mad blacksmith had made for him out of rusted train wheels, which Azad had obtained by bribing the officials of the scrap metal warehouses with jars of delicious goat cheese. The blacksmith, Azad, and his friends and fellow herders brought the bed into his room and he carved his own spot in the corner with a window that looked out onto the distant Turkish plains. Azad and the blacksmith had spent months trying to straighten out the iron rods to create a bed from which Azad could see the border and the guards from the Turkish police, who were well acquainted with him given how often he made obscene gestures at them. They would occasionally respond to his provocations by firing a single shot into the air, after which he was forced to lie low for a few days. He would quietly pass their rifle range and curse at them in songs which the smaller herders would dance and stomp along to. Azad was an indispensable guide, who could lead them across a border whose every secret entrance he knew. He offered his services to all for free. Railroad employees would cross the border behind him, guided by his instructions, and would return a few hours later loaded with sacks of hazelnuts and pistachios and rolls of cheap fabric. Every week, petty traders came from Aleppo and bought these wares in an arrangement which hadn't changed in thirty years.

The long day which we spent in Midan Akbas restored life to Sawsan's face. I looked for the faces which remained in my memory like the first photos of a child opening its eyes to the world and those in it. Sawsan looked for Mihran, who had once offered my mother a part in a play written by the blacksmith, Abu Maksim, about the role of the workers in the revolution to come. He offered her the role of the mother and said proudly that he had drawn inspiration for the character from a novel by his most revered writer, Maxim Gorky. My mother made her excuses, laughing at the craziness of these employees using a play to try to kill their boredom. Abu Maksim was determined to give the role of the Bolshevik revolutionary to Azad, who drew laughter from the crowd at every one of his appearances on the improvised stage. My mother wouldn't let us go to the station, where almost every household in the village had a member employed, to watch the improvised play.

Sawsan couldn't find any of the faces from her memories apart from the mayor, who still sat in front of his house, twirling his luxuriant moustache perfumed with cottonseed oil. He placed his official seal in front of him on the small table made from wooden vegetable crates, and waited for his few petitioners. His seal kept its place although he refused to certify a death certificate unless he had personally seen a body and said a prayer at the funeral procession, leaving many families whose sons had died in distant places frozen in time. In his view, death was the worst possible thing that could happen to someone, even if they were a corpse already.

Sawsan couldn't find many of her old memories, but just being there again made her feel elated at belonging to these villagers. Some of the older people still remembered Sawsan as a small child, bright-eyed, animated, and dressed in clean clothes.

We had planned to leave after the afternoon prayer, but Sawsan was determined to accept the invitation of Azad's family to stay overnight. She wanted to hear the dawn prayer in Midan Akbas. She slept in Azad's bed and I slept on a woolen mattress with clean sheets which Sherine had rolled out for me on the floor. We were fast asleep as if we had never left, with none of the anxiety of a night spent in a strange place. After the midday prayer we ate lunch and hired a pickup truck to take us to the crossroads for the village of Sheikh al-Hadid. We walked through the pomegranate groves as if escaping from the driver, who had asked our names and intentions. Sawsan had taken charge and told him a story that made me admire her for her ability to improvise on the spot. She claimed that she was a Syrian doctor from Anabiya who lived in America, and she was looking over the possessions of her husband's family, dropping in the names of well-known families in the area. She wasn't really trying to make him believe the story; she just didn't want to ruin her enjoyment at visiting her first home.

I balked at the fare he charged, he responded, and then accepted a hundred lira from me. We walked off like tourists wanting to lose ourselves in the paths leading to the olive groves, among the intertwining vines and pomegranate trees which hid us from the eyes of the inquisitive driver. We returned to the crossing and waited less than half an hour before a Chevrolet pulled up and a middle-aged man got out. We greeted him with an indifference that suddenly changed when he politely introduced himself as Dr. Jaafar Mullah Musa and apologized for having startled us; Sherine had told him we were visiting. Jaafar was the son of a Kurdish engineer who had spent more than five years in prison for belonging to the Communist Party. He insisted that we spend a day as his guests, and that was all it took to get my childhood friends back. We were silent as we entered the elegant villa on the top of the hill which commanded views of the olive groves. From the balcony, we could see Midan Akbas and all the surrounding villages, even the distant Turkish plains. He introduced us to his wife, Hevine Sheikh Eisa, a math teacher, who told us she had heard a lot about my mother from her colleagues at Afrin Secondary School.

Hevine welcomed Sawsan and they both tried to remember old mutual friends from Midan Akbas; we were ashamed that we had forgotten so much. We sat down to a sumptuous dinner of goat, mashed potatoes covered in lemon and olive oil, and salad. Hevine was very kind to Sawsan, who recovered her high spirits all at once; she seemed like a new woman, or perhaps the old Sawsan. We heard many strange and amusing stories about Azad's bravery and despotism, and the story of the Kurds aroused Sawsan's interest. She found it reason enough to hate my mother even more, for distancing us from our natural environment.

The following day, after a tour of the villages in Afrin, we went back to Midan Akbas Station. The broken-down car was crawling along and Sawsan was silently, even passionately, watching the trees and the distant mountains. This trip had freed us. She felt it was possible that life offered more than one opportunity to be closer to your true self. I urged the driver on and reminded him that the train left at seven.

In Midan Akbas, the sun was setting over the sunflower fields. The car approached the station and we couldn't believe the wails that rose from the village. Even from a distance we could see that the trains had stopped, the workers were shutting the station gates, and the streets were empty. The sound of weeping and wailing rose from the houses of the station employees, doors slammed, and a man advised us to go back to wherever we came from. Sawsan couldn't believe it when she got out of the car and saw the newscaster weeping on television as he announced the death of the President. She grabbed hold of the only station worker there, who was in the process of closing the last gate, and shook him hard, stuttering out a demand that he refute the news that had spread everywhere within minutes. He shut the main gate leaving her hysterical, releasing bitter sobs I couldn't understand.

She tried to pull herself together and tempt the driver with triple his usual fare to take us to Aleppo but he left us outside the locked station as if we were contagious. Sawsan burst out crying again. I hugged her and sat her down outside an empty café that was usually full of card players and domino matches. The elderly waiter dragged himself over to the ancient television and raised the volume, which had started broadcasting Quranic verses over a picture of the late President with a black ribbon covering the top corner, interspersed with clips of music by Bach. I couldn't take in what was happening. I couldn't believe it. I thought it was a hallucination, that my brain had suspended all rational thought. I sat in the café next to the closed station, and thought that now, at this spot in the world, in this abandoned station, I was receiving news of the President's death. I wondered if we would bury our fear with his corpse.

I thought of Sawsan, who was looking at me anxiously. She asked me to get us to Aleppo at any cost and we found a man and his wife, strangers like us stuck in this remote village, who also had to reach Aleppo. I looked for a hired car and finally Azad's sister Sherine hit upon the idea of a relative who had a small bus that usually took passengers between Afrin and Sheikh al-Hadid. I assured him that everything would be fine and tempted him with the fare we were prepared to pay. He thought it would be an adventure to be out on the road on this night in which everything had so suddenly fallen silent. The bus moved along slowly, with us bouncing and swaying along with it, and the driver never stopped praying for the President's soul in a voice that seemed somewhat insincere to me, as if he were expelling his fear. The man and his wife and all their luggage came with us. Sawsan's sobbing didn't stop until we reached Aleppo a little after midnight.

The streets were completely empty apart from a few cars hurrying on their way. Aleppo was a city of ghosts, deep silence, and fear, which I read in Rashid's face when he opened the door, surprised to see us at that hour. My mother was lost in her ravings. I couldn't believe that we were living in such misery, in this place loaded with losses which didn't need pointing out. The walls were stained from the humidity, and the window panes were thick with filth. The sofas were torn, the dinner table had wobbly legs. We ate the dinner Rashid prepared, and he murmured a few kind words to Sawsan before plunging into a mystifying silence that lasted for days. I turned off the television once and for all, content with the sound of Abdel-Baset Abdel-Samad's Quranic recitation coming from the tape recorder. I couldn't understand why Sawsan was crying for a man who had made our life so wretched, any more than I could understand the sudden silence in that distant village.

Rashid was happy, despite everything. I told him what had happened in the village, and spoke to him about the new president, and the rumors circulating in Aleppo that confirmed that corrupt officials would have their trials expedited and would be thrown into prison without mercy. Rashid nodded and spoke enthusiastically about his wish to pray. His face was gleaming, and for the first time he sat with my mother, who cautioned him against believing this fairytale of the President's death. She laughed at the stupidity of our neighbors who set up a funeral tent where the biggest smugglers, arms traders, and drug dealers in the city held places of honor. My mother concluded that only fools believed the President had died. She begged us in her rare moments of lucidity not to be swept up with the idiots who believed in a trap set by the President to separate his enemies from his friends.

Hidden Paths

"ON MOONLIT NIGHTS, THE WOLVES of love howl and pistachios are pried from their shell," said Sawsan, and waited for a comment from Rashid, who was zealously reading the Quran. He turned a page as if he hadn't heard her and said, "The Quran is not just a book for Muslims, but a book for humanity. We can find all the solutions to our spiritual problems in its pages and in the miracles of its verses."

Sawsan hadn't recognized him when she first saw him. His face was unshaven and his white abaya washed out his familiar features. She quietly wondered about the reason for this sudden transformation, why he never left the house other than to visit the mosque throughout the forty-day mourning period that was announced after the President's death. Rashid explained simply that he felt comfortable in this silent city, adding, "Death is the only just thing in this life."

Rashid didn't reply when Nizar asked about Rashid's enthusiastic attempts at preaching. His behavior was strange, as he tried to guide ladies of the night to repent, volunteering to deliver them to righteous men who would marry them and put them on the right path, or who would secure them honorable employment as seamstresses and maids, or even contentment with living on charity specially designated for reformed women. They would look at him pityingly and leave him to rant and confuse Prophetic hadith with verses from the

Quran so that he seemed like a lost peddler hallucinating in an empty desert. He fell silent and his anxiety increased.

When he went back to work following the period of national mourning, he played with a religious group for the first time. They welcomed him and let him lead the music, given his reputation as a great violinist. He no longer waited for Nizar, and avoided talking with him about hope. Rashid forgot about the compositions in his wardrobe, and almost burned them when he suddenly remembered the day he had contemplated atheism and written out his doubts in a piece entitled "God is Lost." He didn't see the room Nizar had set up for him after he finished his extensive renovations. He told Nizar with unfamiliar cruelty that he would pray for forgiveness both for him and for my mother, who hadn't thought about God's mercy since she was young.

Rashid looked back at his childhood and wept bitterly over our family's deviation from the true path, a family which he had begun to see as burdened with sin. He thought of the days when he would slip into Sawsan's bed looking for the smell of her body. He sought the vines of error he suspected himself of harboring within his anxious soul, and he untangled them in private sessions with Sheikh Abu Bakr, who enjoyed listening to Rashid describe his sins in a calm voice that reminded him of the great historical penitents. Rashid ate dinner at the sheikh's table with a group of young men similar to him, who all spoke about the joy of forgiveness. Death no longer held any attraction for him after he started to attain the certainty that turned him into an ascetic. For breakfast he had a single date with a glass of milk, then he composed religious songs that aroused admiration in his new friends, or he would rearrange a well-known nashid from Medina which welcomed the Prophet after the Hijra. Nizar sensed the spark of genius which had suddenly begun to emerge after years in hiding. Nizar wrote down this vocal chant with its sparse percussion accompaniment and added some pauses, which turned it from a simple nashid into a wonderful piece of music, and Rashid considered Nizar's intervention the beginning of the end of his errors, and a step onto the true path. The sheikh told him not to waste his time, as homosexuals were eternally damned. He advised Rashid in a paternal fashion to distance himself from his dishonorable family and past, and begged him not to take upon himself the heavy responsibility of other souls, as "no bearer of burdens shall bear another's burden." Rashid was tormented when he imagined Nizar burning in hell for eternity.

He woke from terrifying dreams and searched his certainty for new images that would shield him from the old ones, which he longed to erase. If only he could be born again as a child with a clean slate, and the angels would inscribe their wishes on him with secret ink. Images of the faces he had known in his childhood overlapped, such as the image of the father he had longed for, dreaming he would take him to the park and play with him. This happy picture had never left Rashid, and now became mingled with images of his mother who came to him in the dream, mixed up with an image of one of the most famous dancers who had told him mockingly, when he tried to preach to her, that she would write her memoirs that very day and would name all the sheikhs of Aleppo who had tried to seduce her. She went on to say that she had been invited to the farms of rich traders who would perform their ablutions before a sheikh wrote out a temporary marriage contract, and in the morning the same sheikhs would come and divorce them and bless the piety of the husbands she couldn't keep.

My mother's face became confused in his mind with the faces of the female clientele of the cabaret. He couldn't bear to go back after he recited the Shahada with the students of Sheikh Abu Bakr while the world, stupefied, was watching both towers of the World Trade Center collapse. Rashid's friends blessed the conquest of New York, as its executants termed it, and waited until their pictures and biographies were published before lining up behind the sheikh and performing the prayer for those who died on foreign soil, for the souls of the martyrs. A photograph of Muhammad Atta was published on one of the websites that made Rashid feel impotent. He despised himself because he was nothing but a weak, miserable fiddle player. He kept the photo tucked into his books on jihad, and he started to follow news about the rest of the martyrs of the conquest of New York on mujahedeen websites. His friend Sabri al-Effendi broke through the firewall and opened these pages for Rashid and his friends, who followed news of the martyrs avidly. Rashid printed their pictures and looked at them every night like a starry-eyed crush. He felt strength defeating his wish for the gratuitous death he had dreamed of in his existential crises. His skinny body was turned into a pleasant meadow whose exit was as yet unknown.

The dark pot containing Suad's ashes was still on the wardrobe. Rashid paid it no attention amid the transformation which angered Sawsan. She continued to repeat in front of him her fantasy of making love in the light of the full moon as the wolves of desire howled. The approach of her fortieth birthday made her reflect on time. She no longer swayed in flimsy clothes in front of the mirror. She hated the creases on her belly and avoided looking at her dangling breasts. She said to me that she dreamed of a child she would take away from the rubble of our lives and teach the most important dream of living. She surrendered like a train with no brakes, which didn't know the scale of the disaster it would bring with it when it stopped. I looked at her as she sat on her bed and translated articles for a business journal for a fee that wouldn't buy her a pair of socks.

We expected my mother to wake from her coma and stop her perpetual ramblings about coffins crossing the living room and scattering the scent of death in every corner, or her claims that the President was still alive, and she hadn't fallen for his sham death. She would put her finger to her lips to warn us in case the neighbors should hear our drivel, and then she would look at Sawsan and ask who she was. She sat next to Rashid, who kissed her hand and took her quietly back to bed after he changed the sheets which had turned yellow from sweat and let off a foul smell, mixed with that of the tranquilizers lined up nearby on the chest of drawers. She had been so proud of buying it, as it came from a palace whose heirs had demolished it and auctioned off all its contents.

Rashid prayed for death and eternal peace for my mother. He would sit by her bed, open the Quran, and recite verses. She surprised him by asking him in a determined voice to play Schubert's "Death and the Maiden." He didn't tell her that he no longer played those pieces and had stopped playing in Nizar's group, who neither discussed Rashid's decision nor tried to convince him to stay. Nizar in turn renounced worldly noise and sought peace within himself. He enjoyed spending time in his luxurious house where he welcomed old friends of both sexes and rediscovered those evening sessions that everyone called Nizar's Thursdays. They would eat nuts and tabbouleh, listen to music they all knew by heart, and engage in pleasant conversation; anyone would think they were a world away from the city of which nothing remained but old memories they recalled with relish. They were aware they could never go back to those days when the streets were shaded by quinine trees and the scents of spring and the winter rain were too powerful to be ignored.

Nizar, elegant as he remained, had also aged. He kept his memories to himself, and was made desperate by a life he felt to have been a burden. He wanted it to pass quickly and looked in books on Sufism for the meanings of death. He gathered the members of his group and told them in a paternal tone that he was leaving it all to them. He couldn't bear the noise, and wanted to spend the time he had left without obligations of any sort. All of the musicians sensed that it was because Nizar couldn't bear working without Rashid, although he didn't express his horror at Rashid's transformation into a banger of tambourines for amateur groups that toured the villages and praised the Prophet.

Nizar longed to travel once to France, and have one last blowout with his gay friends, to dance on tables and drown in champagne. He looked sadly at the photograph of Michel and his husband at their friend's birthday—he too had aged, and didn't do anything but stay at home or spend weekends at friends' houses in the countryside. Nizar was relieved when Michel wrote to him and told him he wanted to end his days in Aleppo. He complained of homesickness, and the odd phases his husband went through which he couldn't endure any longer.

Nizar was excited at Michel's return and spoke of it as the only solution to his spiritual crisis. He dreamed of spending a cheerful old age with a dear friend, and wrote him a long letter in which he explained how Aleppo had changed. Farmers no longer followed gay men around and threw stones at them; anyone could get lost in the crowds. He waited a long time for Michel to fulfill his repeated promise, but after a while Nizar forgot his invitation to Michel. He passed his time with his friends, velvet-clad women of the upper classes, listening to classical music, or at my mother's bedside, whom he insisted on taking to his house where the quiet might help her regain consciousness. We woke her up and Sawsan was full of enthusiasm at her leaving the house. But then my mother began to curse her for no reason and call her Elena, remembering the woman who had kidnapped my father and taken him away to America.

We were surprised that she remembered Elena, and my father whom she called by peculiar pet names. In the alley she looked as impoverished as the new neighbors she didn't know. No one could believe that this tousle-haired woman was my proud mother.

Nizar was delighted that he had someone at home to look after. He cooked special dishes for her, put up with her cries in the night, and consulted doctors who were the husbands of friends from his Thursdays. He recorded their instructions on colored paper which he hung by my mother's bed and when she was lucid they would celebrate by sharing cheerful memories, ignoring everything that might depress them. Rashid visited her every day at Nizar's house and spent a lot of time there, sometimes sleeping in the room which was always ready for him. In the morning he had coffee with Nizar and they would chat as they had done all their lives. Rashid avoided preaching and Nizar avoided commenting on his face, which radiated foolishness. The disease of longing overcame many families in Aleppo. Large groups would congregate to remember the past, and as they couldn't curse the fear-laden present, they recalled the past as a kind of revenge. They were silent, knowing that their often-repeated words no longer interested anyone but a few researchers who wrote hasty papers for publication in niche periodicals, or books no one read. This history might be turned into TV soaps that excised everything that needed to be said about the past: the disturbances and the military coups and the bloodsucking feudal landowners. The past which was shown on-screen was bitterly disappointing for the sufferers of the epidemic, and they secretly accused the creators of these shows of forging history. They kept silent because praising the past also meant cursing the present, and that could lead to endless questioning in security branches. Or so they thought, and they reflected that they all lived adjacent to the fear that, even after his burial, made the rumor that the President was still alive appear to be a truth circulated in secret.

When only Sawsan and I remained in the house, I had an opportunity to reimagine my parallel life. I thought that many people lived this life, that we were a large group. We had shared the air with our rulers for forty years but never met. We were neighbors who didn't scrutinize each other's funeral biers or borrow each other's dishes, as used to happen in the past. I told Sawsan that when we grew old we would be wonderful, and we would never suffer from this dangerous disease of longing for the past. Everything in our memory had to be erased and its burdens thrown away.

Sawsan liked the idea of not longing for a bygone era; in fact, she said, she hated all eras. I thought she liked the idea because this way none of her victims would ever hold her to account. She praised forgetting, and wearily told me that she would teach her son that his life would start the instant he destroyed the parallel life which so weighed down my soul. I felt oblivion rule our house when I was there alone with Sawsan. She had eventually left her room in Salma's house because she couldn't pay the rent, and we ate our food together and discussed the necessity of leaving the house which had become the principal reason for our depression. We agreed to sell it and travel from this hell to somewhere less cruel. All at once we realized that we were waiting for our mother to die; we were like Jean and so many others, all waiting to be cut off from their pasts.

Rashid made no comment on our dreams, nodding silently. He went out and didn't return before midnight. There was something strange in his reticent piety: fear mingled with the hope of death, as the old fantasy had returned to him. He compared himself to a bird suspended in the sky that would die if it lighted on the earth, and imagined himself suspended with heavenly strings. Suddenly he was flooded with a deep pleasure, which increased when he went away and left us a small piece of paper in which he told us all by name how much he loved us, advised us to look after our souls, and said that he had found himself at last. We didn't understand his few words, until we recalled how he had been glued to the television screen over the previous few weeks, carefully following every news channel. He would open his computer and lose himself in websites that called for the defense of the sacred, inviolable honor of Islamic territories against these new crusaders.

Rashid's anxiety kept him from sleeping, he lost weight, his face went pale, he paced for hours through the empty, quiet streets. He reached Nizar's house and went inside and sat next to my mother's languishing body. He gave Nizar no opportunity to question him and walked home. He needed to think, by himself. He wandered and accidentally collided with passersby, and then turned into empty streets. He got lost on his way home and went to bed exhausted, but sleep escaped him. He thought about his friends who had gone ahead of him to Baghdad, and felt that he was weak and cowardly, afraid of the death he had thought about for a long time. Images came to him of the mujahedeen of New York, and he thought about Paradise; his body relaxed as he grasped the cool banks of the rivers of heaven. He couldn't live any more; he couldn't disappear into the crowds protesting the war; he thought how he had spent his life avoiding crowds. He thought of his loneliness for the first time, and hated my mother, who had fashioned his childhood into entertainment for her stupid guests.

His fate was half decided now. He groped toward death, saw Baghdad close at hand. Standing at Sheikh Abu Bakr's door, Rashid told him calmly that he wanted to leave with the next consignment, to do his duty and defend the lands of Islam against the new crusaders. He added that he needed advice on whether going to Baghdad was in defense of the Iraqi wing of the Baath Party, which he hated, or of the lands of Islam.

He told us there was no need to worry if he disappeared suddenly; he would be in Baghdad. We didn't pay any attention to him because we didn't believe him: delicate Rashid with his sallow and skinny body. But his soul was so crushed he found no better way of saving it than dying in Baghdad.

Nizar wept. In a thoughtless moment he told my mother that Rashid was in Baghdad. I thought of what our life actually was without delicate Rashid; Sawsan was hysterical, and held his possessions to inhale his scent. She thought about killing

Sheikh Abu Bakr, and cursed the Americans and Iraq. When she opened the door to Rashid's room she was shocked to see the dark pot containing Suad's ashes which Rashid had kept beside him throughout his last night, gazing at it intently while he thought about death, and martyrdom, and heaven. In his certainty, he felt great comfort that he would meet Suad there, and laughed at our nonsense and our recent debates about the concept of happiness, or of forgetting, or of our parallel lives. For the first time he felt manly and powerful. He felt our weakness which manifested itself to him in worldly matters, the weakness from which his deliverance had required long years of anxiety, of drowning in loneliness.

My mother gazed fixedly at the ceiling and her tears flowed in silence. She asked Nizar to take her home, and wouldn't listen to his fervent pleas to remain at his house even though her health had improved and she was lucid more than once a day. Her lucid spells had started to last for hours and gave us hope that she would return to her place by the window to drink her tea every evening. Nizar enthusiastically volunteered to pay for repainting the house in case it would improve her state. She wouldn't listen as he begged her to stay away from the alley, which had now become a byword in the local press for crime. The most recent story, which made it into the national news, was about a man who had set his wife and four children on fire, then committed suicide with a kitchen knife as he screamed at his neighbors, who were watching dispassionately, that dying in a fire was more honorable than waiting to starve. He asked them bitterly, "Are there no knives in the kitchens of this city?"

For the first time in his life, Rashid felt he belonged. He needed this feeling to expel his fear after he crossed the border with thirty other fighters in an old bus. They were led by a guide who waited for them in a kebab shop in al-Quwatli Street in Qamishli, which they reached in the early evening. People in the streets ignored these bearded men who sat at the tables in the small restaurant, voraciously eating the leftovers from the kitchen. Rashid felt the calm in the air, the taste of fear, the wariness. He realized that he had made a mistake. He had let their comrade Mudar take charge of everything. The men had met in the mosque courtyard, before taking the bus, and had performed the dawn prayer led by Sheikh Abu Bakr, who kissed them all one by one and wished them martyrdom. Visibly moved, he concealed his tears and waved to them as the bus left. Everyone was silent, looking out at the city. Before the bus arrived at the start of the road to Raqqa, everyone heard sobs coming from a boy of sixteen who was pleading with the driver to stop. Mudar assumed command, told the bus driver to stop, and opened the door for the young man, who stepped off the bus and threw up. Mudar stood up, and in a loud voice he made a speech, reminding them that they were on a duty of jihad, not a school trip; that jihad was an individual duty for every Muslim; that faith was needed for martyrdom. Then he waved his fist in the air, repeating, "Allahu Akbar! Victory to Islam!"

A deep silence settled after Mudar stopped talking. Rashid suddenly remembered him as a small boy, blocking girls as they passed him, walking barefoot on dusty roads. He felt a sense of wonder at this transformation from a mere farmhand and confirmed petty criminal to one of the mujahedeen walking the road to Paradise, which he would certainly reach. Everyone acknowledged him as the prince of their group, and left him the task of communicating with the guides who would take them to the training camps. These had been set up hastily and couldn't contain all the thousands of fighters sent from every country in the world, their stories lost, gone to waste on the streets of Iraq.

Rashid's fear disappeared after they arrived at a large military barracks on the outskirts of Baghdad. The few officers and troops there avoided looking at them directly as they trained them to use the Russian guns handed out along with a few cartridges. On the fourteenth day, they were crammed into civilian cars that hurtled around Baghdad Airport and deposited them there, surrounded by members of the Republican Guard who couldn't care less about these adventurers who had nothing more to look forward to than fighting for their lives amid all this death.

Rashid thought, for the first time, of what death actually looked like. His certainty wouldn't save him now. Images came to him in graphic color and he was horrified to imagine his own charred corpse, or a grave without a headstone for Sawsan to visit and tend its plants. He was besieged by images of every member of his family, including his elegant mother who frustrated him. In among the crowds of troops, he felt reassured. He believed that the American troops would lose the battle and the crows would tear them to pieces before they arrived in Baghdad. He clung to Mudar, who was more convinced each day of having found his rightful place, recalling Sheikh Abu Bakr's lessons about the battles of the first Muslims, who had defeated great empires with their courage and certainty.

Only a few days later, however, they found themselves in the middle of a battle they had thought wouldn't take place for months. They had been relaxed and moved freely around the abandoned airport like any men assured of victory. When the fighting broke out, they tried to coordinate with the officers responsible for armament, but they ignored the volunteers as if they were aliens found by chance amid the ruins. Rashid thought of his fate with resignation, recalling the days when he had thought of death. He felt that the redemption of his skinny body would be hidden in a dark grave, but also that the dead didn't need anything, and had no fear of the President or the mukhabarat.

The thought of redemption possessed him in the middle of the burning wreckage. He was astonished by his tenacious grip on life, and by the burning desire to walk again through Aleppo late at night, on his way home. He was disoriented but practiced the utmost degree of caution, and seeing the burned bodies of American soldiers gave him the additional strength to hang on. For three days he didn't sleep, changing position as skillfully as a fox after he and his companions discovered that they were alone in the battle, as most of the troops protecting the airport had already fled. They had done so in the very first moments of battle, positive that whoever could reach the airport this quickly wouldn't be long in taking up residence in the President's palaces.

Rashid turned into a savage beast with no fear of the death he faced head on. He sprang over the bodies of his friends, recognizing the faces of a few. He reflected that this proximity to death left no time to think of the other life that was lying in wait a few meters away. He wished his memory could become a blank page so he could write his opinion of death which, he was sure, was the only fact that made us into cowards; we fled from it so as not to have it before our eyes, to have to see it when it was so terrifyingly real. He thought wistfully of fleeing, as we had done all our lives from something which clung to us every moment. He wished for a trivial, lazy death, with enough time to say goodbye to his loved ones and examine his memories for the last time. What was the last scene which would remain on the pages of his memory?

This question of the final picture occupied him. He began to select it from among the images which presented themselves in quick succession, so intermingled that all the faces became mixed up. He felt impotence surround him when, on the third day, the scales of the battle tipped toward the American army. The American officers were hysterical at seeing the bodies of their troops flying through the air and felt caught in a trap that was slowly closing, with the desert stretching behind them and the city in front lying dozens of unfamiliar kilometers away.

No one knew the secrets of this battle, nor the number of American soldiers killed. After several months a few testimonies crept out from the ranks of Rashid's companions who, by the fourth day, couldn't get rid of the taste of blood filling their mouths. He walked in the field of death, averting his eyes, all hope of rescue gone. Most of the companions who had come with him he would never see again. The faces of the dead were distorted, their bodies left to rot on the battlefield, the sand ramparts, and the ditches which the troops of the Republican Guard had sweated over. There were only a few of them left, led by young officers who spoke at length about their military honor. They obstructed the American course of action for days before the Americans panicked and bombed the airport perimeter.

On the fourth night, the deadly firing into the airport perimeter fell silent after the decision to strategically withdraw. Rashid was able to cram himself into a car driven by an Iraqi officer with a few other fighters whose accent revealed them to be Yemeni. The officer was familiar with the agricultural roads leading to Baghdad, where they arrived less than two hours later. The officer asked them to get out and flee, after briefly praising their courage.

Rashid couldn't believe that he wasn't dead. He clutched his body all over and felt weirdly comforted. He went into a café in the Karrada district of Baghdad, sold his rifle to a waiter for ninety dollars, and asked for directions to somewhere he could claim asylum. The waiter laughed and pointed to the river and said, "That's where the homeless find refuge." The Yemeni fighters hired a car and left Rashid after he refused to go with them anywhere equally unknown to him.

Alone in the empty streets of Baghdad, his soldier's uniform betraying his loyalties, his long beard attesting to his identity in a way that brooked no doubt, he quickly realized he wasn't safe. He could hardly sit in a café and start discussing Iraqi poetry, which he loved and could recite at length.

Baghdad was deserted, and the American planes dropped bombs continuously. Glowing shrapnel exploded near Rashid, who didn't care. His wish to die had returned. He knocked at a mosque he thought would be a safe refuge overnight, but no one opened the door; it was deserted. Desolation came back to his heart, and he thought of the final image that he had hit upon the previous night. He tried knocking at other houses, but failed to light upon shelter. He would have to sleep in a doorway. He chose a four-story building, climbed to the top floor, and was frustrated to find the door to the roof firmly padlocked. He found a small space next to the door and sagged onto the cold, dirty floor. It wasn't as bad as he had thought, but he needed to get rid of his uniform and beard.

Returning to the café, he found the waiter closing up and tried to negotiate with him to be allowed to sleep there. The waiter wouldn't agree, but he did offer to sell Rashid some jeans and a shirt and to lend him an electric razor for forty dollars. He gave Rashid a cup of tea and told him that the Americans were looking for Arab fighters in the streets; there was nothing for him to do but go further out into the surrounding neighborhoods where his companions were already gathering and regrouping with a few Baathist officers. They couldn't believe the Americans had reached Firdous Square, tied a rope around the neck of the statue of Saddam Hussein, and toppled it—a scene played on television screens all over the world that caused millions of Arabs to weep at the humiliation at the hands of Yankee troops rampaging through the heart of Baghdad.

Rashid's childhood features returned after he shaved. In his loose shirt and jeans he seemed like a young man out for a good time, rather than a fighter who had traveled hundreds of miles to find his salvation. He tried to delay and to convince the young man to let him sleep on a chair, but the waiter asked him to leave immediately, without hiding his glee at the fall of the regime and the destroyed images of Saddam Hussein.

Rashid left the café and went back to the nearby building. He lay down on the dirty floor, and was too exhausted to feel hungry or thirsty. He dozed fitfully for a few minutes, dreaming that dawn would come soon and perhaps he could resume knocking on the silent doors, then he came to his senses and surrendered to the search for his last picture. Images came to him of Sawsan, of my mother and Nizar, the streets of Aleppo, our room, the faces of his jihadi comrades who were now mostly dead, the rest melted away like salt in the streets. He dozed with the languor of forgetfulness, and was woken with a start by American soldiers who had surrounded him and were asking him to get up. He spoke a few English words to the effect that he was homeless and had got lost on the way to his hostel. The Kurdish translator with the troops asked him to get into the large military car, in silence.

He exchanged glances with eight others who were sitting in the vehicle. He didn't know any of them. They arrived at a makeshift prison in one of the barracks where the soldiers were stationed, and where his fate would depend on his ability to withstand the torture and interrogation he faced. He felt homesick for our house, for the sight of Sawsan's sweet face as she slept soundly in her bed.

We all thought about Rashid. We tried to get news of him, and Nizar asked his Iraqi musician friends to look for him, but like many such families we could do nothing but wait. We studied the news and searched everywhere for a trace of Rashid. Everything was lost. We went to the Red Cross and left his picture and our address. Along with the mothers of many lost sons, Sawsan charged into the house of Sheikh Abu Bakr and cursed him. She could no longer bear crying like a powerless woman.

Nizar had to apologize to his friend Michel who suddenly knocked at his door and embraced him warmly, and the two wept from the force of their longings. Nizar apologized for not meeting him at the airport as they had planned, and explained he wouldn't be able to concentrate on anything until he knew Rashid's fate. Michel understood and joined our search. He called French organizations devoted to tracking missing persons in Iraq. He stayed in Rashid's room and looked over his possessions and photo albums. While he waited for Nizar to return, he cooked and washed the dishes and repeated that he had arrived at the right time to support us. Sawsan wouldn't listen to his pleas to slow down and think rationally about a plan to look for Rashid. She left them at Nizar's house with a look of bewilderment on her face. She slept at Salma's house, or Nizar's house, or she would knock on our door late at night before using her key, or linger at Jean's house.

A year and three months passed, and the lack of news about Rashid confirmed that at least no one had seen his body. It seemed likely that he had been killed in the withdrawal from the airport by a bullet from the Republican Guard, who were accused of killing many of the Arab volunteers. We began to lose our zeal for the search, believing that 'missing' was better than 'dead.' I thought about Rashid's body lying under the open skies of Iraq. Would it be buried deferentially, or would it be left for the vultures?

We tried to be patient, and we all seemed to have aged. Nizar let Michel settle into his house and regain a relationship with Aleppo while he stayed beside his sister, whose existence we began to forget, or, properly speaking, to avoid. The two of them spent a long time together, chatting and swapping roles, complaining of a lack of oxygen and cursing the family member by member, before falling silent and thinking about the lost Rashid.

The Dead Mother

I WAS OUTSIDE THE TEXTILE factory when Nizar called and asked me to look for Sawsan. He told me simply that my mother had died. She was late as usual, even for her own death. The news threw me off balance for a few minutes but I didn't understand why I was secretly so happy. In recent days we had supposed that she would return to normal life, as she began to recover her health and tried to walk toward the lettuce fields that had now disappeared entirely, along with any signs that they had existed just thirty years ago. But her body collapsed all at once.

The search for Sawsan on that searing day in June 2004 was the real punishment. As usual, her cellphone was off and her movements were erratic. I left the news for her at Jean's house, who was very kind in offering his condolences to me and my family. I bought four large ice blocks which we would need to keep my mother's body from disintegrating. It was unthinkable to bury her at night, as the bats wouldn't leave her alone. My feelings were so confused that I stopped thinking.

When I arrived at the house Nizar had arranged everything, from the shroud and the roses to the hearse, and he had bought a small space in the cemetery next to my grandmother. At the end of her life, my mother had started to mention my grandmother again, to ensure we understood her ambiguous instructions to be buried next to her. We placed the four ice blocks around her body on all sides and threw every blanket in the house on top of her; she looked like a pile of leaky junk which we intended to get rid of in the morning.

Nariman wasted no time in coming. We were surprised that Uncle Abdel-Monem and his son Hussein came, holding a large collection of Quranic verses. Hussein kept his distance from the female neighbors who had come to offer their sympathies and help while Nizar made the burial arrangements. Everyone exchanged hostile looks, but Nizar refused to leave the duty of spending the night watching over his beloved sister's body to anyone else. Uncle Abdel-Monem was silent, feeling that Nizar was unsettled by his presence and quite prepared to kill him, and he made do with reciting the Quran, with Hussein, by my mother's head.

Sawsan's late appearance at the end of the night made things extremely complicated. She didn't want to sit with a body that meant nothing to her, and she hated looking at what she saw to be the image of her future death. Nariman hugged Sawsan, kissed my head, and generally behaved as if she owned the place; I thought of people who only found time to apologize at the moment of death. She spoke a few heart-warming words about my mother, with whom she had competed in the raising of their children. She added that while we believe it lasts forever, life is a huge joke, and we forget that death lies in wait for us behind every door.

Sawsan didn't respond. She sat in the kitchen calmly acceding to everyone's requests. She had chosen a silent way to say goodbye and kept to it. In recent days she had begun to praise silence when she spoke about humanity's trivial wish to fight over things that had happened years before, and added that people wanted to destroy their enemies even when they were on the brink of death. I asked Hussein, whom I had only seen a handful of times in my life and that years before, to be kind to Nizar, and to head off any clashes between him and Uncle Abdel-Monem. Hussein was kind and understanding and behaved like a man with no fear of funerals. He examined the grave before the burial, which was to take place after the morning prayer. Nizar didn't persist in his wish to bury her after the afternoon prayer; the number of mourners wouldn't increase by much and there was no need for the usual funeral hangers-on.

Everything went normally. I dozed for a few minutes on the same chair Rashid had sat in for the last time before his dawn journey to Baghdad, and heard Hussein repeating "Allahu akbar" in a loud voice as he carried the coffin out with three of our neighbors' sons, when he decided that the appointed burial time had arrived. Nizar watched everything in remarkable silence. He kissed my mother's forehead calmly, objected to nothing, and relinquished his obstinacy. He left the funeral reception to Abdel-Monem so that his presence wouldn't turn the family mourning into a battlefield, and charged Michel with welcoming his close friends and music students at his house. They played a melancholy concerto in her honor, chosen by Nizar after much deliberation. When I heard the music he had chosen I knew that for Nizar, my mother hadn't died; the body we had buried belonged to some other woman.

Sawsan avoided Nizar's invitation to come and live with him. We avoided talking about our dead; the shadows of Rashid's absent face and our dead mother stood between us and widened the gulf separating us. I stayed out of the house as long as I could, loafing around by myself and avoiding Sawsan. Her company had become a burden for the first time in my life, unbefitting the light butterfly she used to be. I suffered from nightmares. Rashid's departure for Baghdad was the death knell for our family feeling, which was too sickly to survive much longer. We avoided meeting and even Nizar couldn't summon up any enthusiasm. He didn't cook, he didn't play, he didn't listen to music, and he didn't care about us.

We all thought of Rashid, who at that time was lying on a dirty sheet in a military prison. He liked how alert he felt, and he composed different stories of his life. Life was appealing to him again, and he thought of going back to Aleppo, writing his music, and presenting it in the greatest concert halls in the world. He dreamed for a moment of going to Paris and working with a great band interested in eastern music that he'd been asked to join, more than once, for a world tour of Sufi songs and the poems of Ibn Farid. He slumped over and knew the questions which tore at him, and which he had avoided for three years, were dangerous. He thought of his existence, his fate as someone who always turned up in the wrong place, his fear which made him long for stability and which led him to be afraid of everything, including his neighbors, Comrade Fawaz's relatives.

He regained his courage and felt strong, confident of returning to his former life. He started to think up a story that would save him from this cell packed with over fifty prisoners. Most of them looked at him with contempt when he stated that he was a Syrian Christian working as a violin player and led the orchestra of a well-known Iraqi singer who had abandoned Baghdad the night it fell.

On the first night he ate voraciously and slept deeply, in preparation for the rounds of questioning. He avoided speaking about jihad with his cellmates, who competed in boasting of their courage in battle. He wished to join in, but remembered the questions which had gnawed at him at the hasty training camp about what it meant to kill and die for Islam, or the meaning of the nation and the Islamic community, the umma. These burning questions were the reason he was so relaxed and sat so confidently on the wooden chairs in the empty room in front of the American interrogator. He was already exhausted from the succession of strange information and stories he had heard from fighters who were determined that they were here in order to fight the new crusaders, unaware of the gallows rope or execution squads waiting for them at dawn.

Calmly, Rashid maintained that his name was Jean Abdel-Mesih and that he was a musician. He commanded interest; the interrogator looked at him and surmised that this skinny creature couldn't be anything but a Christian and a musician, as he claimed. He reiterated his wide-ranging questioning about the Islamic groups which had infiltrated Iraq, and Rashid denied all knowledge of them. His consistent answers ensured that his bouts of torture remained light. It didn't compare with the experience of his companions whom the Americans carried away, thrown onto filthy blankets or gurneys unconscious, their wounds oozing blood and pus, and crowding the place which was already too small for its clientele.

Rashid looked away and despised himself. He heard the groans of his companions and thought of salvation. He no longer believed that Paradise was a lovely place of eternal life. He tried to hide his story from those around him as they repeated the name Mudar, now Abu Qatada, who appeared on Arab television screens threatening to burn the earth under the Americans' feet if they did not unconditionally withdraw from Muslim Iraq. The prisoners exchanged accusations about why they had fallen into captivity and paid no attention to the directives of their leader, Amir Abu Qatada, who had warned them against trusting Iraqis who would deliver them to the Americans for a few coins.

When Rashid met the Kurdish interpreter again, he seized his chance and spoke to him using the Kurdish which remained in his memory from when he was young and his mother would leave him with her Kurdish neighbors until she came back from school. He casually mentioned the names of famous Kurdish singers and sang part of a Kurdish song by Muhammad Shekho. He succeeded in rousing the interpreter's interest; ignoring the guards, the interpreter asked him about his life in Midan Akbas and Afrin, about his father, Elias Abdel-Mesih, the president of the Rail Maintenance Department, a mechanical engineer and a graduate of the Université de Genève.

Rashid used everything he had to create a story he knew needed to be convincing. The small cracks in his story did not attract the attention of the interrogators, who were interested in it but did not have time to verify every detail, owing to the large number of prisoners and the psychological pressure that they themselves were under. Hundreds arrived every day to be stuffed into the barracks, which had been converted into a crude military prison, and they received erratic military decrees that added to their anxiety over the quagmire of Iraq, which was turning from a military pastime into a nightmare reminiscent of Vietnam.

During the first month Rashid felt relaxed and wasn't asked to repeat the details of his story. He began to feel that he really was that Christian who'd been abandoned when the famous Iraqi singer took off and left his musicians lost in the prisons and streets of Iraq. He solidified his relationship with Bihram, the Kurdish interpreter who had graduated from the English department of the University of Suleimaniya and could find nothing else to do than put on cloth armor and work as an interpreter for the American interrogators and soldiers bent on taking revenge on Baathists.

His relationship with Bihram and the American interrogator John Mercavel gave him simple advantages such as more time outdoors, or work distributing food to the prisoners. He expected to be released, and the expectation became a certainty after he buckled and agreed to write daily reports on the other prisoners; they held no new information for the interrogators but they confirmed his willingness to help. After a year and three months of imprisonment, the opportunity he had been waiting for arrived. John summoned him and suggested that he play with the military brass band which was coming to celebrate Thanksgiving.

He demonstrated his skill at leading a band. The players, all soldiers, listened to his instructions and called him *maestro*. He chose old songs he used to love, such as Bob Marley, and some swing numbers. He demonstrated his skill at playing the trumpet, and any lingering doubts about his innocence were dispelled when the celebrating soldiers and officers asked him to replay "My Way" and "New York, New York." His dexterity returned and his fingers glided over the violin like silk; he felt they were his only chance to escape before he was transferred to another prison.

The following day, John congratulated him and apologized for his incarceration. They returned his eighty-two dollars, his watch, and his clothes. Rashid didn't want to leave prison without seeing Bihram, who wasn't due to come in until the next day, and John let him sleep on a cot in an office that night, understanding his wish to say goodbye to his friend. Bihram congratulated him on his release, and thought hard for a few minutes before agreeing to the favor Rashid asked of him: safe passage to Suleimaniya. It was the only safe place for him, as he knew someone there who had played with him in a concert by Iraqi and Syrian musicians five years earlier, hosted by the Assyrian church in Aleppo. The concert had been led by Nizar, who with Rashid's assistance had collected a trove of Syriac and Kurdish folk music. Rashid had been nineteen then and longed to found his own group, which he dreamed would tour the world to show off the treasures they'd come across in the houses of Qamishli, Raqqa, and Hasaka. Nizar and Rashid led the nomad life of touring musicians for four consecutive months in the company of Kurdish musicians whose leader was a Baathist from Amouda who hated rehearsals, preferring to improvise using the Sufi music he had inherited from his family.

On his last night in prison, Rashid recalled Uncle Nizar's friend Kamiran, a Sufi with stage fright. Nizar had gotten used to the chaos his Kurdish friend aroused and no longer minded when he didn't show up for things. He was the subject of many stories which his friends laughed over, which mostly involved him sneaking out of concert halls crammed with people waiting for him to take the stage. He would look at the crowd in terror, and skip nimbly out of the back door, leaving the organizers bewildered.

Bihram, protected by an American patrol, brought him to Firdous Square, which was guarded by Peshmerga troops, where a Chevrolet was waiting to take four young Kurdish politicians in the direction of Suleimaniya. They offered him tea at the rest stops and continued a boisterous conversation in Kurdish which meant nothing to Rashid. After reaching Suleimaniya, they were surprised when he asked for their help in looking for a Kurdish musician known as Juan Khalil. One of them knew him and took him to his house. Juan was surprised by this skinny young man who was exhausted from traveling and a little peculiar. He remembered that they had played together on that day five years ago with musicians who had generously hosted him. He looked over the pictures in his album and recognized Rashid from his picture, where he stood next to the elegant Nizar.

Juan listened to a new story Rashid composed about an Iraqi singer living in the Gulf who had brought him to play at a party for the daughter of an important official some weeks before the war. Rashid had been taken for questioning by the Iraqi security officials after the singer fled. He immediately asked Juan to ensure he reached Syria, and to arrange a passport for him; Rashid said the singer had stolen his own when he fled.

Rashid concealed his role in the airport battle. He slept that night in Suleimaniya at the Kurdish musician's house, who had no choice but to arrange for Rashid to travel with a band leaving for Vienna via Damascus Airport in two weeks. He spoke with officials from the Democratic Party of Kurdistan who trusted him, and he added Rashid's name to the list of travelers as the bandleader. They supplied him with a fake passport, which was only to be brought out if the operation to smuggle him over the border failed. Rashid couldn't believe that everything was this easy. Once he'd crossed the border at Qamishli, he went to a lahmacun restaurant next to the Qasimlo mosque and asked to borrow the owner's cellphone, who didn't hesitate for a moment to hand it over to a clearly honorable client who had generously paid twice the amount he owed for his flatbread topped with spiced mince. Rashid dialed Nizar's number, the only one he remembered by heart. Nizar couldn't believe it when he heard Rashid's voice. He burst into tears before pulling himself together and arranging for a luxury private car to convey him to Aleppo.

We couldn't believe the man standing at the door was Rashid. His skinny face reminded me of Sawsan's on the day she returned from her travels, loaded with worries and her face pale from hunger, and I wondered what it was that happened to us when we tried to leave this house. We flung ourselves onto him and wept. Sawsan couldn't believe her insomnia had come to an end. She grabbed hold of his body to reassure herself that this emaciated young man was her beloved brother Rashid. We all sensed that he regretted everything, and couldn't embrace us as he wanted. The memories he'd replayed on his way from Qamishli to Aleppo disappeared and suddenly he wished he had stayed in Iraq as one of the mujahedeen in Abu Qatada's army. He thought at first that this was due to exhaustion. He didn't answer any of our questions and asked to be alone with my mother, and quietly we told him that she had died.

He remembered the last time he had sat beside her bed, before he went to Baghdad. He had looked at her face deep in its coma and was choked by the pervasive smell of decay that came from her, whose source we couldn't trace. He noticed she had added iron bars and strong bolts to the window. When he took her hand and kissed it, she opened her eyes and warned him not to believe that the President had died, or we would be ruined. She addressed Rashid using his father's name and resumed her silence, staring blindly into a corner of the room. He had stayed until after midnight, certain it would be the last time he would see her.

He went into her room where nothing was left apart from a few odds and ends we never got around to throwing out. We could hear him sobbing, and Nizar couldn't bear it. He tried to enter the room to bring Rashid out, but the door was locked from the inside and Rashid wouldn't respond to his pleas to come out and have dinner. He heard the ghost of his mother's voice scolding him for taking so long to return to her bedside. He saw the shade of a slight smile. He heard her singing a village song the children of Midan Akbas would often sing when they left school. He wished he could speak with her one last time, or ask how she was, even though it didn't need to be asked; her pus-filled body and mottled skin belied it. To him, she had long since seemed like a woman left by the side of the road, someone who everyone passing by wished would hurry up and die.

Rashid left my mother's room at midnight. He was surprised to see that we had waited up for him; Nizar was lying on the sofa, and Sawsan was translating a text about how important the Internet would be in the years to come. I tried to tell him about how worried and afraid we had been, how Sawsan had been frantic, thinking about him every morning and evening and going to see mujahedeen who had returned from Iraq to ask about him, accompanied by other grieving mothers who were not slow to knock on our door and throng about him after the dawn prayer the next morning. Rashid sat in the living room and had no replies to the women's questions or their wrangling for news. They were astonished when he said that he had left their sons and his companions before he went to Baghdad. A woman accused him of lying and reminded Sawsan of Naji al-Maliki, a friend of Rashid's who had told Sawsan that her brother had been among the few undefeated fighters who stayed in battle and swore on the Quran that they would either be victors or martyrs. She left, astounded by his flagrant lie.

His image as a fighter, one of the brave mujahedeen, was a burden. He was surprised before the afternoon prayer to hear Sheikh Abu Bakr knock on the door and ask for a few minutes alone. The sheikh told Rashid he had to repent for his heretical conversion to Christianity, leaving aside the matter of the reports he had written on his fellow mujahedeen. The sheikh's gaze on his clean-shaven face carried an accusation and a hatred that choked him. Coldly, Rashid informed him that every detail that had reached him was a lie. He went on to say that he had fought as no else had, and felt no need to prove his heroism. He concluded by accusing the sheikh of selling him and his companions to the Syrian and Iraqi mukhabarat who had treated them like disposable scraps.

The sheikh was taken aback at Rashid's tone, especially when he added that he really had thought of renouncing Islam, and his companions would settle their scores with the sheikh even if it was years after his betrayal. The sheikh gathered his wits, then laughed derisively and asked Rashid's permission to leave, regretting the opportunity he had offered to Rashid before he revealed his true colors. He left calmly, refusing to acknowledge Nizar, who gave him a sardonic look. Nizar spat on the door behind him and asked Rashid to come and live in his house to escape the mujahedeen mothers who hadn't stopped knocking at the door for days.

Before my mother's death, the three of us used to sit in our rooms on rainy nights and weep. My mother coughed loudly from time to time, groaning like an old horse spotted all over with mycosis. I thought of all the years we had lived through without sensing Rashid's anxiety. We had thought it was normal when he said that he couldn't bear anything, or when he spoke of the fear he had lived with all his life, or the degradation of being forced to play pop songs to drunks. The city stole his dreams.

Rashid had felt he was suffocating after the President died and his son was made the new President. He thought he would spend his whole life being desperate and afraid. He told me he wouldn't wait until the grandson of the late President was ruling over us. He couldn't bear having to be courteous to drunks when they would suddenly think to demonstrate their loyalty to the dead President at the end of the night. The dead President was present in every detail of our lives. We couldn't continue living forever in these parallel lines.

Rashid deeply regretted returning from Baghdad. There, he had had the opportunity to be brave, to fight and kill in the name of an ideal he didn't believe in but which gave him a sense of belonging in a group that felt no fear. Occasionally, he imagined himself as the leader of a gang of kidnappers that haggled over its victims' lives with their families. He tried to recover the moments when he'd sat in the café of the bus depot writing new music, but his hand stiffened so that he couldn't form a single note of the piece he wanted to write to glorify his comrades in the airport battle. The insignificant phrases he wrote convinced him that he could no longer call up the choir of violins which used to invade his mental horizons. He was not skeptical about his feelings of impotence. He recalled his old experiences years before when he would go home with dancers from the cabaret after work, having sex and fleeing love. Women held no attraction for him after several of these experiences, which he deemed nauseating. One morning he'd asked us if any of us had thought about having a family. I was too afraid to say that I had often thought of what it would be like to be married and have five children with whom I would spend all my time playing. We spent the winter of 2005 avoiding discussing the future.

In the elections for the new President, back in 2000, familiar images had filled our lives. Party members came out trumpeting its story over the past thirty years and beyond. They published the same disgraceful tracts all over the country. Doctors, lawyers, journalists, traders, deputies, university students, and high-school students were all coerced into dancing dabka and screeching into microphones. A new image of the dictator was produced, one that Syrians already knew well and avoided looking at so as to keep on their parallel paths, heading toward whatever God had in store for them.

Rashid thought of the image of the Dictator. The memory of Baghdad ate away at him again. He could no longer endure merely existing. Nizar was the only one who knew that Rashid would not be able to cope with life. He grew convinced that it meant nothing to Rashid to live just to see the shame of the Syrian people growing slowly, like the inexorable pace of the freight train my grandfather had died beneath. Violence gripped the streets around us, and to him they were an accurate reflection of the country as a whole: a chaos where screaming microphones broadcast village songs all night, men spied on women, killers hid in the long, winding lanes and bribed poorly paid policemen to look the other way, retired soldiers looked for work as waiters, sons of villagers dreamed of volunteering for the mukhabarat. The alley was witness to the destruction of my mother's dreams, and the idea of this alley grew to encompass the length and breadth of the country. Rashid spoke about how he had felt as a fighter, but said little about his overwhelming nausea while fighting. He had discovered the cowardice rooted inside him, and spoke about the bliss of trying to resist it. He told Nizar that he had almost overcome it, the sensations of a warrior settling in its place.

Everyone around me thought of the images of power which lead a person into a labyrinth of delusion. I thought that I was the opposite of everyone else in that I liked being happy. I watched my weakness grow, turning me into a silent being, fearful and hopeless. I slept on the same bed for thirty years, went to the advertising office of the textile factory and stayed there as long as I could. I translated trivial publications and spent my time timidly watching the girls at work. I became a terrified dove; I didn't think and I didn't dream. My only enjoyment was sitting in the Muntadi Café overlooking Saadallah Jabri Square, reading old newspapers and playing chess with my friends, employees at the textile factory. I would lose so they would be happy at winning, and gradually the bliss of accepting defeat grew inside me. I avoided listening to angry people whose anger only grew. Signs of deviance and hysteria began to appear on the faces on some of the café regulars. They would lose their heads and curse the authorities, then they would heap abuse on the President and his family, and then they would disappear and melt away like a grain of salt. No desires, no dreams. No future, no past. These were the principles of happiness which I fervently believed in. I convinced myself that living in the present saved people like me, who were without hope.

I was afraid my world would collapse, and I would end up like the pleasant man in the accounts office whose name I didn't know, but whom I would say good morning to when I collected my pay. He didn't raise his eyes from the statements, and he worked seriously and silently. I saw him trying to dance at parties of allegiance to the President, making a concerted effort before giving up. He was like me in my inability to shout, and turned a deaf ear to the banalities of his colleagues, who competed to demonstrate the greatest loyalty and veneration of the President before informers. He told me once, without showing fear, that they disgusted him and added, "They live a dog's life, happy licking shoes." When I missed him one day, his colleague told me he had killed his wife, his two children, and then himself, and explained, "He found out his wife was a whore and the children weren't his." But I believed it was something else—he couldn't bear his life any more. The silence and the shame which were integral to his image were also Jean's. He had composed a small book entitled "On Shame and Its By-Products in Syrian Life."

On Sawsan's fortieth birthday, we all gathered in my mother's room at Rashid's wish. We celebrated calmly, without fuss, and made do with a plate of fried potatoes and tabbouleh generously prepared by Sawsan herself. Rashid wanted to ask my absent mother why she had given birth to us, and to rebuke her for an idiotic act whose price hadn't been hers to pay. I discovered a harsh side to Rashid which appeared clearly in his final days. He no longer prayed or went to the mosque and cut off all contact with the religious music groups who pleaded with him to return after a surge in demand from the old respectable families of Aleppo. They had exchanged the deep-rooted Aleppan tradition of qudud music for religious mulid festivals, performed by singers clothed in white and perfumed with a nauseating odor of rosewater. Rashid said this music was plagiarized from pop songs, adding, "How can believers steal from the songs of infidels in cold blood?"

That night, Sawsan's eyes were sparkling. She got up after an hour to blow out the candles and cut the cake which Nizar had brought from the best bakery in Aleppo when suddenly she let the knife fall from her hand and went into her room. We were left listening to Rashid and Nizar who were chatting fitfully, in overlapping phrases that spoke of our childhood. Irritated, I went to my room. I didn't like the way that Nizar told stories from my childhood, which I still considered the only happy time in my life even though my ill-omened birth was a perpetual reminder of the Party's coup. I occasionally wished to forget that date but everything was a constant reminder of it. Before going to my room I saw Sawsan wearing a short, pretty dress. Her body was still beautiful. She was carrying her suitcase and she left without saying goodbye.

She knocked at Jean's door, who hadn't been expecting her, and asked him to take her for dinner at a nice restaurant, so she could celebrate in a way that was more appropriate for her birthday. Jean was bewildered and felt Sawsan's subtle invitation to be a foolishness he was no longer prepared for. They drank excellent wine in Wanis and Sawsan asked him to tell her about the women who had passed through his life. She was surprised at his bashfulness, which reminded her of his old, more innocent image. For a moment Jean recovered his longing for those days, reached out his hand, and took hers under the table. They were both shocked at the fact that it was the first time he had ever done so.

That night she went to bed with him. She told him plainly that she wanted a child, and if she became pregnant she wouldn't give it up. Jean thought about the lunacy that had squandered his happiness for almost a quarter of a century. Sawsan summoned up everything that was left of her memories, her dreams, and her passion, and she succeeded in igniting Jean's desire. They were like lovers who had lost one another years before. Jean was powerful and Sawsan passionate; tenderly she embraced him, and like a child he fell asleep in her arms.

Their repeated meetings ignited the passion in Jean's body, and his craving for love came back to him complete, gushing, powerful. Sawsan was once more that woman who gave lethal bliss to a man who had waited for her for years, finally convinced of his mistake in thinking that the past was dead. They never discussed what Sawsan had said that night; he wasn't able to take her lunacy at all seriously. He couldn't live with anyone other than his mother, and he was addicted to reading her French children's stories suitable for her level of speaking. She had improved over recent years and her mind remained clear despite her ninety years. Sawsan moved some of her clothes to his house and spent the whole winter with him, and took prodigious care of his mother. She flung open the windows, washed the sheets and curtains, and repaired the tables and chairs. She ironed Jean's shirts, arranged his papers, and tried to see if it was possible to alleviate the house's immovable smell. Jean didn't object but he didn't like the windows being open all morning to expel the smell he had grown used to over the years. He couldn't spend the rest of his life with her, but he surrendered for the time being, certain that she would leave him in a few months after his sexual desire reverted and waned.

Sawsan left Jean's house for a few days. She sat contentedly in her room and joined me in looking over my mother's photo album. She neutrally examined each photograph and did not avoid the pictures of my mother, whom Sawsan increasingly resembled with the passage of time. All she needed was my mother's dark suits and she'd be the picture of the stern teacher. Sawsan missed no opportunity to avenge her resemblance. She looked at my mother's pictures, arranged with care in her sumptuous album, and immediately did the opposite in her perpetual attempt to escape this likeness. She cut her hair short like a boy, and put large hoops in her ears. She still had a few remnants of the jewelry she had bought from an African man in Arles on a rare trip with Munzir. He had been determined to read her fortune for free, and when he told her she would have a wonderful life she squeezed Munzir's hand hopefully and kissed him on the lips. She bought many accessories as a way of offering money to this man who had refused payment and given her hope that she would be happy despite all the trials she would pass through. She bought leather bracelets, silver rings and hair bands, a collection of hoops in strange shapes, and found the leftovers of this pile to be helpful in escaping her likeness to my mother.

Jean found her short hair exciting. It aroused him on the first night, and he exulted over his full erection and the blood pumping through his veins. A week brought his frigidity back despite Sawsan's euphoria at sleeping in his arms. Jean didn't have the strength to be frank with Sawsan, to tell her that in his eyes she had become a parasite he cared nothing for. He burst out in anger when she moved some pieces of furniture from the places they had occupied for fifty years, fled the house, and only came back late at night so he wouldn't have to see her. He realized that she was making herself wake up early in order to make breakfast for his mother, before she went to the nearby translation office and worked until late in the evening. She understood everything. She began to stay away for longer at a time, trying to save their relationship by causing him to miss her, but he didn't. She admitted that she didn't like this new image of Jean and no longer missed him either.

At the end of winter 2005, she stayed away for more than two months. He didn't call, and neither did she. She was content to pass through the house for a short time while he was out in the evening to look in on his mother, who reflected on time and how this girl was still searching for something which had altered with the passage of the years. In a lucid moment, she thought to herself that the girl's voice had aged; certainly she had grown older, despite her agile movements and the moans which issued from Jean's bedroom.

After an absence of two months, Sawsan asked Jean to wait for her one day. She opened the door with her key and put it down on the dining table, which Jean had returned to its old place in the corner of the living room. She sat down and coolly told him that she was pregnant, in her second month. She was silent and the evening shadows which settled over the old furniture made Jean realize that he hadn't chosen anything in his life. He hadn't even chosen the French language, or his wife Colette; she had chosen him, and even now he didn't know why he had agreed to be married to her. She hadn't aroused him, and he never liked going out with her to the cinema or to Geneva's endless receptions.

Jean slumped over and thought before articulating his decision to Sawsan. He was sure that the first and best decision of his life was when he resolved in a moment of courage not to repeat the Party song and was dismissed from teaching. The second was to lie with fallen women who were content with a little cash and who meant nothing to him. He gathered his courage for the third time in his life and told Sawsan that he wouldn't marry her, and the baby meant nothing to him. Curtly, he asked her not to move the furniture around. He added, after an apology, that he would pay for the operation if she wanted an abortion.

She didn't for a moment consider letting her child slip into the sewer of some secret clinic. She was relieved that Jean didn't want it, and didn't try to convince him or even discuss it. She knew that she wouldn't be able to bear anyone else interfering in the life of her child. She liked her new image, which had been hidden in the shadows of her old image. She thought that Jean wasn't as bad as she had thought, even though he lacked gravity when he was having sex and was prone to laughing. She knocked on Nizar's door, but Rashid opened it and told her that Nizar and Michel had gone to Kessab, in the mountains, and would be back in a few days. She almost told Rashid everything then, but stayed quiet and sufficed with the cold coffee he offered her, before he turned his attention to the investigative report in *The Guardian* about Arab fighters in the Iraq War.

Rashid didn't notice when Sawsan left. He thought my mother's death had made a reunion half impossible for us. She wasted no time in looking for a father for her child. She contacted Nizar, who waited for her in the main square of Kessab with Michel, who seemed like an old man to her. He sensed her worry and told her to behave as if Michel weren't there. She hesitated when she saw Nizar's happiness at celebrating with his life-long friend but Nizar, as usual, could read her thoughts, as indeed he could for all of us. He poured her a glass of wine and took her to her room where she sat down opposite him, and was shocked when she told him calmly, "I want a father for my child." For three days, Sawsan stayed with them and listened to their dreams. She saw them embracing tenderly in bed, living without desire, eating their breakfast, and walking for an hour in the mountains. They went to the beach, swam sedately and swapped stealthy kisses, and returned with fish they bought from fishermen on the beach. She observed the changes of her body and tried to sense her baby. She watched Nizar, who wasn't ready to talk about it. She was afraid that this time he would abandon her and leave her to her fate. She couldn't hold out much longer; she felt that she was weaker than she had ever been, without a future, without admirers or lovers, without a family. Just a woman seeking a father for a baby that had not yet formed into a being with a right to this mountain air.

Nizar arranged everything cleverly. Michel had told him that he felt like a stranger during the months he had spent in Aleppo, and added with a plea that if they wanted to live together, they had to think of getting a house in the Kessab mountains. Michel was miserable about Aleppo and his family, who had paid enormous sums to forge his death certificate. Nizar said calmly, "Yes, we have to think about leaving Aleppo. The mountains are perfect for our old age. We can plant vegetables and raise a goat and make cheese, we can listen to the music we love with the volume turned up high. We can swim in the winter." They delved deeper into this dream the more they imagined that they really could establish a place where their friends would be welcomed from every corner of the earth.

Nizar couldn't tolerate living in a city where murderers roamed all around, where men with long beads and short robes carried knives in their pockets. At the other end of the scale, the mukhabarat spied on people and bargained with them over their livelihoods in operations of regulated looting. All he could do was move to this enchanting place which he had always visited. He had spent more than ten years there, if he added up all his visits and the weekends he had spent in the house of his friend Mona al-Shazli, who gave him a key to her house on the day she bought it. Winking, she gave him his own bedroom overlooking the valley, so he could howl away with his lovers.

He asked his friend Washma al-Biluni to sell him a piece of the land she had bought there years before when she dreamed of building a country house; she still sometimes spoke about it to Nizar on his Thursdays. She said she wanted a country house built entirely in natural materials, without any chemicals, and a room with a Jacuzzi and a glass ceiling where she could undress and see the clear sky in summer and the rain in winter. She had needed Nizar's offer to spur her on to completing her lifelong project. She welcomed Nizar's suggestion to share six acres overlooking the sea at Samra. They both began talking enthusiastically about their project with a mutual friend, a talented architect who dreamed of a distant place where he could write a multi-volume history of Aleppo. He had wanted to take revenge on the Party, and derided its new regional branch building as a Gestapo HQ occupied by people who hated beauty.

Nizar's enthusiasm for his project brought on a fever among his friends. They all began to design furnishings worthy of the imaginary place which Michel had sketched on cold nights in Paris. Michel couldn't believe that this miracle was nearing completion. It was an image of old age which was worthy of him and his lifelong friend Nizar: they would be a complete family caring for a small child and plaiting colored ribbons in its hair. Michel told Nizar and they looked at the moon. Yes, a complete family: a mother cooking for the lovely child of two fishermen, returning from the sea at dawn with an abundant catch.

*

Rashid continued to clutch onto life in our house. He wouldn't listen when Nizar tried to convince him to go back to work and lead the group, or to live in the house which Nizar would leave to Rashid when he went to his new house in Kessab. He read what he had been afraid of in Nizar and Michel's eyes. Nizar was astonished at Rashid's harsh tone when he asked about Sawsan, whose arguments we hadn't found convincing when she had left the house with a small suitcase leaving all her things behind. She was looking at the house as if she were leaving it for the last time, and didn't reply to our questions. It was too late for us to behave like a family. She said Rashid hadn't thought about us when he was thinking about dying in Baghdad, and she didn't mention my mother, as if she hadn't existed at all. She said she would go to Paris with Michel and wouldn't be back for at least a decade. She asked us to forget her and tear up her pictures. She cursed my father and my dead mother and wouldn't stop chattering as she looked for justifications to leave us without feeling guilty. Sawsan was the only one Rashid had missed, and she was leaving him forever.

Rashid slumped on his bed and mused that the only reason a person had not to burn their family tree to the ground was the delusion that they would grieve for each other. He reflected that Sawsan wouldn't be sad if something happened to him, and took comfort in the idea of a family where none of its members cared about death. We both tried to imagine our new lives. Rashid told me that we shouldn't treat him as if he were ill; he was at the utmost limits of happiness at everything that had happened, and happiest of all that our mother had died while he was in Iraq. He tried to gather the details of the day of her death; his memories were scrambled but when he thought hard he remembered that on that day in June 2004 he had been in military prison, missing Sawsan and thinking of her grief if he should be tortured to death. He had also thought of the pieces of music that sheltered him from madness, where the violins entered slowly, joined by the piano which came in timidly like a distant voice from the unknown. He realized that on the day my mother died, he was pretending he had another family name and another mother. The discovery didn't cause him sleepless nights; in fact, he stayed in his room and didn't get up for several days.

He was lost between certainty and doubt, between images in his memory and notes of the music he wanted to write about death and betrayal, about the taste of fetters and whips in American prisons, about the misery in the eyes of his companions when they looked at him and despised him as a spy, a worthless being who played music for the pleasure of the occupiers.

He was seduced by images, mixed with others now grown faded, of a father lost and wandering through icy cities, a mother begging to die. Everything was mixed with the lassitude of death, which once more appeared to him as a salvation with no trustworthy alternative. He was comforted when the page of death appeared to him, white and uncontaminated by delusions about life or music. He was surprised at his attachment to life when death was so unbelievably near. He asked himself if the real reason he had returned across all that distance, and invented stories which everyone believed, was to be buried in a grave for an indifferent family to visit. His warmth toward Sawsan didn't leave him for a moment. He came to the conclusion that he had returned because of her, to smell her old perfume. When she had hugged him he sought out that old perfume and was frustrated when he smelled nothing but a worn-out body, something like desiccated fig.

Nizar brought food to Rashid's bed, opened the window, and spoke enthusiastically about a piece he had composed, full of swift movements that spoke about the glory of being alive, which had been inspired by the commingling of sounds and voices in the souk. He tempted Rashid with trips to have lunch in Kafr Janneh, or to walk for hours through the Kessab mountains and the beautiful cactus groves found there. He told Rashid about the new house, and Rashid nodded, tasted the dishes which Nizar had prepared with such artistry, asked carelessly about Sawsan, and fell back to sleep. No one knew the daydreams which possessed him: stairs that the murdered would climb in order to throw themselves into a pyre, all young men with fresh, blooming faces who saw their fingers chopped off by their executioners and thrown into acid where they dissolved and left no trace. He remarked that he didn't dream of women, and his few adventures in that direction had never laid bare his virility.

Yet, during those nights at the training camp in Baghdad, he had been besieged by sexual fantasies. Before he fell asleep, he saw images of women he had worked alongside for years without being the least aroused by them. An image of Sawsan came to him as if he desired her: beautiful as a wild horse, wearing the delicate, white clothing she used to wear before she left for Dubai as Munzir's lover, sitting on her clean, fragrant bed. He fled from it and wished he would die, as these dreams in which he yearned for Sawsan were so painful. Recently she seemed more fleshed-out than she should be, and she often spoke of how much she wanted a child to frolic with on the shores of Latakia.

Shortly before her fortieth birthday Sawsan had accepted invitations from prospective bridegrooms, who initiated each session by dictating a never-ending list of conditions. Sawsan was possessed for a moment by a maudlin weakness. She looked into the face of each interlocutor and felt nauseated by the utterings pronounced with masculine confidence. She pulled herself together and reflected that she was nearly forty and her life had been spent in one long delusion. She had tried to stop time but was shocked when it continued slipping through her fingers.

Her walk no longer aroused men. She was like a maid, or one of the depressing public-sector workers. Even Jean surprised her; it had been a long time since he called a woman with any resemblance to her. Her current image marred his pleasure and made his penis limp. She was astonished when Jean adopted a pitying tone with her, when he himself had become an old man. He was no longer the "man of romance" Sawsan and her school friends had dreamed about; they had masturbated for the first time over an image of him approaching them gently in their beds, where he kissed their navels and their nipples before entering them with a delicacy that gradually built to boundless passion.

Before Rashid went to Iraq, she told Jean spitefully that he had become a stupid man, no good for anything but wasting his money on third-rate prostitutes. She soon regretted what she had said and apologized sincerely at their next meeting when they reviewed their, by that time, platonic friendship. She went to see his mother, who, despite being over ninety and completely blind, hadn't been deserted by her cheer and sharp wit. Sawsan spoke about how her son Jean had introduced her to French, when he translated some texts for her by Surrealist writers like her friend Orhan Misar.

Sawsan begged him to accept an invitation to dinner at Nizar's house, who said that Rashid needed some noise and affection to bring him out of his silence.

Jean arrived, and he brought a girl, who demonstrated great decorum in the role of fiancée of Monsieur Jean. We all spread out around the table and Rashid stuck close by Sawsan. After a few glasses of wine Jean's tongue loosened up and he spoke about strange things with Rashid, such as music manuscripts discovered by a French priest in a church in Arles, composed by priests who had committed mass suicide at the beginning of the sixteenth century. The church tried to cover this up and claimed they had contracted food poisoning from old provisions which had been kept in the cellars for fifty years.

Nizar was courteous to everyone, and served naqaniq sausages prepared with a broth and olive oil. He played some classical pieces, and Rashid joined in for one of them, but our warm applause and encouragement didn't persuade him to stay with us for the rest of the party. He made his excuses and went back to his room, and a deep silence prevailed. We spoke very quietly until late in the night. Sawsan was grateful for Jean's presence, and overlooked his having brought this woman.

I wondered about Sawsan's wish for us to appear once again like the family she had left. This was the image of us that she was determined to revive after our return from our visit to Midan Akbas. She wanted us to have a childhood that could be remembered, a life that could be lived, full of the surprises of a simple life, such as a fiancé knocking on our door with his mother to ask for the hand of our sister, irrepressible Sawsan, after praising our wholesome reputation and noble upbringing; anything, in fact, that would make us feel hopeful, like all families whose women ululated loudly at any happy occasion, however trivial.

Sawsan's time had passed, just like my mother's had. There wasn't enough time left for regret. My mother used to hate being alone in a room with Sawsan, who looked at her like a heavy inheritance she wanted to throw off and be freed from. For her part, Sawsan was afraid of her future image when she discovered too late that she bore such a close resemblance to our mother, the same dark, almond-shaped eyes with the same long lashes, the soft skin and well-proportioned figure. She thought of escaping this future of hers but couldn't bring herself to do anything so desperate. She packed a suitcase and asked Salma again about happiness, then scolded her for the ridiculous men who suggested she should get to know them better.

Sawsan didn't want to admit that what remained of her body would no longer be considered tempting; her breasts had withered, and her stomach was flabby despite her corsets and strict diets. She thought of Hiba, who was still slender and sweet as a lettuce leaf. Sawsan dreamed of comfort and love, repeating that great love could only be found on the open road. She vowed that the man who stirred her would see Paradise with his own eyes. When she remembered her old daydreams, she was depressed. She had hoped for a good man who would give her children, quickly, before she reached forty; she no longer had time to have two, but told herself she would be happy with one. She sighed like a princess who had lost her throne in a moment of pleasure. That cruel look returned to her. She wouldn't be deserted like my mother was, or lost like Rashid, or resigned to my fate like me. She wanted to be a female version of Uncle Nizar, who began to spend hours in her company, and they would talk as they prepared dinner together. Sawsan began to be convinced that dreams roosted in physical places and we couldn't carry them with us in our memories, any more than we could relive the events they came from. So her dreams had the force of a scent which receded with time.

Sawsan no longer cared about us. She left us for the last time, after hastily packing some clothes and giving a kiss to Rashid, who was still reliving the war and prison. Michel was waiting for her in the car that would take them to Aleppo Airport, where they would leave for Paris as husband and wife to record the birth of Sawsan's child.

Rashid spoke about his experience morosely. He described his weakness in the face of death and his cowardice before the interrogators, in contrast to his companions who had openly expressed their wish to kill every American soldier on every inch of the land of Islam. He was silent on the weight of his guilt, and the jumbled intermingling of his unstable worlds. Sometimes he got up and performed his ablutions, then raised his voice in prayer, closed his eyes, and implored God for mercy and forgiveness; he sat on the prayer mat like an old man, his eyes letting the tears stream forth. At other times he threw the Quran aside, tearing at its pages and repeating that anyone demanding worship should be more merciful and just, and his eyes bulged as he sank into silent hysterics. He joined Uncle Nizar to play at three elite private parties held by music lovers at the house of a European consul. The invigorating atmosphere in the house and the silence of the crowd reminded him of his reflections on salvation through music.

He took out the music which he had never told Nizar about, and tried to play one piece. He didn't like it, but he didn't rip it up. The only thing which calmed him was sitting by my mother's empty bed for hours at a time; the place we wanted to escape gave him some reassurance. When I saw his pale face and vacant eyes, I thought that he wanted to sit close to death, to see how the soul rose and slipped out of the body. We used to think that he was suffering from the shock of the war, and kept telling him that he would forget in time and return to the projects and dreams which he had often, if briefly, spoken of, such as his wish to move abroad and live in a place where the neighbors didn't knock on the door to borrow salt, and he wouldn't see women shelling seeds and sitting in front of their doors to watch the passersby and make insolent comments. He spoke in awe about the life of European musicians who played in clean theaters, and whose work wasn't hampered by Party members who loved speechifying and talking since time immemorial about imaginary enemies like "the feudalists, " "the bourgeoisie, " "the imperialists." Even a mention of these time-worn tropes elicited a sympathetic reaction from audiences, just like "the working class" who now went barefoot.

Rashid remembered those golden years when he slept in the day and worked at night, and wasn't forced to see the streets crowded with people and always wonder why they were hurrying. He remembered his meetings with Sheikh Abu Bakr, and his certainty that his search for salvation was the reason for his restlessness. He didn't regret going to fight in Iraq, but he remembered his discomfort at sleeping in the barracks with fifty other fighters and being forced to share food with them in the morning. He remembered that during his military service, he had been happy to hear the morning fanfare and fool about with the other conscripts, but within a few weeks his delirium returned to him along with his horror at being an individual within the herd.

Was it possible for a man to live independent of anyone else? Rashid used to believe that this could be the answer to complete happiness, but despaired over his attachment to his inscrutable family.

Before Rashid went to Iraq he spent most of his time in my mother's room. He seemed like a servant with a bowed back, waiting for a sign and ready to comply with any order, but my mother requested nothing but death. She complained how hard it was to breathe the heavy air which infiltrated her lungs like sharp stones grating against each other. She used to ask Rashid, "Does air have a sound?"

A smell of mothballs seeped from the wardrobe when Rashid opened it, and it brimmed with old clothes whose elegance had once been the envy of many. He spotted a mouse, which was stiff and seemed to have been dead some time. No one had noticed it. He cleaned out the wardrobe, burned the mouse, put the tattered clothing back in order, dabbed my mother's body with cologne, and sprayed cockroach repellent into the corners of her room. In a lucid moment she asked him to take her to Nariman's house, so he helped her to bathe and chose her a long broadcloth jacket, one of Nizar's beautiful gifts, whose hem had been spared by the nibbling mice. Rashid asked me to go with them, and we went out like any family going to visit relatives. I was surprised when she reached the alley and asked Rashid about the mulberry tree that hadn't been there for more than twenty years.

Nariman opened the door and was astonished to see us. She kissed us warmly and told us that her mother had died. She was raising her niece, as her brother's wife had left him when he decided to devote himself to worship and move to be near the Prophet's grave. A charity offered him a small, humble room which he shared with an Afghan man who sewed clothes for the poor. Nariman's house had retained some of its legacy; although the sofas and curtains had aged, they were clean and smelled fresh. She offered us coffee and sweets, and looked doubtfully at my mother, who seemed normal enough, as she apologized for not attending the funeral for Nariman's mother. We were heartened to see my mother reliving shared childhood memories with Nariman and laughing shyly. Nariman's niece left and seemed somewhat spoiled and silly to me; I saw no need to be courteous to her. I used to think that my mother deserved a house like this for her old age, and I was struck by a peculiar fatigue when I realized that we were no longer children and were nearing old age ourselves. The trains were now an old memory, the subject of incomplete and patchy stories, and when we saw an old train we said, "That is a piece of our childhood," without any sense of affection.

During the short time we spent at Nariman's house I observed that we had all paid the price of our parallel lives. I thought to myself, "What if we had lived in another time?" Such as the time my mother and Jean's mother spoke of, or the time to come a hundred years from now? What would be different? Would it change this fear which nested in our chests, making it easy for mice to slip inside and breed? I was sickened when I imagined my body filled with mice. I occupied myself looking at the ornate panels; my mother and Nariman had once boasted that they would leave one to each of their relatives. On our way home I thought about my mother, who was holding on to Rashid's arm like a small child.

I spent my nights with Nizar, listening to Rashid getting his memories off his chest. He unburdened himself of the thoughts and daydreams which had not left him since his return from Iraq. He began with a weak voice and scattered thoughts, but presently the details were gathered together and the narrative straightened out. He relived his alienation amid the fighters who shouted and congratulated each other on nearing their goal of heaven. Rashid was surprised that they craved death, which he had thought of for years. He wondered about the difference between dying for a cause or in a car accident. Did death have a taste? Nizar was nodding, encouraging his old friend to throw off his burdens and be free of the thoughts which weighed down his soul.

Rashid spoke confidently about death of a different flavor. He was eloquent in praising a voluntary death, when a person chose the right moment to end their life and was freed from the nightmares, holding out against fate. He wondered simply why he had to live through so many repetitive years, only to reach one of the miserable destinies awaited by those who grew old without attaining happiness.

A few times, we saw Rashid going out with women, or speaking like a normal person about wanting a family, wanting children he would carry to the closest clinic when they fell ill at night; children who would grow up with no regard for time. They would go to school, think about killing their father, and rebel against the old ideas. It was a stupefying discovery for me that none of us had seriously thought of starting a family, as if it were normal that we were all alone. We all thought that Sawsan was the only one who would have children and in better years to come we would share in bringing them up and spoiling them. I tried to draw a picture of this hypothetical family, but no image which suited Sawsan was any help to me. I realized that I didn't know what that imaginary family looked like. The years had passed and we still dreamed of sitting quietly around the dinner table, conferring about trivial affairs such as pooling our small salaries and lending them to Rashid so he could buy a bedroom set and a suite of sofas for the house he had bought with a bank loan. But Rashid's serene face and unequivocal words about death dispersed the few images I had been able to form in my daydream.

We spent hours next to Rashid as he retraced the faces of his companions. He talked about Baghdad, and returned dozens of times to the scene of the River Tigris and the unknown bodies floating on its surface, which no one bothered to bring to the banks. No one had time to bury the dead; you had to have a family if you were to be buried, and a headstone if your grave was to be defended. The corpses remained floating on the river, recalling his first questions about why they had died. These unknown people were killed for many different reasons, in a place which had stopped asking why. He tried to grasp the last spark of life: perhaps they had been killed as a result of a tribal feud, or American troops had killed them and thrown their bodies into the river, or they were killed because of sectarian struggles and revenge killings. Eventually, Rashid concluded that he didn't care, as long as the idea of Paradise was a delusion required by the weak to give them the strength to set their sights on the passage over the isthmus, over the moment of separation between life and death, that single moment between the final breath in and the final breath out, before a deep tranquility reigned and all questions reached a conclusion. He added, "This is what death really is, not the completion of memories."

He rose at dawn and walked steadily to his room. Nizar remained in his chair, sunk in silence. He was wounded by the questions Rashid had cast at us so simply, like someone spitting out a peach pit. I was besieged by that terrible scene at the deserted station when we received the news of the President's death. I had looked at Sawsan as she wept for her executioner, and for a moment I felt like crying bitterly for my dead mother.

Nizar wept in silence as the dawn crept slowly in. A moan, quickly cut short, gave me the feeling that we were the guardians of souls which were trying their utmost to slip away from their bodies. I felt depressed and confined by the rank smell of the house. Before I got up to go to bed, I heard Nizar saying quietly that Rashid wanted to die, as if he were telling me simply to cover up well, because this cold would gnaw at your bones.

I opened the door to our room and my head swam. Rashid's body was dangling from the ceiling like a filthy lightbulb. Nizar saw him from the open door and sobbed. He had known that Rashid would die, and had waited for dawn to be sure that his dear friend had fastened the noose securely, so there would be no doubt that his death would be as simple and clean as pouring out a cup of water onto the parched earth.

Author's Acknowledgments

ALL THANKS AND ESTEEM MUST go to my friends Dr. Osama Ghanam and Ilham Maad, and my dear friend Yasmina Jraissati, for everything they have done for me during the writing of this book.

Notes

Hamid Badrkhan: Syrian–Kurdish poet born in 1924 in the village of Sheikh al-Hadid in Afrin District, Aleppo Governorate. He wrote in Kurdish, Turkish, French, and Arabic. His diwan, "On the Pathways of Asia," is published by Dar al-Hiwar. He died in 1996.

Khaireddin al-Asady: Famous writer and the most important historian of Aleppo. He was born in 1900 in Aleppo and died there in 1971. He published a collection of poetry called "Songs of the Dome" and a complete history of the city of Aleppo in the form of an eight-volume comparative encyclopedia.

Louay Kayali: One of the most important Syrian artists of any era. He was born in Aleppo in 1934 and committed suicide in Paris on 26 December 1978. He is buried in Aleppo.

Orhan Misar: One of the earliest Arab Surrealists, he was born in 1914 in Istanbul. He died in Aleppo in 1965, where he was also buried. He is well known for his diwan called "Surreal," published in 1948.

SELECTED HOOPOE TITLES

The Longing of the Dervish
by Hammour Ziada, translated by Jonathan Wright

A Beautiful White Cat Walks with Me
by Youssef Fadel, translated by Alexander Elinson

Time of White Horses
by Ibrahim Nasrallah, translated by Nancy Roberts

*

hoopoe is an imprint for engaged, open-minded readers hungry for outstanding fiction that challenges headlines, re-imagines histories, and celebrates original storytelling. Through elegant paperback and digital editions, **hoopoe** champions bold, contemporary writers from across the Middle East alongside some of the finest, groundbreaking authors of earlier generations.

At hoopoefiction.com, curious and adventurous readers from around the world will find new writing, interviews, and criticism from our authors, translators, and editors.